SONG IN THE RUINS

SONG IN THE RUINS

MANJU MOHAPATRA

Black Eagle Books
2022

 Black Eagle Books
USA address:
7464 Wisdom Lane
Dublin, OH 43016

India address:
E/312, Trident Galaxy, Kalinga Nagar,
Bhubaneswar-751003, Odisha, India

E-mail: info@blackeaglebooks.org
Website: www.blackeaglebooks.org

First International Edition Published by
Black Eagle Books, 2022

SONG IN THE RUINS
by **Manju Mohapatra**

Cover & Interior Design: Ezy's Publication

ISBN- 978-1-64560-297-2 (Paperback)
Library of Congress Control Number: 2022943030

Printed in the United States of America

To my Parents — The Past

To Phoenix, Mena, Oscar and Frida — The Future

To Rabi — Always

Acknowledgements

I'm grateful to Katie Herman for editing the book and to writer Howard Norman for taking the time to read the manuscript.

My heartfelt thanks to my friends Indira Tripuraneni, Kasturee Mohapatra and Jagannath Rath for their enthusiasm and encouragement. I'm indebted to my daughter-in-law, Sarah Sandoval-Mohapatra, and my friend's daughter, Mukta Mohapatra, for their much-appreciated time and suggestions.

My gratitude goes to Satya Pattanaik and Black Eagle Books for giving my novel a home.

Last but not least, I want to thank my husband, Rabi, no matter how inadequate it may be, for his unwavering support in this lonely endeavor.

*"Someday, somewhere—anywhere, unfailingly, you'll
find yourself, and that, and only that, can be the happiest
or bitterest hour of your life."*

Pablo Neruda

Part One

Chapter One

It was late afternoon when the bus pulled over and dropped him on the side of the road extending toward the horizon. He could tell that the road was newly paved, its top pitch black and still shining in the afternoon sun. The bright rays from the sun hit him at an angle, and the saffron bandana only partially protected his face. He stood there until the bus disappeared from view, leaving behind a trail of smoke.

Then he walked slowly with the help of a walking stick, a small saffron-colored bag hanging from his shoulder, not sure which way to proceed. He looked in the direction the bus had come from. He could see the thatched huts in a mango and coconut grove, their shapes waiting to melt into the approaching dark. He pulled out a piece of paper from his pocket and studied it as he looked around and saw the outline of the riverbank. His long-forgotten memories nudged him in that direction. He thought that path should lead him to a village.

He had been traveling for the last three days, from San Francisco to Mumbai, another flight to Bhubaneswar, the capital of this state in eastern India, and then the four-hour bus ride to this village. In spite of his long journey, he felt his spirit up—revived by the river and the memories he did not want to respond to. He could see himself, a young boy skipping along the bank on his summer vacations. His mother getting worried about his turning dark from the hot sun, while his grandparents were happy to have him for a long stretch and said, "Let him be." However, Sukhatma tried to suppress these happy recollections, just like any other reminiscences of his past life.

He walked on the road, his wooden sandals clicking against the hot asphalt, while counting the beads strung on a thread. The hot afternoon air vibrated with his chants: *"Om Tat Sat, Om!" You are the supreme absolute truth, O God, all that is!* After going a hundred meters or so, he left the main road where it bent and started walking toward the river. The river was closest to him at this point.

It was May. The riverbed was already parched from the fierce summer heat. He left his sandals and his bag, which held his few belongings, under the shade of a gulmohar and moved closer and closer toward the water. The dry and hot sands burned the soles of his feet, but soon he was standing in ankle-deep water. It felt warm to the touch. Bending down, he cupped his hands and scooped a handful of it on his face and drank some at the same time.

He got out of the water, but instead of climbing up the bank to reach his belongings, he sat on the sand, his bare back burning in the setting sun.

Away from the crowd and the road, he sat there in perfect solitude, in unison with the river, counting the beads as they rotated between his fingers, and chanting, *"Om Tat Sat, Om!" All that is*. Decades had passed since he'd had any connection to this place. The numbness from the long journey snuck upon him. He lay down on the wet sand, his feet touching the water, and closed his eyes.

"Mohan, you are back?" he thought he heard someone asking him. "It is good to come back and find your roots, isn't it?" he heard a voice say, carried over time from another world. The voice was soft and fleeting. He tried to remember who Mohan was, and whom the voice belonged to. However, it was beyond him to respond to any of that knowledge. Swami Sukhatma's world was supposed to be devoid of any earthly bondage.

***

"Mohan, you are back?" His mother was standing outside their one-story brick house, her face glowing with happiness. She said this like a question even though they had received the telegram about his coming, and she had been preparing for days for this visit. Now that he was standing in front of her, it felt like a dream. "It is good to come back to your roots, isn't it?" she said, trying to hide her joy, afraid that the evil eye would cast some unforeseen fate on the happiness she had prayed for day and night for the past five years.

She looked him over from head to toe. His skin seemed lighter than she remembered. He had been fair like her since the time he was a baby, but the long winters and the less scorching sun in America must have made his skin even fairer. She didn't like the way he wore his hair; it was somewhat long, as if he hadn't had it cut in a while. Then she thought about the long hours he must have worked to earn his degree. In spite of his unkempt appearance, he looked sharp in faded blue jeans and a short-sleeved white shirt. She made a mental note to send word to the village barber to come and give her son a respectable haircut.

He had come home after five years in America getting his doctorate in engineering. She knew that his degree had to do with building things—tall buildings that would rise to the sky, like the buildings she had seen in pictures of New York City. She hoped that with all the knowledge he had gained in that foreign land, her son would build up India from nothing. She smiled at him, not knowing what to say. He stood there tall and handsome.

"Let us go in, silly me. You've been standing here like a guest," she said, while wiping his sweaty face with the end of her *saree*.

"Ma, you look good." Mohan touched her feet for blessings as he said it. "Where is Baba?" he asked, looking around for his father. He was about to step inside a house he had never been in before but remembered to take off his shoes and line them up on the veranda with his parents' slippers.

"Your *baba* has gone to talk to the priest. He will be here any minute."

"Ma, that isn't necessary," he said, knowing that his mother had asked the village priest to come to the house to pray to the family deity for his welfare. This was nothing new. Although, they had lived in a nearby town while he was growing up, whenever his parents had brought him to this village to see his grandparents, his mother would send word to the priest ahead of time to come and pray for her son. It had happened at least once a year. Sometimes, even when Mohan wasn't present—when he started a new class or a new school or when he went to America— his mother would ask this priest to worship the invisible god for her son's protection.

"The priest must come and pray, now that you're back after so long," she responded. While his mother went to the kitchen to check on the mutton curry she was preparing for lunch, Mohan inspected the new house. It had been built while he was in America, after his father had retired from the police service. The parcel of land on which his grandfather's thatched house stood had been divided into two equal portions after his death—each part belonging to one of his sons. His uncle and his family remained in the old house, but next to it, his parents had built this new one and retired in the village.

Unlike the old house, this house was made of bricks. It had three bedrooms, a drawing room, a kitchen, and a room with a latrine and a faucet that protruded midway between the floor and the celling. A bucket with a plastic mug hanging from it stood under the faucet, and he could see a small hole at the bottom of the wall to carry water outside. All the rooms opened onto an interior veranda, and on one end of it, near the kitchen, there was a small table with four wooden chairs with backs decorated with intricate designs of tree branches with little birds on them. It was a modest house, but his father must have poured his life savings into it.

Though the house wasn't large, it was much bigger than the government-provided living quarters where Mohan had grown up. The quarters were assigned by rank, and as a constable, his father had been allotted the smallest unit. Since Mohan had no siblings, the three of them had managed in the two rooms, plus a small kitchen and a bathroom with a latrine, without complaint. One of the two rooms, the bedroom, had been his parents'. The living room had been his, where he had slept and studied and, on summer nights, looked through the open window at the sky covered with stars.

Mohan stood on the exterior veranda of the new house waiting for his father to come home. There was no wall or fence between the old house and the new. From a distance, he could see his uncle outside lounging on a cot. He didn't see his aunt or his cousin, Murari, and his wife. They must have known about his coming, but no one had come to greet him yet. With a heavy heart, he went back to the drawing room. He wondered what was the matter with his uncle's family. He decided to visit them in the evening.

His father came back within half an hour. Before

Mohan could bend down to touch his feet, his father hugged him, the way people hugged each other in America. "You are all grown up now, in these five years," his father told him, looking at him up and down. "Five years is a long time," he said as he took his sandals off and placed them with the others.

Hearing them talking, Mohan's mother came out of the kitchen. "Did you get to see the priest?" she asked his father while straightening the chairs around the dining table. "Lunch is ready. Manu, go and wash your hands." She got an uplifting feeling by calling him Manu, his childhood nickname, every now and then, and reminding him to wash his hands before eating, although, he had been away and living on his own for so many years.

"The priest cannot make it this week. It has to be next Monday," his father said as Mohan followed him to the bathroom, where he got a mug of water and motioned Mohan to hold out his hands under it while he poured. "You'll be here for a while, Mohan?" he asked as he washed his own hands. His mother extended a towel for them to wipe their hands.

"For a month." He didn't tell them that he would be going back to America after that, that he had accepted a position as a postdoctoral fellow at a university in California. He knew they expected him to come back home, to India, now that he had completed his higher education. They probably assumed he had already secured a job somewhere in the country. He would tell them his plans later. He didn't want to crush their happiness so soon.

Mohan and his father ate while his mother served them. She kept bringing out dishes from the kitchen and kept telling him to have some more of this or more of that. This was how it had always been. In the past he had never given any thought to the fact that his mother didn't eat with them. Now it seemed peculiar that she had eaten all by herself all those years.

"Why don't you eat with us?" he asked his mother.

"Well, who would serve us if we needed more of something?" she replied and poured some more water into his glass. "Maybe, after you get married, I can join you two, sometimes." A thin smile spread on her face as she said this.

After they were done eating, his father went to take a nap. Mohan decided to stay at the dining table to keep his mother company. "I hope you stay with us for more than a month. It felt like ages while you were there," his mother said after taking a few bites. "I know you must have a nice job that pays lots of money lined up in one of the big cities. India needs people like you. India needs tall buildings, like in New York. They will hold so many people, so many families." Mohan was struck by her naivety. One could build as many skyscrapers in India as one wished, but the masses would only be able to stand under them, bending their necks backward to gauge how tall they were. They wouldn't be able to afford to live in them.

"I already have a job in California, another place in America." he admitted, because he didn't want to lie. He wished he could have held off telling her until she had finished her lunch.

"You are going back?" she asked, her hand freezing in the middle of picking up some food. She sat quietly, not eating. "How long you will be gone this time?" she asked after a while. Before he could respond, she said, "Like so many others, you are not coming back, are you? We were thinking about your marriage."

"I've met a girl in New York. I like her." He said this without looking at his mother. "Why don't you finish your lunch? Then we can talk." He got up, avoiding her eyes, and headed toward the bedroom where his mother had taken his things. As soon as he lay down, deep slumber overtook him and when he woke up, it was already night. He could hear his parents arguing in the next room.

***

After Mohan had left for his room, his mother had thrown her unfinished lunch into a big pail and fed it to the cow. She had remained quiet the whole afternoon and evening. She hadn't said anything to his father about what Mohan had told her. It wasn't for her to inform her husband about his own son. Let him feel the heart-wrenching pain of hearing the news from his son firsthand, as she had. Her only child was about to desert them, returning to a foreign land they knew nothing about.

Nevertheless, as she lay next to her husband in the dark night, her broken heart couldn't hold back the words. He tried to shake off what she was telling him, but he couldn't ignore his pain at the news that his son was returning to America.

"He'll be back again. Let's not worry yet," he told her, trying to muster the strength to believe his own words.

"You are lying to yourself," she told him. "What is it that you don't understand or perhaps refuse to understand? He won't be back after he marries a foreigner."

"He said that? that he is marrying this American? He sounded perplexed. "I thought you said he just told you he is in love with someone. Maybe you are assuming too much. We don't even know if she's a foreigner."

"I've never seen anyone so blind," she said with rage in her voice. "Why is he going back do you think? Don't you think they both would have come back if she wasn't a foreigner?" To her, her husband's calm seemed like indifference to her agony. The fact that he didn't express the same pain she was feeling only added to her hurt.

Even before Mohan had arrived, she had known that her son wouldn't stay much more than a month's time. She hadn't expected him to come and settle down with them, in this house, but she had thought he would at least settle somewhere in this country. She didn't want him to return to a land that was beyond her imagination, beyond the dark waves of vast oceans. Her son had written to them at the beginning of his time in America that when the sun rises over New York City, it is about to set in their small village. She was bothered by the idea that they'd hardly share any waking hours. Moreover, if he lived in America, he wouldn't be home during Diwali or Durga Puja, and her hope of visiting him and his family every so often was dashed.

***

The rest of the night, Mohan could not sleep, even after his parents had stopped arguing. He hadn't admitted the truth about his feelings to himself until his mother brought up marriage, and now he realized he could not imagine marrying anyone else other than Sophie.

Next morning, when Mohan got up, he knew that the dynamics of his family were forever altered. Until now, his parents had been like conjoined twins—living as a team, pouring all they had into family life. Now he could see they each felt alone in their sadness, not able to grasp the other's pain or understand their son.

***

The month passed quietly. The priest didn't show up, presumably because Mohan's parents had told him not to come. Now there was no need for him to look at Mohan's horoscope, etched onto the surface of a palm leaf. Some unforeseen hand had already guided Mohan's fate and planned his future with a foreigner. His parents knew that when their son got married, they would have nothing to do with it. They wouldn't even be present.

His parents became cordial but distant, acting more like friends or hosts to a guest. His mother cooked and cleaned without complaint. His father left at odd times of the day to supervise the men and women working in the family's rice fields. He would come home to eat a quick lunch and go back again into the hot midday sun. They felt a bitter satisfaction in knowing that Mohan observed their hard work and felt he had no right to show his sympathy for either of them. To them, the fact that he had ventured out on his own, to find someone to marry, justified their bearing.

Any time Mohan went out of the house, people asked him the same questions: Had he come back for good? What about getting married? He didn't want to say anything about Sophie, because he didn't want them to taunt his parents about their son marrying a foreigner. Besides, since he and Sophie hadn't planned to get married, he was sure his parents hadn't told anyone about what they assumed his plan was.

The rest of the month, he went for long walks on the banks of the Murudi River and spent time under the shade of the bamboo groves, the places he had spent his time when he visited his grandparents as a child. His leisurely strides along the river took him among the *kashatandis* swaying in the breeze and under the *gulmohars* blazing with flowers the color of blood.

He sat on the banks of the river, and he could see schools of fish swimming by him and some herons flying in circles in the distance. He could hear the squeaking from the wheels of bullock carts approaching and after a while disappearing on the road on the other side of the river. Every now and then, he heard the *ting, ting,* of bells from a bicycle or the honking of a car or jeep. He saw the silhouettes of tribal women, baskets on their heads, moving down the road in either direction. In the evening, throngs of men returned home after a hard day's work in their paddy fields. Their chatter filled the air.

The first time his parents had brought him to his ancestral home in the village to show him to his grandparents was right after his birth. He had heard the story many times. His father had been a constable at the district headquarters, which was an hour by bus from the village. That particular time, instead of taking the bus, his father had gotten permission from the police department to take the jeep assigned to him for official duties. Children, big and small, had come running out of their houses to see the jeep as it drove down the dirt road leading to the village. Some of them had run after it, stopping at his grandparents' house when the jeep stopped there. They were more interested in seeing his father, a policeman, than the new baby. They stood at a respectable distance when his parents emerged from the jeep, his mother proudly holding him for everyone to see. Then she disbursed packets of sweets to the waiting children in honor of his birth, which they ate quickly, not knowing whether this treat was to celebrate the bundle she was showing off or just a nice gesture from the policeman and his wife.

The neighbors came by to see the baby, his mother had told him, not wanting to leave, as if the baby belonged to all of them. They peered into his face and said that he had his grandmother's nose and his grandfather's long torso.

They forgot to mention any resemblance to the parents, which the parents didn't mind.

Things had changed since he was a little boy visiting the place with his parents during summers. Back then the villages had had no paved roads, no electricity, and no hospitals. Politicians had come and gone, handing out crisp ten-rupee bills to get votes from men and women who were so happy to get the free money that they forgot to ask them how they were supposed to get from place to place, how they rid the darkness from their homes, and where they should take themselves or their children when they got sick. The money would be spent in a few days, and the politicians would disappear until the next election. Time had seemed to fly over these places without altering them, leaving them in the dark.

However, this time around, when he had passed through the same villages as in years past on his way here, he had not recognized any of them. Now they looked so beautiful dotting both sides of the Murudi River, claiming their place on the face of the earth beside new paved roads. He had passed schools where children dressed in uniforms kicked balls during recess. He had seen "Hospital" signs at various places where the bus had stopped. Almost all the villages had electricity now.

Nevertheless, Mohan could not wait to leave the stifling environment of the village. Despite the modern improvements, everything seemed broken to him here, including his relationship with his parents.

The morning of his departure, the first thing his father said to him was: "Is it true that you have arranged your own marriage?" His father didn't look at him when he asked it.

"I have found a girl, if that is what you mean,"

Mohan replied. This was the closest he had come to voicing his decision to marry Sophie aloud. He had waited for his father to ask this for the whole month. Now he felt an emptiness echoing from his answer. He felt as if over the last month, his parents had steadily transferred their hopes for him from themselves and given them to him to do with as he pleased. He was now the sole owner of his life—a life without their blessings.

"What is she? A Christian? I hope not," his father said, keeping his voice emotionless.

"She is Christian," Mohan answered, knowing that this answer meant he would be shut out of their lives forever. Yet he couldn't lie to his father.

"I have nothing to say to this. But there is no need for you to return to us anymore," his father had said this in a firm voice. "The white Christians ruled us long enough. I don't want a white person or a Christian in this house," he said, turning to walk away as he spoke. These were his last words to his son.

His father left the house to attend the paddy fields. Mohan knew that his father could never allow him to bring Sophie to visit this house. His parents would be so ashamed to see her in a western dress, not covered by a six-yard saree. As a Christian, she won't be allowed to enter the temple to worship their family deity. She was already unholy from eating meat from cows. No amount of penance or ritual could convert her into a Hindu. His father had made up his mind to give up his son rather than deal with the humiliation presented by him. He had to keep up appearances in the eyes of neighbors.

Before he set out on the long journey back to the place, he would try to make his home, Mohan touched his mother's feet, asking for blessings. She put her hand on his head and blessed him. Like the first time he had left for America, his mother had packed food for him to eat on the way. She stood there on the veranda with a distant look, wondering what the future held for each of them. She hoped that once Mohan arrived in America, he would realize his folly and come back home. It would be fine with her even if he married someone from this country over there, even if he stayed in America. At least then they could think of going and visiting their son and his family in that foreign land.

As he started to walk toward the road, leaving his parents' house behind, Mohan felt an urge to turn around and say good-bye to his mother once more, but he was afraid to look back. What if his mother had already gone inside, leaving him alone and exposed in front of the villagers? As long as she stood there, nobody could deny his connection to this place or his past life.

When Mohan reached the bend in the road, he looked back abruptly. His mother was still standing there, a small figure melting into the walls of the house, raised hands waving at him. He didn't know whether he would ever see her again, but he saw the omen he had been hoping for. He knew that someday he would come back to this place. He turned right and walked through the bamboo groves.

He saw the bus coming, surrounded by its own smoke and dust. With emptiness in his heart, he climbed into it. As the bus wound through the village and crossed the river, the paddy fields came into view, stretching on both sides of the road. He looked this way and that, trying to get a glimpse of his father. Finally, he spotted a big umbrella. His father was stooped under it, his back toward the road. Mohan kept looking in that direction until the whole scenery became a speck in his memory.

Chapter Two

With a broken heart, Mohan came back to America after a month-long visit to his parents. His father had barred him from setting foot in their home. According to his parents, he was committing the worst possible offense a son could commit—he was probably going to marry a foreigner, who also happened to be a Christian, without consulting them. Once the thought of his parents had kept him alive in a faraway land. He had imagined his mother standing outside their home and waiting for him, his father working in the paddy fields, thinking about his son's future. Now Mohan was a stranger among his own people, and the place and the river he had left behind would recede from his heart, making room for his new life in America.

For the past five years, while in America, he didn't have time to think about hopes and aspirations. In the jumbled configuration of what was expected of him, his desires had seemed too abstract and unfathomable. As the past years unspooled in front of him, the silhouette of his unlived life came into focus and he was resolved to give an undeniable shape to his dreams.

***

It was the last week of August 1969 when Mohan arrived in New York's Kennedy Airport for the first time. Once he got down from the plane, he followed the long, zigzagging line to customs and waited behind the yellow line, his Indian passport in hand. Mohan was hungry and thirsty. He had eaten little during the long Trans World Airlines flight, which had departed from Bombay in the middle of the night. As the line inched forward, his excitement about going abroad for graduate education was mixed with apprehension about the new country. Everything he read about this place—the long winters, the snow and the food—sounded so different than what he had been accustomed to in his first twenty-two years. He thought about what he'd left behind—family and friends, his life nurtured by the familiarity of his surroundings. He would miss his mother's home-cooked meals, and hanging out with his friends during the summer breaks. Looking around at the crowd, he felt lonely all of a sudden. However, he told himself that he would just have to concentrate on his coursework, and time would pass, and he would return to his familiar life.

Mohan had traveled for almost two days by train to reach Bombay for his flight. His mother had packed some food she had made for him in small polythene bags—puffed rice and mixed vegetable fritters, fried cauliflower and potatoes rolled inside *chapatties*, some *besan ladoos*—food that wouldn't perish in the dead heat of Indian summer. She had poured *lassi* made out of buttermilk into a glass bottle and placed it standing upright in his handbag. She had urged him to eat well, to look after himself, and to write to them when he arrived in that foreign land of America.

After the train left the platform at Bhubaneswar, Mohan opened the food packets and spread them on his lap. It was past noon. He took a bite from a chapatti roll as he stared out the window. Suddenly, he felt tears collecting in his eyes. As he pulled out the handkerchief from his pants pocket, a hundred-rupee note fell from it. In spite of his protest that the note was useless in the country he was going to, his father had put it in his hand and looked away. His mother had taken the note, wrapped it in the handkerchief, and put it in the pocket of the pants he was going to wear. The faces of his parents rushed past him along with the landscape as the train gained momentum and took him farther away from the place where he had grown up.

Mohan tried to chew the bite of chapatti slowly, but he felt a lump in his throat when he tried to swallow it. He put the food back in his handbag and took a few sips of lassi. It was too thick. All he wanted was a glass of water. He thought of the water his mother kept in an earthen pot with a long narrow neck. The porous pot kept the water cool even in the hottest summer months. When he visited home during the college breaks, his mother always kept more than one of those pots filled with cold water, so that they would never run out.

It took the train a day and a half to reach Bombay. Mohan tried to sleep, but people kept jostling past him to get off and getting on at various stations on the way. The hawkers calling out, "*Chai, a Babu chai*" kept waking him from a dream-filled sleep, and every time he woke, he was struck again by the feeling of missing the place and people he had left behind.

It was late afternoon when the train arrived in Bombay. It passed through enormous slums as it approached the station. Naked children, stray dogs, and half-clad women in petticoats roamed outside broken tin houses with tin roofs. They didn't look up to see who had come to their city or who was about to leave. Mohan hadn't seen slums like this before. He wondered about the day-to-day lives of the slum-dwellers, and the poverty they lived in made him sad.

When the train stopped, people swarmed out of it like bees, pulling their belongings in a hurry, pushing and elbowing one another. Mohan waited until the compartment he was in cleared somewhat, then climb down the couple of steps to the platform. He inched his way out, trying to locate the taxi stand. He saw a sign for the restrooms. He hadn't used one on the train for the last eight hours. He made his way and opened the door to the men's room, but the stench of urine propelled him back. He decided to wait until he reached the airport.

The sun was going down when the taxi pulled up at Santacruz International Airport. It had taken almost an hour to cover the distance of eighteen kilometers from the Central railway station to the airport. Mohan handed the driver the hundred-rupee note his father had given him and almost snatched the change as he ran to the arrival gate. His stomach was hurting, and his full bladder was about to burst open. A police officer holding a gun with long bayonet stopped him at the gate and demanded to see his passport and ticket. Once he was let into the airport, Mohan spotted a sign for the restrooms in the distance. He took quick steps in that direction, and he'd barely unzipped his pants when a stream of urine flew into the urinal.

It took a long time to go through the luggage check-in, customs, and security clearance. Men in khaki sat with an air of great importance in their respective booths. They asked for documents, scrutinized them from various angles, and stamped the pages with undeniable authority. After they were done, they returned the passports and all other relevant documents to the passengers, as if they were giving them back their destinies.

It would be a while before Mohan's plane took off. Mohan found a corner seat in the waiting room and opened his carry-on bag to check the food his mother had packed. The buttermilk *lassi* had turned to curds in the heat. A faint sour smell was coming from the packet containing the chapatti rolls. They must have gone bad too. Mohan got up to throw out the spoiled food. He was tired, sleepy, and hungry. He bought a bottle of water at a stand, and when he returned, to his chagrin, the rickety chairs were all occupied. A few inconsiderate men had pulled two or three together and were sprawling on them.

Mohan sat down on the floor, his back against a wall, and opened his bag again. From the fresh aroma of the *besan ladoo*s, he could tell that they were unspoiled. He ate them one after another, washing them down with the water he'd bought. He decided against buying any food at the airport so as not to spend the few dollars he carried with him. He would need the money once he arrived in New York.

The intercom kept announcing flight numbers and boarding gates, and after each announcement, the waiting areas became a little less crowded. After a while, Mohan found an empty seat and settled there to wait until his flight time. The thought about his parents and his friends back at home occupied his mind. His parents must have felt really sad about his going away to a country they had no knowledge of. He had told them he wouldn't be able to visit them from America very often. They knew from the price of his plane ticket how expensive it was to travel between that country and India. He told himself that it would be a matter of just four or five years before he returned home.

Finally, five minutes after two in the morning, the intercom announced the boarding for the TWA flight to New York. Passengers stood at the boarding gate, some trying to cut the line and go ahead, as if the plane would leave them behind if they stayed in their places in the queue, observing some basic decency. Mohan stood toward the end of the line, holding his Indian passport with the boarding card tucked inside it. To an observer, he wouldn't have seemed nervous exactly, but one could tell that he didn't have the air of confidence of a seasoned traveler. His small carry-on bag was lighter since he had disposed of the *lassi* bottle and spoiled food. The long journey with little to eat had made him weak in his limbs, but he stood with patience as the line crawled forward.

By the time he boarded the plane and got to his assigned seat, the overhead luggage compartments were overflowing with the belonging of other passengers who had been ahead of him. His was a middle seat, and the old man already occupying the aisle seat swung his legs outward to let Mohan pass. Mohan was able to squeeze his small carry-on underneath the seat in front of him and sat down. Streams of passengers kept entering the plane and kept eyeing at the overhead bins, but the stewardesses had closed all of them by then, since they were full to the brim.

A man who looked younger than Mohan came and stood in the aisle waiting for the old man and Mohan to get out so that he could get in. Once he sat down and stashed his bag under the seat, Mohan and the old man returned to their seats, and Mohan fumbled for his seat belt. The younger man helped him find the belt closer to him and then clicked his own belt closed.

It was four o'clock in the morning, Indian time, when the plane rolled out of its gate. The window shutters were all pulled down. Mohan longed to take one last good look at the country he would be leaving behind for years to come, but he hesitated to ask the young man to open the shutter. All of a sudden, the young man lifted the window cover a bit, like he could read Mohan's mind. Amid the morning fog, Mohan saw lights in all directions—low light posts lining the runway, light from various airport buildings, and once the plane took off, the lights of Bombay twinkling below like stars.

As he leaned back in his seat, Mohan wondered if his parents were already up or whether they had slept at all. He had always felt the burden of being the only child. Now that he was leaving them for so long, his worry for them settled inside him like a stone. They were not that old, but he was afraid that the weight of his absence would crush them.

When he was growing up, sometimes Mohan had the feeling of responsibility that came with being an only child, something he had no control over. He missed having a brother or a sister, but he played with his cousins when they got together during summer breaks. His parents were always generous about his bringing friends home. His mother fed them day and night without complaint, to make up for the sibling he lacked. Only much later, when he was in college, did he learn that soon after his birth, his mother had been pregnant and she had almost died in childbirth, and the baby was stillborn.

The stewardesses in his section of the plane, a young white woman and a slightly older black woman, started serving beverages from a rolling cart. Mohan asked for a Coke and tried to stay awake until the snacks were served, whereas the passengers on either side of him had already fallen asleep, their heads lolling to find comfortable positions. Mohan assumed that they hadn't had to travel for two days to get to Bombay, and their families must have fed them heartily in preparation for the journey.

After about half an hour, the cart came rolling by with snack boxes. Mohan had not had a proper meal since he'd left his parents' home. The stewardess handed him a box with a big V on one corner, indicating a vegetarian snack. He ate the vegetable cutlet, sandwiched between two pieces of bread, as he sipped water from a plastic cup. He could barely keep his eyes open by then. Before long he was asleep.

When Mohan woke to a gentle tap on his shoulder, the interior of the plane was filled with bright morning sunlight. He had slept well in spite of the cramped space he was in. The young man in the window seat was half standing, waiting to get out. Mohan got up and let the man pass. Then Mohan glanced around and saw the older man standing on the other side of the aisle talking to someone. Mohan followed the younger man and stood in the queue for the lavatory. The food carts had started to roll again, the stewardesses handing out breakfast, and the burnt aroma of coffee filled the air.

Mohan and the other two men in his row returned to their seats before the arrival of the cart. Mohan looked at his watch. It was noon Indian time. He subtracted four and a half hours from that. It would be seven-thirty in the morning in London. In two hours, they would be in London. There would be a three-hour layover there, and then from London to New York, it would be another eight hours. He subtracted another five hours, and his scheduled arrival time of three-thirty matched his calculation. The plane would be flying west, moving with the sun.

The passengers on either side of him seemed refreshed from the long naps they'd taken, and they tried to talk to each other over Mohan while he tried to eat his breakfast of leathery scrambled eggs and a bun. The orange juice smelled like a certain medicine, but he couldn't say for sure which one. The other two passengers had already finished their breakfasts, and that was the topic of their discussion—how bad the food was, how these foreign airlines never served proper Indian food.

The seat-belt sign went on as the cart rolled between rows of seats. Empty boxes and glasses were being collected. Finally, the stewardesses had to sit down and put their seat belts like everyone else. The passengers on either side of Mohan sat quietly, looking straight ahead. The plane circled over London at a low altitude. Mohan leaned a bit to the left. He could see the earth below—a tangle of fields, houses, and roads.

When the plane landed, the older man stood to get his suitcase from the overhead compartment. He tried to pull it out, but his short stature and the weight of the luggage made it hard. Mohan got up and helped him out. The younger man had collected his belongings from under the seat in front of him and moved into the queue to exit the plane. The two of them moved forward in the line little by little and exited without saying good-bye to Mohan.

The flight from London's Heathrow to New York's JFK Airport was uneventful. Half of the plane was empty. Mohan had all three seats to himself. After a lunch of pasta, which he barely ate, he stretched himself on the seats and fell into a deep sleep.

By the time he woke up in New York, it was mid-day. The customs line for incoming passengers at JFK moved at an even slower pace than the customs line at Bombay's Santacruz Airport. Finally, Mohan proceeded to the booth, which was occupied by a white man. He looked at Mohan and then at all the documents, including his admission papers to the graduate school, stamped the passport without any fanfare, and let him go. Mohan liked the way the customs officials worked. They did their duties without exerting undue authority on anyone, not intimidating the people they relied upon to build this country of immigrants.

Once Mohan collected his single piece of luggage from the conveyor belt, he felt lost. Until then, his journey to this faraway land had been all taken care of by the logistics of travel. He had known where he had to be when, and on the plane, like everybody else, he had been fed, no matter that he didn't like the food. He had a seat assigned to him, and regardless of the time, he had fallen into deep slumber between meals. He had eaten, drunk, and slept like a newborn baby, but now he would be required to find his own way in the new world he had landed in.

He followed the signs for ground transportation and stepped outside into a sunny day. There were taxis, buses, and hotel shuttles waiting to take passengers wherever they needed to go. Everything seemed so disciplined—the drivers behind the vehicles waiting in line to pick people up, the people waiting in line to get inside the vehicles. There was no hollering or stampedes. Like machines, the drivers got out, shoved the luggage into the bellies of the buses or the trunks of the taxis, and motioned the passengers to get in.

Mohan took a bus to the Jamaica train station, where he boarded a train to Long Island. The train passed through the outskirts of the city before heading into the suburbs. Cars, people, and stores were everywhere. He felt as if he were in Bombay again, except for the fact that Bombay had mostly brown people. Here, they were all colors and shapes and sizes. By the time he arrived at the Port Jefferson station, it was almost evening. A fellow graduate student had offered to let Mohan stay the night with him. He woke up in the middle of the night in a strange room, thinking his parents were asking him something. Once he realized that they were half a world away, he went back to sleep.

Chapter Three

It was the first snowfall of the season and the first ever for Mohan. By the time he woke up that morning, big drifts of fluffy snow had covered the ground. It wasn't December yet, but he had heard that winter in Long Island could be brutal. A northerly wind was blowing from the sound, and gusts of wind pushed the snow in all directions. Snow had covered the clumps of pine trees, and in the semidarkness of the morning, they looked like white ghosts.

Mohan had gotten a one-room apartment on top of a beauty salon in Port Jefferson, just across the road from the port. His advisor had helped arrange the room for him. He would have preferred to live on campus but had been told that no on-campus housing was available. People who lived all around the State University of New York at Stony Brook, in places near and far such as Port Jefferson, Sound Beach, or Miller Place, advertised houses or small parts of them to be rented by members of the university community. Mohan was glad that the place he was living was connected to the campus by public transportation, in case he missed the campus shuttle.

He raised the blinds on the window facing the port. It was completely empty that early morning. He wanted to go back to sleep but had to finish his morning rituals before the customers showed up at the beauty salon. His landlady and the owner of the shop, Francesca, an elderly matron of Italian origin, was fussy about any noise or smell of curry coming from upstairs while the salon was open. It didn't bother Mohan most of the time, because during the weekdays he was at the university, all day. By the time he returned in the late evenings, the last customers were about to leave.

On Saturdays, he stayed in bed a little longer and woke up to the sound of Francesca vacuuming the salon before it opened. Soon after, her daughter, Julia, would park her car, a blue Chrysler Valiant, behind the fading green building that housed the salon and the two upstairs rentals. Mohan was told that the other unit was bigger. It was a regular one-bedroom apartment with a separate bathroom and a combined kitchen and living room, and it was rented only to couples with children, whereas his one room contained everything—a little sink, a stove, and a small partition with a toilet and a shower.

He had heard noises coming from the other apartment—the crying of a toddler and the mother trying to hush the child in the morning, toy cars racing across the floor and hitting the walls, and the father yelling repeatedly in an unfamiliar american accent, "This is the last time I'm telling you!" Sometimes the child's loud shrieks penetrated the wall and seemed to go through Mohan's head like arrows. Sometimes at night, Mohan woke up to creaking noises and soft moaning coming from the other side. All this took place when the salon was closed.

Mohan had not run into the other family yet, but he knew for sure that they were not from India. The aroma of food being cooked sometimes wafted from the other apartment. It was not the smell of cumin, coriander, or curry powder but something more delicate and subtle. He cooked the same dinner day after day—rice with vegetables and a piece of chicken thigh, sprinkled with salt and curry powder he bought at the supermarket, which tasted nothing like curry powder back home. Often, he craved something different, and he wondered about what his neighbors were cooking.

On that snowy morning, Mohan stood near the window watching for the university shuttle. Usually, he could see it from quite far off as it rolled down the hill. That morning, he could not see very far because of the snow. As he was watching, he heard the child start crying at the top of his lungs. The mother tried to placate him by saying something softly, but the child would not stop crying. Then Mohan heard the father's impatient and severe voice: "Stop, now." But the child kept wailing and repeating what sounded like "Out."

It was almost opening time for Francesca and Julia. The child hadn't let up with his screams. Mohan was familiar with his temper tantrums by now. He wondered how the mother managed him the whole day when the salon was open. Surely the landlady didn't put up with that kind of commotion coming from overhead during business hours.

There was no sign of the shuttle yet. It had stopped snowing, but there was what looked like a foot of snow on the ground. A ferry had arrived at the port, and flocks of people disembarked as usual, but nobody was waiting at the port to get on. Mohan saw a big yellow truck coming down the hill, pushing piles of snow to one side of the road. Near the port, it turned around and went back the opposite way, and piles of snow gathered on the other side of the road.

Now that the main street was clear, cars entered the port, and people were dropped off and picked up. Mohan stayed near the window waiting for the university shuttle. The child was still crying to be taken out.

Mohan heard the neighbors' door open, and out of curiosity, he walked away from the window and headed to his door. He stepped out and started to descend the stairs but turned back once he saw a man going down ahead of him. He ran back to his window and parted the curtains slightly to get a look at the man, his neighbor.

The man was walking away from the building. He looked short and stocky under layers of winter clothing. His head was covered with a hood to protect him from the blowing snow. He walked a small distance down the main road and then took a side street and disappeared from view.

There was still no sign of the shuttle. Frustrated, Mohan abandoned the thought of going to the university that day. For a few moments, he wondered what to do. Then he tore a piece of paper from his notepad and sat down to write a letter to his parents:

Dear Ma and Baba,

Hope you are both in good health and spirits. My classes are going fine. Did you go to town to see Durga Puja this year? It has started snowing here. It has been so cold, and from what I hear, the cold weather will continue until the end of April. Not to worry. I have bought myself a really thick wool coat. It will easily last the next five years. Ma, I'm going to try the *chana masala* recipe you sent in your last letter, since it looks like I will be stuck in the apartment for today. I send my *pranam* to both of you.

Your loving son,
Mohan

This would be his second letter to his parents in the four months since he'd arrived. Mohan wanted the letter to be matter-of-fact. He didn't want to tell them about his busy schedule at the university or how little time he had to cook a proper meal. He didn't write about his lack of social life either. He didn't want them to worry about him. The post took almost a month each way, but he was always happy to get the news from home, even though it was a month old.

He folded the letter neatly and went to see if he had the right kind of spice to cook *chana*. He found some curry powder his mother had packed, but he would have to wait until the salon closed in the evening. By this time, the child had stopped crying.

That snowy day was the first time since he'd left India, that Mohan had some time to himself. He made a cup of tea and opened the small cupboard to see if any sweets were left. Everything his mother had packed was gone, and he settled for a shortbread biscuit. As he sipped the cup of tea, he heard slogans and went to the window. A group of young men and women were marching from the direction of the port in the snow, protesting the Vietnam War. More protestors were getting down from the ferry and joining them. A group of school-age children was in the middle of building a huge snowman, their backs turned toward the protestors.

By now, Mohan was used to frequent demonstrations on and off campus. He could feel that America was in the throes of social and moral upheaval. The women's liberation movement was growing. On his way home from the university, Mohan often saw bras hanging from tree branches, which had made him blush in the beginning, though now he had grown used to it. And the year before, Martin Luther King Jr. had been shot dead, and racial tensions were high. Even though Mohan had been in India at the time of the assassination, he remembered how gloomy the university campus felt that day. He had felt an affinity toward King because of the Gandhian philosophy of nonviolence he'd followed. And then, there was the antiwar movement.

Mohan had read that the hippies were mostly blamed for the social revolution that was taking shape. Just as he landed in USA, their movement had reached its pinnacle at the Woodstock music festival. Over four hundred thousand youths had gathered to listen to famous musicians, including the Indian sitar star Ravi Shankar. Mohan's father had even written to him asking about the huge gathering at the concert, which he had read about in the newspaper. Mohan didn't like the hippies' tattered clothes and long unkempt hair. To him, the hippie ideal of free love seemed unchaste. He thought the hippies were wasting their time without any direction.

But as he watched out the window, Mohan didn't see any hippies in the crowd. The protestors all looked like ordinary college students, young people whose futures were hanging in a balance as the war continued. The Nixon administration was planning to draft young people by random selection. Mohan watched the nightly news on the small television that had come with the apartment. The television anchors reported about the My Lai massacre in Vietnam, and men walking on the moon in the same breath.

As the protestors waited at a red light to cross the street, a man in a bulky coat caught Mohan's attention — it was his neighbor, whom he had seen descending the stairs earlier. Mohan marveled why the man would involve himself with the protest when he had a wife and a child to take care of. His son had probably been crying to be taken out to play in the snow, as other children were doing. Instead, his father had left to join the protest. Mohan watched the man with intense curiosity as the light turned green and the group crossed the road and headed in the direction of the university.

Mohan left the window and tried to relax on his one rickety chair with the cup of tea. He pulled out the midterm exams from his backpack and tried to grade them. These were from an engineering class that was a requirement for architecture students. He had finished grading two problems for the whole class, and three more problems were waiting. Methodically, he began grading and adding the numbers. He needed to finish the grading that day. The next day, Professor Gutenberg would decide how much to curve the exam and enter the grades.

It took him a while to go through all the problems. Once he finished, he put the exams back in the backpack, and as he was getting ready to boil water for another cup of tea, he heard the neighbors' door open and steps descending the stairs. The small child's chatter penetrated the walls. "Out . . . out, Mama. Dada out." Mohan could tell that the boy was in a good mood. He went back to the window and observed the mother holding her son's hand and proceeding toward the pile of snow left behind by the other children.

Mohan watched her as she bent, her back toward him, to help her son build a little snowman near the big one. Then, all of a sudden, he heard the boy scream as he kicked the little snowman, breaking it up into crumbly snow. Unperturbed, the mother started to make another one, a much bigger one—a big round belly, a head on top of that with no sign of a neck in between, and two little stumps as hands. Mohan could see the smile on the child's face. He wanted a big snowman like the other children had left behind. The child collected two sticks and handed them to his mother, who in turn stuck them into the stumps so that they looked like arms.

After they were done, the woman turned and faced the green building. Mohan moved away from the window but kept watching her from behind the soiled curtains. She took the cap from her head and put it on the head of the snowman. The child took off his own hat and gave it to his mother to do the same. She hung it on one of the arms.

Now Mohan had seen the whole family for the first time—first the husband alone, then the mother and the child. From a distance, in the fading evening sun, the woman looked young. She was medium built with an oval face. Dark brown hair covered her shoulders, and some small strands fell over her cheeks. She wore brown ankle boots on top of her jeans and a short black coat. Her face was strikingly white above the coat.

Mohan felt like a thief, watching the woman from his window. He slowly turned and went back to the chair. The sun was about to set. He put a pot of water on the stove to make rice. He would have to wait to cook the canned chickpeas and spices until Francesca closed the salon doors, which wouldn't be for at least another hour. As he picked up an engineering book from the bed to study for the course he was taking, he heard the happy voices of the mother and son climbing the stairs.

After a while, Mohan switched on the small television and began chopping onions for the *chana masala*. Soon after, he heard Francesca pull the front door of the salon shut with a bang to make sure it was closed. By now, from the intensity of the sound, he could tell it was her. As soon as he heard the mother and daughter walking away, their voices getting fainter, he put some oil in a pan. Once it was hot, he dumped the chickpeas, onion, and curry powder, everything at the same time. The smell of raw spice filled the small room, and he headed to the window to open it.

Frigid air from the sea blew in, and quickly he decided to pull the window back down, but it got stuck at an angle and wouldn't close.

For almost ten minutes, Mohan struggled to close the window. The heating in the room worked constantly, yet it felt as if he were inside a refrigerator. Then he noticed his neighbor—the man—approaching the building. He couldn't decide whether to call Francesca or ask the man for help. Finally, Mohan opened the door and stood on the landing to catch his neighbor as he climbed up.

"Hello," Mohan greeted the man.

"Your window doesn't close, either?" the man replied. "You will soon learn not to open the fucking thing." Saying this, the man stepped past Mohan into his room and went straight to the window. Instead of pushing it from the top, he jiggled the bottom of the sash at both ends until it was back in line with the frame. Then he slowly pulled it all the way down and pushed it hard from the top to make sure it was sealed.

Before Mohan could thank him for his help, the man said, "If I were you, I would leave this thing alone. What are you cooking?" He looked toward the cooking range. "Man . . . it smells good."

"I was trying my mother's chickpea recipe," Mohan replied. "I'm not sure how it is. Would you like to try some?" He hoped that the man would say no. Mohan thought he would say that his wife was waiting to have dinner with him. There was no noise coming from the other side of the wall. Mohan thought the child must have been tired and gone to bed.

Without answering, the man went and sat down on the rickety chair and looked at the television, which was still on. "The moron is at it again," he said it, dragging the chair closer to the set. It was one of Nixon's speeches pushing for a draft lottery for the Vietnam War.

Mohan put some rice on a plate, topped it with chickpeas, and handed it to the man with a fork and napkin and a glass of water. "By the way, I'm Mohan," he said. He had decided he should share his food with the man since he was grateful for his help.

"I'm Chris. Oh hell . . . this is so good," he said, still keeping an eye on the screen as he turned halfway toward Mohan. He didn't ask Mohan to join him. In any case, Mohan had only that one plate.

"Your son is very cute..." Mohan volunteered to keep the conversation going. In his next letter to his parents, he could write about the man, who was enjoying half of what Mohan had cooked without even acknowledging that Mohan probably wanted to eat it.

"It's my wife's son," replied Chris, collecting the last morsels of food with his fork and licking it. After drinking the glass of water, he wiped his mouth with the paper napkin and got up to leave. "Thank your mother for the recipe," he said, heading toward the door.

"Thanks for your help," Mohan said, walking after him to see him out. He felt weird about the whole encounter with Chris. His swearing and offhanded remarks hadn't seemed funny to Mohan at all. The revelation that his wife's son wasn't his child seemed strange to him. Chris had taken the food for granted, as if it had been owed to him in exchange for closing the window. No thank-you, no goodnight.

After he'd closed his door, Mohan realized that Chris had left the soiled plate on the chair. He took it to the sink and soaked it in soap and hot water for five minutes before rinsing. The rice and the chickpeas on the stove were cold to the touch. He dumped the rice into the chickpeas and warmed them together. Then he sat down on the bed, legs stretched out, with the dinner. He decided not to write anything to his parents about his neighbor. They would think of him as a bad influence on their son because of his unrefined manners and the fact that he had married a woman who already had a child.

It had been a long day. Mohan ate slowly while watching the *CBS Evening News*. In his student days in India, he had paid little attention to the news, but now it made him feel more informed about the outside world. He liked the anchor of this program, Walter Cronkite, whose dignified presence had made all the troubling news bearable.

President Nixon was about to give another press conference on the Vietnam War. People were eager for the war to end, but instead, that evening, Nixon announced the executive order for the United States Selective Service to randomly select people to serve in the war. Mohan thought of the kids as young as nineteen years old, who now must be afraid they'd be sent to fight on the front line. Drafting such young kids seemed cruel and pointless to him. Mohan knew that he was safe as a noncitizen on a student visa, and after he finished his graduate work, he would be back in India. At the same time, he didn't like the chaotic atmosphere of his host country, with its constant protests and student walkouts. That night he fell asleep feeling uneasy about the future.

Within the next week, the United States Selective Service conducted two lotteries to draft young men, aged nineteen to twenty-six, and Mohan saw more unrest spread throughout the country. At the university, students walked out of classes on a regular basis. Mohan tried to focus on his work, leaving for campus early and coming back late.

He hadn't come across his neighbors again, but it seemed to him that Chris screamed at the child with more vigor now in response to his crying demands, and the mother's efforts to pacify her son sounded more urgent. Now instead of hearing the couple's lovemaking, he heard them arguing, sometimes waking him up from sleep.

As Mohan got busy with the final grading and preparing for his own exams, he started coming home quite late at night. Sometimes he ate his evening meal at the university cafeteria rather than taking the trouble to cook at home. The streets and the neighborhood were quiet when he got down from the shuttle. The customers at the beauty salon were long gone, and usually no sounds came from his neighbors that late, not even their arguments.

During the Christmas break, in the silence of his room at night, Mohan felt lonely. He realized he missed the child's crying, the man's yelling, and the woman's soft voice trying to comfort her son. He knew his neighbors must have gone somewhere.

Then, right after Christmas, they appeared one morning as Mohan was heading out to the nearby grocery store to buy food. The university was closed for the winter break, and he had nowhere to go. The students he knew at the department had all left for home to spend Christmas with their families. That morning he had tried to study for his qualifying exam, which was almost a year away, but hadn't been able to concentrate. He hadn't eaten much of a breakfast because he didn't have much food at home.

As Mohan opened the outer door, a cold wind beat against his face. He pulled his hood over his head and proceeded to cross Main Street. Right then, a boat docked at the port, and people started pouring out into the cold air. The grocery store was two blocks down. On his way, he met Francesca, who greeted him in a hurry and continued toward the salon. As Mohan walked quickly, he saw his neighbors—the husband dragging a big suitcase and the woman carrying her son—coming from the boat. Chris waved at him from a distance, and Mohan waved back.

After lunch, Mohan wrote a letter to his parents asking about their health and his uncle's family. His father had written about his uncle's son, who had been admitted to college that summer but had dropped out for no reason. While growing up, Mohan had always sensed a jealousy from his uncle's family. Because Mohan's parents had lived in the town, his uncle's family in the village had felt inferior, and this had manifested in many ways. His uncle's family attributed every success of his father to his living in town, though Mohan's grandfather had given equal opportunity to both his sons as they were growing up. The display of envy became more apparent as Mohan kept doing well in his studies and continued with higher education.

Mohan told his parents about the snow and the cold and wrote that things were fine with him. Everything at the university would remain closed until the day after the New Year. Classes wouldn't start for another three weeks. He didn't write anything about his neighbors. He heard their usual commotion coming from the other side of the wall, and the place felt normal again.

Chapter Four

It was almost the end of April, and the piles of snow blackened by pollution from cars had finally all melted. Mohan could not wait for the cold weather to go away. In a little over a month, the spring semester would be over, and he would be working on a research project under a professor during the summer. Life had been all routines since he'd arrived from India. It consisted of teaching, grading, taking classes, shopping, cooking, and, if time permitted, writing letters to his parents. He hadn't been to New York City yet.

With the improved weather, the beauty salon downstairs filled with patrons, and Mohan could hear them chatting away. On his way to the university, he saw them coming and going. Most of them were elderly ladies whose lips and nails were always painted. In the beginning, they had looked comical to him in their thick makeup and dresses that covered their bodies like pillowcases. But now Mohan had gotten used to seeing these ladies and liked the way they carried themselves. There was an air of dignity about them. Age hadn't robbed the wills of these women to live as they pleased. Back at home, ladies in that age group shunned fancy sarees and any makeup. They were defined by their place in the family, mother-in-law or grandmother. They stepped aside to let the younger generation revel in everything lavish and ornate. Mohan thought about his mother, how hard she worked, and felt sad about her. Nevertheless, he thought that his parents loved each other and they were happy.

Sometimes, mostly at night, Mohan thought about the couple next door. He had met the whole family once, at the grocery store. Chris had introduced his wife. Her name was Sophie. She had been holding the hand of the toddler, and she had simply said, "This is Andy," and gone back to selecting apples. Mohan had noticed Chris leaving for a day or two, then, reappearing again. He assumed that Chris was going to participate in protests. Even though, he thought that Chris must be associated with the university, he had never seen him on campus.

Mohan thought about the family's dynamics. The first time they'd met, it had been clear to Mohan that Chris didn't care for the child. Mohan wondered how he had met his wife and why they had gotten married. They could not have been married long if the child had already existed by that time. What bothered Mohan most was that lately he could hear them arguing more and more. He would put his ear to the wall when he heard them. Their voices were too muffled for him to make out what they were saying, yet, they had the sharpness of metal grinding against metal. These weren't typical husband-wife fights.

Then it happened one night. They started arguing, like most nights. First, the voices were low, then they got louder and louder. Their argument had woken Mohan up, and he heard the child crying. They got quiet, and it sounded as if the child went back to sleep. After a while, they were at it again, arguing bitterly. Mohan was fully awake this time. There was nobody to hear them other than him, and if it occurred to them that he was listening, neither of them cared.

"I saved you! Don't you realize?" Chris was screaming at the top of his lungs. Each word penetrated the wall and landed on Mohan's side.

"You married me to dodge the draft, didn't you?" she shot back. "Now you're safe, even though you don't like the child. So, what's the matter with you?"

"I should never have married a pregnant whore," Chris said. There was a thud, as if he had punched the wall. Mohan put the pillow over his head and lay still. There was nothing for him to do. He was too new to the country to help anyone. He wished he hadn't met Chris, hadn't met any of them. He felt scared. What if Chris became violent?

"Get out!" Sophie shouted. "Get out, before I call the police." Mohan heard their door open and the noise of things being thrown out. The child had started crying again. Someone stepped out, and the door closed. Mohan heard Chris banging against the door for a while and shouting to be let back in, then, there was the sound of him going down the stairs and leaving.

After that, Mohan couldn't sleep. It was clear the husband and wife didn't care for each other. Each had gotten married to do a favor for the other, and the marriage had been doomed from the beginning. Mohan felt sorry for the child. From their first meeting, he hadn't liked Chris. Mohan had known he had a crude manner, but the way he'd called his wife a whore was beyond Mohan's imagination.

After a while he got up and sat on the edge of the bed. He felt thirsty but didn't want to turn on the faucet for the fear of being heard. He tiptoed to the window and stood in the dark, looking out toward the port. The area in front of the marina was empty, except for some parked cars reflecting back the light of the streetlamps. There was no sign of Chris. Mohan went to the sink and got a glass of water. Everything was quiet on the other side of the wall. He thought that the child must be asleep, since he wasn't crying. Mohan went back to bed but couldn't fall asleep till early morning. He thought that he heard a soft sobbing coming from the woman.

***

In the beginning of May, instead of ending the war in Vietnam, Nixon began sending troops to Cambodia. Combined with the draft lottery, this new development enraged the draft-age college students. Antiwar protests heated up on campuses across the country, including Stony Brook's. One day on his way to the cafeteria, Mohan encountered a group of about two hundred students marching down the campus's main road, bringing traffic to a halt. At the front of the crowd was Chris.

Mohan hadn't seen him since he'd been kicked out of the apartment next door, and he was surprised to encounter him on campus. As Mohan stood facing the oncoming demonstrators, he heard sirens behind him. When he turned around, he saw two police cars heading toward the crowd. He decided not to go to the cafeteria and walked fast toward the library. That was when he heard Chris call at the top of his lungs, "Wait! Wait! Mohan, wait!"

Mohan started walking faster, pretending not to hear Chris. He didn't want to get involved with him, or with the police. Hearing his name in that crowd was unnerving. He walked faster and faster, but Chris caught up with him and tapped his right shoulder from behind. "What's the matter with you, man? I've been yelling like crazy. Couldn't you hear me?"

"What do you want? With all this noise ..." Mohan said, trying to hide his annoyance with this man he hardly knew.

"Can you give this to Sophie?" Saying this, Chris handed a creased and folded piece of paper to Mohan.

Before Mohan could respond, Chris had run back to the crowd.

That was when Mohan heard a police officer shouting through a bullhorn, telling the crowd to disperse. Instead, the marchers moved closer to the first police cruiser. Mohan hid behind a big bush and watched from there as someone threw a bottle onto one of the cars. The policemen threw tear gas canisters into the crowd, and people started running all over. Mohan's eyes were stinging, and he ran into the library to wash his face in the bathroom.

He was still clutching the note Chris had given him when he reached the bathroom, and he put it in his shirt pocket. His heart quickened at the thought of being the messenger for a man who could be in trouble with the police. Mohan felt tempted to read what was on the paper and flush it down the toilet. He pulled out the folded note and examined it. As he was about to open it, he felt his heart racing faster at the thought of the disgusting act he was contemplating, and he put the paper back in his pocket. By the time he left the library, there were more police cruisers around the campus, and people were being handcuffed and put into vans.

In the evening, on his way home, Mohan thought about the note. From the shape the piece of paper was in, he tried to judge as to when Chris had written it. The note could have been written a long time ago, or it could have been written on a crumpled piece of paper Chris had found lying somewhere. He could have called his wife, but having been thrown out of the apartment probably made him ashamed to contact her directly. Somehow, Mohan felt indifferent toward both of them, his sympathy reserved for the child.

As he climbed the stairs to his room, Mohan saw

the mother and son emerging from their apartment. She hesitated for a moment when she saw him, then turned her back to lock the door. Mohan stood on the landing and waited for her to turn around. The child stood quietly besides his mother, looking at the floor. Once she was done locking up, she saw Mohan still standing there, and a visible annoyance spread across her face.

"Hold my hand," she said to her son and proceeded toward the stairs. It was clear she didn't like being in the enclosed space with Mohan.

"Your husband gave this to me to give you," Mohan said, pulling out the crumpled piece of paper and handing it to her. He stepped past her to unlock his door.

"Where did you see him?" she asked, as he was about to enter his room.

"He was on the campus, protesting," Mohan replie

"Were you protesting too?" she asked.

"No, I just ran into them on my way to the cafeteria," Mohan answered.

She opened the letter right there and read it silently. Mohan watched her face but couldn't tell whether her expression conveyed anything of importance.

"Thank you," she said without looking at him and proceeded down the stairs with the little boy by her side.

As he entered his room, he picked up a letter from the floor. Francesca always took the trouble to come up and push Mohan's mail under the door when an aerogram arrived for him, in spite of his protest that he could collect it from the salon. "The salon will be closed by the time you are back," Francesca had replied the first time. "I don't want you to wait the whole night to read your letter from home," she had said later. Mohan felt obliged for the favor and didn't know how to thank her.

He switched on the television and opened the letter. His parents had written that they missed him. Not even a year had passed—there were at least four more to go. They asked if he could visit them sometimes in between. They had mentioned consulting the priest about an auspicious day to break the ground for a new house. They would need a bigger house by the time he was back, and they were planning to move to the village after his father retired. Mohan's grandfather had left his two sons his home and the farmlands in the village. They also mentioned that they were looking around for an eligible girl for him. They wanted to know about his preferences when it came to that matter.

As Mohan put the letter down, a sense of apprehension overtook him. He could not imagine marrying a total stranger and letting luck work it out. Then he thought about his parents and his uncle and the people he knew back home. They had all married that way. Again, he reflected that his parents seemed happy. If they weren't, he could not point his finger at any indication of it. At the same time, his neighbors here must have known each other for some time before they got married, and it made him nauseated to think about their constant bickering. He wasn't even sure if Chris was coming back. What if he ended up in a marriage like that? He decided to keep quiet and not to respond to his parents regarding his marriage. That could wait until his graduate work was finished.

A few days later, four students protesting the Cambodian invasion at Kent State University in Ohio were shot and killed by National Guard soldiers who had been mobilized to the campus. In response, more violence erupted at universities throughout America. On the Stony Brook campus, protestors burned down the barn, used as storage space by the university, and set the Humanities Building ablaze with Molotov cocktails.

That whole night, local news channels kept broadcasting live footage of the unrest. Mohan tried to prepare his lessons for the next day's class. The uncertainty of the situation made it hard for him to focus. He kept listening to the news to find out whether the campus would be closed the next day, but it was too early for the university's president to decide anything.

Mohan was familiar with riots from back in India. It seemed to him that, even after India was free from the British imperialism, it had not been able to free itself from the evil within. People burned and looted their own country in the name of religion and caste and every inconvenience that came their way. They could not let go of the mentality of being ruled. They did not ask, "Ruled by whom or what?" They were still stuck with the divisions left over from British rule. He saw riots between Hindus and Muslims and upper-caste Hindus taking advantage of untouchables.

He sympathized with the antiwar protestors' desire not to let Nixon destroy Cambodia and Vietnam. He thought that in war, there were only losers, and they were usually the innocent people caught between the power struggles of multiple factions. The atrocity of the Vietnam War unnerved him. He was afraid that America would now do what Britain had done for centuries— dominate and break the spirits of countless individuals in less fortunate countries. Here in the States, unrest hung in the air like fog, pervading the normalcy of everyday life. Despite his sympathy with the protestors, he found it distressing. He wished he had come to this country at a different time.

Late that night, as Mohan was about to fall asleep, he heard someone knocking on his door. He got up and looked out his window. Everything seemed calm, as if the neighborhood had no sense of what was going on around it. Thinking that he had been dreaming, he went back to bed, but then he heard the pounding again, this time sounding urgent. "Please open the door," said the voice of the woman next door. "It's me. I need help."

He went to the door with a sense of unease. He wondered what kind of help she needed in the middle of the night. Other than the campus, he wasn't familiar with this place yet. He didn't even drive. The moment he opened the door, she walked in, pulling her child behind her. The child was in pajamas. "I have to leave my son with you for a while. It's Chris." She let go of the child's hand as she said this, then turned and hurried down the stairs. The child, who was half-awake, started yelling, "Mama, Mama!" and ran after his mother and out of the room. Mohan heard the exterior door slam and a car stopping in front of the salon, then, quickly pulling away. He picked up the child with both hands and brought him back into the apartment. The child kept screaming.

Mohan looked at the crying child, and anger at the woman took hold of him. He didn't know her well to be asked to babysit. He didn't know where she had gone or for how long. He had no telephone number where he could reach her if the child didn't stop crying or, worse, if there was some kind of emergency. As he pondered the situation, the child continued crying at the top of his lungs, calling for his mother. Then he started kicking the door.

Mohan was at a loss as to how to quiet the boy down. It occurred to him that the child's cry might draw some unnecessary attention to the place. Luckily, the salon was closed. However, he was sure that the crying would be audible from as far as the port. He inched toward the child and asked, "You want a cookie?"

The child spun around like a raging bull and kicked Mohan in the shin.

"Stop it! Right now!" Mohan screamed as he bent and rubbed his leg. The hard edge of the child's shoe had hit him and it hurt. He wondered if the boy went to bed regularly with his shoes on. Mohan got hold of the child's right foot and tried to untie the shoelace. As soon as the shoe came off, the child picked it up and threw it at the wall with all the force he could muster. He was still wailing. Mohan pulled the other shoe off.

"Andy want shoe." The little boy tried to wiggle his foot back into his left shoe, sobbing. By this time, a good fifteen minutes had passed, and the crying seemed to be tiring Andy out. He stopped for a brief moment, looked around the place, and started again.

Mohan pulled out a plastic jar of cookies from the cupboard, opened it, and put it in front of Andy. "Want a cookie?" he asked again.

Andy wiped his face with one hand, trying to take care of the tears and the snot at the same time. Before Mohan could get a napkin to wipe the boy's face, Andy dipped his hand into the cookie jar and helped himself with one. Mohan looked at the jar. He wouldn't be able to eat from it now. The rest of the cookies would go to waste. At least he felt relieved that Andy wasn't crying anymore. The child seemed somewhat calm.

Mohan felt as if he had been in crisis mode since the woman and the boy had shown up at his door. He didn't know how to control the child's behavior and had no experience dealing with children. He had been so consumed with the child that he had forgotten about the woman, who had thrust him into this difficult situation.

Now that Andy was quiet, helping himself to cookies, Mohan began to think about the situation once again. Every time he heard a car passing by, he waited eagerly for the front door to open and the woman to reappear. Half an hour passed that way.

"You should go to bed now," Mohan told Andy, walking him toward the only bed in the room. By this time, Andy had devoured half of the cookies.

"Juice," the boy said, looking around the room with curious eyes. Then he went and stood near Mohan's notebooks and said, "Draw Mama." It was quite obvious that instead of feeling sleepy, he was waking up to these new surroundings. Before Mohan could answer, the boy had pulled out a loose piece of paper from one of the notebooks and was searching around for something to write with. "Pencil. I want a pencil." He put his hand in Mohan's backpack and started reaching around.

Mohan pulled Andy's hand out of the backpack. The child started whimpering. "You draw when you get up," Mohan said as he went to the fridge to get some orange juice for the boy. There was hardly any juice left, so he watered it down and handed it to the child. This whole affair of the mother leaving her son at such an hour and the child's demands were getting Mohan exasperated. He felt desperate to get Andy to sleep.

Andy took small gulps of juice. "I want a pencil," he repeated.

"No, Andy. You may not have a pencil," Mohan said, his voice harsh. "What did I tell you? Not now." He had sympathized with Andy when he'd heard his demands through the wall but felt irritated now that Andy was making them to him. Momentarily, all his sympathy shifted from the boy to Chris.

Nevertheless, he felt sorry for Andy for being left with a stranger in the middle of the night. The boy had finished the juice by now and was tipping the glass all the way back, trying to get the last drop. "Want milk?" Mohan asked.

Andy nodded without looking at him.

Knowing that he would not be able to sleep until Andy fell asleep, Mohan switched on the TV and took the empty juice glass. As he poured milk for the boy, he realized that he didn't have that much milk either. He wanted to save some for the next morning's breakfast, so he added water to the milk he'd poured and hoped that Andy wouldn't ask for more.

"Here," Mohan handed the glass to Andy. "How old are you?" he asked, though he wasn't really interested in knowing the answer. Two hours had passed by now. He wondered again when the mother would be back to collect her son.

"I'm this old." Andy raised three fingers, folding his pinkie and thumb down. He took a sip of milk. "I don't like this," he said, spitting a mouthful of milk on the floor.

"Don't do that," Mohan snapped. He wiped the milk up with a paper towel. He thought that the child was testing his limits. He held the glass close to Andy's mouth and said, "Now drink it." The boy looked at him and started to cry again. Mohan picked him up and put him in the bed. Andy started howling, and Mohan let him. After a while, the child's wailing turned into sobbing, and then he fell asleep. Mohan went to the window and looked out. There was no sign of the woman. He sat in his chair and closed his eyes. Before long, he fell asleep too.

It was almost morning when the woman knocked on

the door. Mohan's body had slumped into the chair like a rag doll, and his head was resting on the table. He felt disoriented as he tried to figure out the origin of the sound. His head was heavy as he lifted it to change its position. The soft and intermittent knocks seemed distant, as if in a dream, and Mohan tried to sleep again. Then the knocks became louder and more insistent. He sat up with a startle and heard the woman's voice: "It's me. Please open the door." He opened the door and looked toward his bed. He had forgotten about the child who was sleeping there.

"Sorry for all the trouble," the woman said as she walked into his room, again without waiting to be invited. "I'm Sophie," she said and extended her hand, as if suddenly remembering her manners, though Chris had introduced them months earlier.

"Mohan," he said, shaking her hand. "Hope Chris is okay?" he inquired halfheartedly. He wanted her to take the child and leave him alone. It was too early in the morning for conversation, and his body ached from sleeping on the chair the whole night. He didn't care to hear about where she'd been and was afraid that if he acted too interested, she might ask him to look after the child again while she went out. Nevertheless, Mohan could tell that she had hardly slept for many nights. There were dark rings under her eyes, and her hair and clothes were disheveled. It felt awkward to Mohan to stand there not knowing what to say.

"I hope he behaved," she said, looking at the sleeping child. Then she saw a blanket spread on one corner of the floor and apologized for the inconvenience, assuming that Mohan had slept there the whole night. She noticed that there was no couch or other bed in the room.

"It wasn't bad," he lied. He didn't want her to know that he had slept in the chair because the floor would have been too hard. He picked up the blanket and placed it on the bed.

"Chris is in jail," she volunteered. "A friend of his drove me there." She related these facts without looking at him, and this seemed enough to explain her current state of affairs. He thought that Chris had been bound to end up in jail sooner or later. Given the circumstances, her indifferent tone didn't surprise Mohan. Yet he also realized Sophie must have cared for Chris to leave the child with a stranger to visit him at the jail in the middle of the night.

"Did he say how long he will be there?" asked Mohan. He didn't want to get stuck babysitting Andy in the coming days. He was too busy at the end of the semester, and looking after the child again would be too much for her to ask of him.

"No. There's going to be a court case. A policeman is hurt." Saying this, she picked up the sleeping child and headed toward the door. Mohan followed her and stood in the doorway. "He wants me to post bail for him," she said as she opened the door to her apartment.

Once Sophie had disappeared with Andy into their apartment, Mohan decided to sleep a little longer before going to campus. As he lowered himself onto the bed, it felt wet and there was the undeniable stench of urine. He got up and opened the window. A stream of sunlight came into the room with the fresh morning air. After blotting the mattress with paper napkins, he spread the blanket on the floor and lay on it. Sleep had deserted him by then, but he stayed there for a while trying to comprehend the predicament Sophie was in.

Later that day, Mohan got the full account of Chris's situation from the campus newspaper. He was accused by law enforcement for throwing a Molotov cocktail at a police cruiser, and one of the policemen was being treated at a local hospital with life-threatening injuries. Chris was being held at the county jail. A judge had set the bond at one thousand dollars.

There was a detailed description of the offender. Chris was a graduate student in the political science department who was active in organizing student demonstrations against the war. He often traveled to other universities to participate in protests. Over the course of the last two semesters, there had been complaints to the department chair about his negligence of duty, and there was a very good chance, that there would be a hearing among the faculty to expel him from the university. The article didn't mention anything about his personal life. No mention of Sophie.

***

By the end of the month, exams were done, students were leaving for home, and things were winding down for Mohan at the university. At last, the weather had warmed up, and the trees were covered with new foliage. More people were taking the ferry at Port Jefferson not only as a means of transportation but also to be on the water and enjoy the coastline on both sides of the Long Island Sound. The beauty salon became livelier with chatter as the outside temperature inched upward.

A few weeks had passed since Sophie had left Andy with Mohan. He had seen the mother and son going out or coming in with bags of groceries. As Mohan had expected, Chris had moved back to live with them after being released from the jail. He greeted Mohan when they ran into each other as if nothing had happened. Things seemed calm— Mohan didn't hear any intense arguments between the couple, and Chris screamed at the boy less. He remained at the apartment most of the time. It felt as if there was a long overdue harmony in the apartment next door.

But this state of calmness was only temporary. One day, as Mohan skimmed through the campus newspaper, he came across a picture of the wounded policeman, who had succumbed to his injuries that morning. He was young, in his twenties, and was survived by his parents and a younger brother. Mohan's heart felt heavy at the thought of the demise of such a young life. Then he read that Chris would be standing trial for the policeman's murder. Living next door to Chris made Mohan nervous—not for his own safety, but because of the unrest Chris brought to the place.

When Mohan returned that evening, he saw a police car parked outside the building. Some officers were talking to Francesca, who was nodding and shaking her head. As Mohan unlocked the front door and was about to climb up the stairs, he noticed one of the policemen heading toward the door. Mohan stood at the entrance, realizing that the officer was coming to question him. He knew that Chris must have taken off. The man in uniform asked him how long he had known Chris and if he knew where Chris was. The officer wanted to check Mohan's room. Mohan led him upstairs, and the man checked under the bed and inside the bathroom and then left.

The chatter of the child could be heard from the other apartment. It was obvious to Mohan that Chris was gone for good, leaving Sophie and Andy behind. It felt unsettling to live next door to someone whose life had fallen apart, probably more than once. He didn't like the fact that he knew Chris or that a police officer had questioned him, but there wasn't anything he could do about it. In any case, he planned to inquire about more suitable housing closer to campus once his present lease expired.

Chapter Five

A few days after the babysitting incident, on a Sunday, as Mohan was about to cook his midday meal, Sophie knocked on his door. He opened the door with much reluctance. Sophie greeted him with a smile. "I made pasta for us. I thought you would like to try some," she said. Andy stayed back near the door to their apartment.

At first, Mohan didn't know how to respond. He still resented the unexpected situation he had been forced into the night she left Andy with him. He wasn't expecting anything in return. He just hoped not to babysit again. However, out of politeness, he extended his hand to take the dish she was holding and said, "There was no need for this."

"It is something little. Hope you like it," Sophie said shortly, and before Mohan could thank her, she turned around and went back into her apartment with Andy.

Mohan liked the pasta dish made with cheese and some spices he did not recognize. It was so different than the food he cooked. He wondered if it was difficult to prepare. He could have asked her for the recipe but decided against it.

A few days had passed since Chris's disappearance. Sometimes, Mohan saw Sophie from a distance, holding Andy's hand and walking by the sea, near the port. Andy skipped by her side happily, not missing Chris, who had no patience with him. Neither Sophie nor Andy showed any explicit sign of a loss in their lives created by the absence of Chris. If they came face-to-face with Mohan, the child averted his eyes, while Sophie greeted Mohan with a friendly "Hello." If Mohan wasn't in a hurry, she tried to make small talk about the weather or the campus. Slowly, it began to seem to Mohan that he was getting used to being there.

Mohan went to the department every day except Sunday and stayed there until the last bus left the campus. On his way home, he could see the light coming from Sophie's apartment, and as he opened his door, he'd hear her reading stories to Andy. After eating a simple meal of rice and curry, he would switch on the news as he lay on his bed and think about the lives, such as his neighbors', that were affected by the war in some way.

Sometimes at night, when he lay in the dark, he thought about Sophie. He wondered whether she had loved Chris when they met or whether circumstances had made her marry him. Mohan wanted to know about her family and where they were now. Had they disowned her, as a family would have done in the same circumstances in India? Whatever the answers were, he liked her independence from her husband. Back at home, boys and girls married without having met each other, and things were different. Once married, the wife was tied not only to the husband but also to his family, for life, the way a bullock was tied to the cart.

Then, one evening, when Mohan returned home, he found Francesca and Sophie standing on the landing. As Mohan climbed up the stairs, they became quiet. He went to his room, and from behind the closed door, he heard Francesca telling her, "I know it's difficult. But we need the rent." She sounded polite yet firm in demanding the money.

Mohan waited there to hear her response. "We still have a few days. Chris will do something by then," she said.

"What about the month after?" Francesca asked. "He's in Canada for all you know. Chris won't be back." Francesca walked down the stairs as she said it, then stopped halfway and said, "Don't you have anywhere to go to? At the end of June, you have to vacate it." Mohan heard the exterior door and Sophie's close at the same time.

That night, Mohan remained awake for a long time. It was apparent that Sophie and the child had nowhere to go, but it wasn't for Mohan to get involved in her affairs. The most he could do was offer to help her with the rent for a month. Then, as Francesca had asked, what would happen after that? He was a visitor in their country. He would go back as soon as his studies were finished. The urge to help her and the fear of entanglement kept him up, and when he finally fell asleep, he dreamt that he was back at home and his mother stood at the entrance with someone who looked like a young woman whom Mohan had never seen before.

The next morning, on his way to the university, Mohan posted the letter he had just written to his parents. Like before, he hadn't written anything about Chris, Sophie, or the boy. Now that Chris was out of the picture, it made even more sense to him not to write anything about them. In every letter, his mother wrote that she went to the village temple once a week so her son would be spared the evil eye. In the next sentence, she would write they had seen so-and-so, who would be a good match for him. Mohan easily understood what his mother meant by the evil eye.

His days were spent reading research papers written by others and solving problems given to him by his advisor. Now that he had done well in his qualifying exam and had been offered a research fellowship, he could write his doctoral thesis in another four years and return home. Nevertheless, when he got back to his room in the evenings, his heart felt heavy for no apparent reason, and he tried to make himself disappear behind the closed door. He felt like a thief, tiptoeing around someone's misery, even though it was not his fault and nothing was required of him.

A fortnight had passed without any incident since Chris left. Then, one Sunday afternoon, as Mohan was about to finish cooking his customary meal of dal, vegetables, and rice for the next couple of days, he heard Sophie open her door. Mohan stopped stirring the cabbage and strained his ears to follow the descending footsteps of the mother and son, but instead of descending, they stopped on the landing, and he heard soft knocks on his door. First, he thought of not responding. After all, he might not have been home. But the aroma escaping from his cooking would give him away. After a few more knocks, he opened the door with hesitation.

Sophie wore a sleeveless, summery white dress with black polka dots. Her hair was cropped to the neck. Mohan noticed that she looked thinner. The dark circles around her eyes were still there. Andy was wearing a jumper and held his mother's hand as tightly as he could.

"I've found a job at the campus cafeteria," Sophie said, after a moment of awkward silence. "But . . . it won't start until the fall semester." She looked down the stairs as she said it.

Mohan waited anxiously to hear what she was going to say next. He had a broad knowledge of her problems but felt disquiet with her assumption that he knew about them. It was apparent from her demeanor that she wasn't just parting with information.

"Meanwhile," she continued, "I'll be working at

ShopRite . . . mostly in the evenings." This time she looked at him expectantly, as if her working there depended on him. ShopRite was their main grocery store, a few blocks up on the main road on the other side of the street. "Mohan." She paused after saying his name for the first time. "I was thinking . . . If I could leave Andy with you during those hours . . ."

That was exactly what Mohan had been afraid of, a request to babysit Andy again. While standing there, he had prepared himself with an easy answer: "With my research demands, I won't know when I'll be back at night. You cannot depend on me." Mohan said this without a pause, hoping that he didn't sound impolite and Sophie would understand and make other arrangements.

"My shift will be from seven to eleven," she said. "I thought you'd have had a long day by then. It is only for the summer."

Mohan didn't reply to this immediately. It would be impossible for him to do what she was asking. He didn't want to be tethered to a child after a whole day's work, particularly after his last experience. At the same time, he didn't want to say no to her face. "I really don't think it is possible, but I'll think about it." He said this and turned around, pretended to make sure the stove was off, even though he knew he had turned it off.

"I'll be starting this Wednesday. When will you know?" she simply asked.

"Well, you just told me. I've to think about it." Mohan felt irritated at her question. It might have been that she had no one else to help her out, but he thought it was an extraordinary favor she expected from him. Moreover, he couldn't understand how she would pay the rent working a few hours a night.

"I got the job this morning," she said. "I took Andy with me to the interview. You should have seen him . . . Sat quietly the whole time." She looked down at Andy as she said it, and a thin smile spread across her face. Then, she looked up at Mohan and said, "We must go now," and went down the stairs with her son without pressing him any further for an answer.

Mohan sat down to eat his freshly cooked meal, but his hunger had suddenly deserted him. He felt conflicted. His resolve to say no to her would make him appear small and petty. If he wanted to, he could watch Andy. He would be home just before she left for work and could do his own things while tending to the boy. After all, the child wasn't so young. Mohan would set his own rules this time. He could even teach the child a few things.

Nevertheless, he knew that it might not be that easy. The thought of what might lead from a simple arrangement to a heartbreaking complication unnerved him. Every letter from his mother had warned him about such dangers, no matter how implicit the warnings were. What if he fell in love with Sophie? Or what if their passion for each other, the physicality of it, came to know no bounds, but without any love? Either way, he would be condemned. His parents might not know, but his heart would know it. Again, he could set his own boundaries and remain well within their walls. He didn't think of himself as weak when it came to such matters.

After much deliberation, Mohan decided to help Sophie out. It would be just a deed of kindness. It would earn him good karma, and God would pay him back with more kindness. That was what his mother would have said, if it were a different situation, and if it weren't for someone with evil eyes.

During the rest of that summer, Mohan left early in the mornings so that he could have the whole day to himself. His advisor, Prof. Thomas, was out part of the summer, giving lectures at various conferences, but he had given Mohan a big project to work on throughout the whole summer. Each evening Mohan returned home just before Sophie was about to leave. She had asked him to babysit in her apartment, so that she didn't have to carry a sleeping child back to his bed. Moreover, they had both agreed that Andy would be at ease in a familiar setting with his own things.

The first day, Mohan had tried to arrive a few minutes early. Sophie stood at her door holding Andy's hand and waiting for him. As Mohan climbed the stairs to reach the landing, she kept repeating, "Be a good boy" to her son. Then she planted a kiss on the child's cheek, saying, "I love you," and let his hand go. Andy started screaming. Mohan took his hand without saying anything to Sophie and led him back into the apartment.

Andy cried, "Mama . . . Mama," and tried to pull himself away from Mohan. Mohan let go of the child's hand. To Mohan's relief, Andy wasn't crying hysterically like the other night. The child went and sat on the floor, sobbing and looking at his toys at the same time.

It was a sparsely furnished apartment, littered with toys. There were stuffed animals on a blue sofa made of fabric that looked like cheap velvet. Toy cars were lined up on and under a rickety table dividing the kitchen from the small living room. Three chairs were kept haphazardly around the table, and it held action figures: Planet of the Apes, Wonder Women, and some other figures Mohan had no idea about. He threw a stuffed bear and a Mickey Mouse on the floor and made room for himself on the couch.

"Don't do that!" Andy screamed at Mohan. "They are mine." As he said this, he put the things back on the sofa and gave Mohan an angry look. His crying had stopped all of a sudden.

Mohan assessed the situation. Andy wasn't crying at that moment, but anything could trigger a tantrum. He thought that the child must be disciplined as long as he babysat him. He remembered his own early childhood.

His mother was the one who had disciplined him. If he didn't like the food one day, she had said, "No matter. You will eat when you are hungry." Eventually, he had eaten the same food with little protest. He hadn't had many toys to mess up the house with, but if he didn't clean up after himself, he didn't get to play with them for a day or so. If he didn't write his alphabets and finish the simple additions, and subtractions she had given him, she told the little kids who came to play with him, "You all keep playing. I'll send Manu as soon as he is done." Mohan had tried to throw tantrums, but it hadn't worked.

Mohan assumed that Sophie let Andy do whatever he wanted, and he had probably never liked Chris because he disciplined him. He wouldn't listen to Mohan either. However, he decided to try anyway. "You have to listen to me, you understand?" Saying this, Mohan put the teddy bear and the Mickey Mouse back on the floor and occupied the empty space. Then he saw a big cardboard box containing some wood blocks in a corner of the room. "What are these?" he asked the child to divert his attention.

"These are bocks." Andy inspected the box as he said it, glancing back at the stuffed animals. "This mine," he said emphatically as he dumped everything on the floor and looked at Mohan combatively.

"Now, can you put the other toys in the box, please?"

Mohan asked Andy, ignoring the child's look and gathering the cars from under the table. Then, one by one, Mohan put them in the box. Andy watched him intently. After a while, he climbed up on a chair and dropped the cars from the top of the table onto the floor, as Mohan was about to finish. "Now you get down from the chair," Mohan said, as he looked at Andy. He was more determined now to make Andy pick up the cars.

"I don't like you," Andy said and looked the other way.

"Okay. That's okay with me. Just put them in the box." Mohan chose not to take offense at the child's words. At the same time, the boy's defiance made him firm. He repeated the commands a few more time to no avail. Andy sat there pouting. With utter helplessness, Mohan tried to ignore him and spread out a couple of papers from his backpack to go over. He decided that it was not his job to teach manners to the boy. He was there to help the mother out. He was thankful that the child wasn't screaming, as he did the other night.

Andy sat on the floor, moving the action figures around with his little hands. Then all of a sudden, he started throwing them at the wall. At first, Mohan pretended not to notice; then he snatched the figures from the boy's hand and started putting everything in the box. "Mine. Give me back. Mama!" Andy howled. Mohan picked him up and put him on a chair.

"You sit here," Mohan said to Andy as he sat on another chair next to the child. He was thinking about ways to handle him. Then he remembered how his father had rewarded him for his good behavior when he was a child. The rewards had been small—sometimes an orange flavored candy, at other times a pencil with a little eraser at the end. Nevertheless, Mohan had always looked forward to those little presents. The thought made his mind less burdened, and he asked Andy, "You hungry?"

Andy nodded. He had stopped crying. He stood on the chair and pulled a covered ceramic pot in one corner of the table toward himself.

"Wait. It'll fall." Mohan got hold of the pot and looked around for a plate.

"Up there," Andy said. Mohan saw the small blue and green plastic plates in one of the cupboards. Andy waited as Mohan got a small plate and put some macaroni and cheese from the ceramic pot on it. Andy pointed toward a drawer, where Mohan found small forks and spoons. The child ate while moving the action figures with his left hand. Mohan let him do that. He thought that he could get some work done while Andy kept busy on his own.

"Mommy said, 'Share,'" Andy said when he was almost done eating, and pointed his index finger at Mohan.

"I'm not hungry," Mohan replied. He'd had a grilled cheese sandwich at the university cafeteria, and he was going to eat his dal and rice once he went home.

"All done," Andy said after a few more minutes. He slid down the chair to the floor and dumped the box full of toys on the floor again. Mohan told him to put them back, but he didn't pay any attention. "I'm not sleepy," he volunteered. "I want to play. I want Mommy."

At the mention of the mother, Mohan panicked, thinking the boy might throw a tantrum. However, he replied in a strong voice, "Absolutely not. It is bedtime."

"Read me this book," Andy demanded. He was holding *Green Eggs and Ham* by Dr. Seuss. Mohan read the beginning, then, proceeded to the end skipping the middle.

Andy pulled the book away from him and said, "You don't read like Mommy. You don't know the story."

Mohan read the story quickly from beginning to end. "Now you have to sleep," he told Andy.

"I want to pee," the child said and ran toward the bathroom. Once he was out, Mohan tucked him into a little bed next to the full bed in a hurry, lest the child demand something else.

"I'm right here. Okay?" Mohan said, closing the door halfway as he stepped back into the living room. When he didn't hear any sound coming from the bedroom, he breathed a sigh of relief. It had been a long evening, and he was totally exhausted. He opened his backpack and tried to concentrate on his project.

As soon as Sophie opened the door at ten past eleven, Mohan picked up his backpack and was out of the apartment. When asked how things had gone, he answered her that it had been okay and went into his own apartment. He resisted the impulse to let his frustration demoralize him.

The next day, Mohan went to the campus bookstore and bought the cheapest pack of colored pencils he could find. He would have to use these to entice Andy to listen to him.

That evening, things went a little better for Mohan. The colored pencils helped. He promised Andy one of them, a blue one to write with, if he listened to him. With the pencil, Mohan gave the boy a piece of paper as well. If he insisted on something, Mohan asked for his pencil back. When Andy went to bed, he got to keep the pencil and paper with him. The next day, when Mohan arrived to babysit, Sophie mentioned to him that Andy slept with them next to him. At the end of the week, Mohan told Andy that the pencil was his to keep.

At the beginning of the next week, Mohan gave another pencil, a green one, to Andy. Before giving it to him, Mohan made a deal with Andy once more—that he had to put his toys away and not throw them at the walls. As Mohan took his papers from his backpack and spread them out, everything around him seemed quiet, until he noticed that instead of writing on the paper he'd given him, the boy had written all over the table.

"What have you done?" Mohan jumped up and snatched the pencil away from Andy.

"Give me back!" Andy howled.

"I gave you the paper to write on," Mohan said as he poured some dishwashing liquid onto a wet paper napkin. He rubbed the green marks with it. Andy watched him intently, crying and stopping intermittently. After a while, most of the marks came off.

"Can I have it?" Andy looked at Mohan expectantly.

"If you do this again, you will never have another one." Saying this, Mohan handed the pencil back to Andy. He felt irritated but less despondent than the week before. The child's behavior had taken a positive turn over the last few times Mohan had babysat, no matter how slight it was. Andy's temper tantrums were less frequent. He looked forward to owning another one of those colored pencils, along with the box full of toys and cars.

As the weeks passed, Mohan got used to Andy. It wasn't easy to entertain a child. However, he made an effort to do a couple of things with the boy. He crawled around with him to collect the cars. At times, he asked Andy to count them as he put the things into the box. The child could count up to ten. After that Mohan counted, eleven . . . twelve . . ."as the toys were put into their proper place.

For the next three months, Mohan settled down to

the routines he had taken on. He arrived on time and left as soon as Sophie returned. Every evening, Andy told him that he was supposed to share his food with Mohan, but Mohan always answered that he wasn't hungry. It wasn't that difficult to babysit the boy, he told himself as the three months neared their end. Andy now looked forward to his coming in the evening. His whole demeanor changed when he saw Mohan, and he was eager to please him. He said "Thank you" and "please" and had quickly learned the numbers while putting his toys back in the box. In return, Mohan had given him an array of colorful pencils.

Nevertheless, Mohan had made a conscious determination not to feel any emotional connection to Andy. He did not want to be a crutch for the child. Once or twice, Sophie had mentioned that the boy asked for him over the weekends, to which he hadn't answered anything. He had considered the babysitting to be a big sacrifice on his part, and he looked forward to the arrangement being over.

It was the last day of work for Sophie at the grocery store. Mohan climbed up the stairs and noticed that Sophie wasn't waiting at the door, as she always was to leave in a hurry for her job. The smell of food being cooked drifted through the door. He could hear Andy's revved up cars racing on the floor. He rang the doorbell as he transferred his backpack from his shoulder to his hand.

"Hi, come in," Sophie said as she opened the door. Mohan noticed a faint smile on her face. She had pulled her short hair into a ponytail from which strands were spilling onto her neck. She wore a bright yellow dress.

"I didn't know you weren't going in today," Mohan said and was about to turn toward his door.

"I quit a day early," Sophie replied.

In a way, Mohan felt relieved that the three months were finally over. He would now go back to his life, and he could come and go to the campus as he pleased. He hadn't written to his parents the whole time he'd been babysitting. That was the first thing he planned to do that night.

"I have cooked dinner for all of us. If you don't mind, I would like to invite you." Sophie looked at Mohan expectantly as she said it. It had been a last-minute thought. She wanted to thank Mohan for his help.

"Well, um . . ." Mohan searched for words to decline the invitation. It had been just business between them, and it was over. He didn't want anything on a personal level. At the same time, he realized that it would be rude on his part to tell her no and replied, 'There was no need to take the trouble."

"It's no trouble. I just want to thank you for all your help." Saying this, with her hand, Sophie motioned Mohan to come in. Unlike the other times he'd been there, the place looked clean and organized. On the small dining table, she had placed some yellow roses in a vase. He had seen the flowers growing abundantly, like wild flowers, behind the building.

"I didn't think you was coming," Andy said as he left his cars on the floor and ran toward Mohan. "Mommy got this for me." He raised a red car in his right hand as he said it.

"How many cars do you have now?" Mohan asked him.

"I can count." After saying this, Andy started counting the cars one by one. "Twenty-one," he said, after counting and recounting, and then went back to playing.

"It is all vegetarian," Sophie said as she served a simple meal of pasta and salad. "I didn't know whether you eat meat." They ate without much conversation. This was the first time someone had invited Mohan for dinner. He felt awkward in her presence.

"Chris wanted me to join him in Canada," Sophie said while clearing the dishes from the table. Mohan didn't reply to this. Probably they were in touch by mail, he thought. After all, they were married to each other. It was not his place to say anything.

"Chris left a note for me before he fled. It had an address in Canada . . . but I haven't heard from him since he left," she volunteered. She let the dishes soak in water and put scoops of ice cream in three small bowls. Andy was busy with his cars, but his mother's words had not escaped him.

"We are not going. You told me..." he said it, over and over, as he came and took a chair as soon as he saw the ice cream.

Sophie remained silent for a while, then, replied, "We'll see."

After the ice cream, Mohan thanked Sophie and got up to go. She pulled out a small envelope from one of the kitchen drawers and handed it to him, saying, "This is something really small. I don't know how to thank you."

"May I open it?" he asked. He was really surprised that Sophie had gone through the trouble of buying a card and writing him a thank-you note.

"Yes, of course," she replied while taking the empty bowls to the sink.

Mohan opened the envelope, and inside the card were tucked five ten-dollar bills. He took them out and put them back on the table. "This isn't acceptable. I cannot take it." He said it firmly and moved toward the door. He hadn't expected to be paid. He had always thought that he was doing her a favor just for a few months. They had never discussed anything about money in exchange for his help.

"I'm much obliged for your help, but I don't want you to feel pity for me." She looked directly at him while she said this. "I'll be fine. I'll have to be, for Andy's sake." Then she collected the bills and held them out to him. "You must accept it, Mohan. I'm really grateful to you. Please."

Once inside his room, he read the card: "Mohan, I can never thank you enough. Sophie." Carefully, he put the money back in the envelope and put it under the clothes in one of his dresser drawers.

That night, sleep eluded Mohan. He parted the curtains and looked out the window. Aside from the occasional sounds from the passing cars, the neighborhood was quiet and empty. The beam of light from the lighthouse kept pulsating at regular intervals, breaking the monotony of the port. The water at the shoreline reflected the lights from the pier, and the vast sea stretched into the dark from where it wasn't visible anymore.

He went back to the bed and lay there, scared of his emotions. They seemed alien to him because his mind had never entertained them before. New, shapeless feelings lurked inside him, growing moment by moment, and as he tried to suppress them, they took the decisive forms of a woman and a child. No. It could not be. He tried to convince himself.

Chapter Six

Mohan's first year in America was over with the fall approaching and a new class to teach. In another four years, he thought hopefully, he would be back in India among his own people. He received letters from his parents asking him to visit them. Sometimes they complained about the long intervals between his letters. He wished they knew about the struggles and the chaos everybody was going through due to the war.

Often, students walked out of classes to participate in demonstrations, leaving the instructors to cope with the fallout. Mohan thought that they had a moral obligation to protest against the war. Yet it felt unreasonable to him that he had to repeat the materials in class over and over because half of the class wasn't there at any given time. When they were there, students protested about the grades they got and the unfairness of the tough exams.

Nevertheless, Mohan tried to be as reasonable as possible. He felt empathy for the young students who felt obliged to be part of the process. With the draft hanging over their heads, they dared not drop out of college and, at the same time, could not ignore the unrest around them created by the war. Conscientious objectors to the war headed for Canada before they were drafted, but not all young people wanted to flee the country, uprooting themselves from their families and friends.

Mohan offered extra discussion classes to help those falling behind. Now that he didn't have to look after a child in the evening, he felt he had more time, and he spent those hours helping the students. He hardly saw Sophie, or the boy, anymore. By opting for the extra responsibilities, he had successfully managed to avoid them. By the time he returned home, the lights would be out in her apartment. He hadn't been to the campus cafeteria since she'd started working there.

Then one day, just before Thanksgiving, Mohan saw Sophie and Andy waiting for the same shuttle he was planning to catch to bring them home. The campus was closing that day for the break. After a couple of hours of intense activity of parents picking up their children and some of the students crowding the campus roads at the same time to drive home, the place looked deserted. Mohan had decided to go back to his apartment and work on his project. As he walked toward the stop, Andy saw him and waved, nudging at his mother. He was enrolled at the day care on campus.

"Hey, hi, Mohan. Haven't seen you in a while," Sophie greeted him after she turned around and saw him. Mohan noticed that her hair had grown longer. She was wearing slacks and a turtleneck sweater to ward off the November chill.

"Just busy. Trying to finish my first paper." His advisor had given him the project in September, but between teaching and grading, he had not been able to devote as much time to the paper as he'd intended to. "How is your work?" he asked Sophie.

"It's okay. They point at the food they want, and you put them onto their plates. It is boring, day after day, but I like it better than being a cashier at the supermarket. I shouldn't complain." Then she thought for a while and said, "I like the crowd. They make me think about my days in college. It's good." Mohan noticed an ease and resilience in her voice. She was navigating rough terrain on her own, and he could tell that she was proud of it.

Mohan thought about women back in India. Women left behind by their husbands either went to live with their parents or stayed with their in-laws and, either way, faced humiliation. The stigma of an abandoned woman knew no bounds. Her status in society was worse than that of a widow. At least, in some cases, a widow was the beneficiary of the sympathy that was bestowed on the dead husband, but no such consideration was given to an abandoned woman.

He remembered the girl, Rumi. She was his age. His grandfather had brought her from his village when she was ten or eleven to work at Mohan's parents' house. Mohan's father, being in the police, had objected to hiring such a young girl, but his mother had said, "Let her stay. She is much better off here." Rumi's mother had died when she was born, and her father had remarried soon after that. She had gone to the village elementary school, and after that, her father and stepmother had kept her home to take care of their growing brood. Now they wanted her to be employed at some suitable household and earn a wage before it was her time to get married.

During those two years the girl worked at their house, his mother gave light chores to Rumi. She set the dinner table, cleared it, watered the flowering plants in the garden, and folded the clothes that were washed by the dhobi. Sometimes, on the weekends, Mohan was asked to dust the furniture with her, which he resented tremendously. "I'm not being paid for this," he would call out to his mother, being watchful that his father wasn't around to hear him. In the evenings, when Mohan did his homework, Rumi would sit in a corner and watch him.

Then, after two years, one day when Mohan came home from school, he was told by his mother that he would be helping her out with setting the table and dusting the furniture since Rumi had gone home with her father to get married. Mohan laughed at the thought of Rumi getting married. He wondered whether she was marrying someone her own age. He missed her for a few days, but after a while forgot about her absence.

Not long after that, maybe within a year, his grandparents visited them. Mohan was in high school at that time. It was a Sunday. After a sumptuous lunch of rice, goat curry, and sweets made by his grandmother, Mohan went to his room to finish his homework. His mother and grandmother remained on the veranda and exchanged news. All of a sudden, his grandmother started whispering. Mohan tiptoed to the closed door of the veranda and stood behind it.

"Is that so?" Mohan heard his mother responding. Then she added, "It is sad." Mohan became more curious and kept his ear close to the door.

"Her husband beat her. Poor child. He forced himself on her, I hear," his grandmother murmured. "She had no choice but to return to the village."

"Well, she can come back here," his mother said.

"No, no. Don't make that mistake. Manu is growing up. You know what

I mean." His grandmother kept quiet after saying that. Then she raised her voice for everybody to hear and said, "It is getting hot on the veranda. Maybe I should go in."

Mohan retreated to his books and thought about Rumi. There was no doubt in his mind that they had been talking about her. He was almost thirteen but couldn't understand what his grandmother had meant by Rumi's husband forcing himself on her. Later, when he realized the meaning, it felt horrible and he felt woeful about it.

***

As they waited for the bus, Andy stood quietly to one side, holding his mother's hand. Every now and then, he glanced at Mohan and then looked away. "The bus is coming . . . the bus . . ." Mohan heard Andy saying again and again, bringing him back to the present.

"Mommy, can he come to Coney Island?" Andy asked his mother. Mohan sat two rows behind them in the bus and waited for Sophie's response. He would come up with some excuse if Sophie invited him. He had to finish writing his paper. Not only that, he did not want to go out with Sophie.

"I don't think so, sweetie," she replied, to Mohan's relief.

"But, Mommy . . . why can't he?" Andy insisted.

"It's all planned this time. I'm sure he has other things to do," Sophie told her son, and handed him a chocolate chip cookie. Andy seemed disappointed but didn't persist.

By this time, the bus had arrived at their stop, and Mohan followed Sophie and Andy as they got out. She slowed her pace so Mohan could catch up. "I received a letter from Chris," she told him.

"He must be all right," Mohan responded, trying not to sound indifferent. It had been almost six months since Chris ran away, leaving Sophie and Andy behind.

"He wants me to join him," she said, lowering her voice so that Andy wouldn't hear her.

"Are you going to?" Mohan asked, even though he thought that it was unlikely she would go.

"No. It is better this way," Sophie answered, as Mohan opened the door and they all started climbing the stairs. Then mother and son entered their apartment and locked the door.

Nevertheless, Sophie had decided to visit Chris during that Christmas break. She asked Mohan to tell their landlady, if he was asked, that she would be back right after the New Year. The day before Christmas, she took a Greyhound bus with Andy and headed to the address in Canada Chris had provided. To Mohan's surprise, they returned two days later.

***

Sophie had informed Chris that they were coming, and of their arrival time, but he wasn't there at the bus stop. Finally, after much searching and waiting in the morning hours, mother and son took a taxi to Baldwin Village, which was close to the University of Toronto. The place where Chris was living was surrounded by the so-called student ghetto, which had been a breeding ground of the 1960s youth movement. It made sense to Sophie that Chris had fled there, because the place was a central location for draft dodgers.

The taxi pulled up in front of a dilapidated two-story brick building, one of many, lining Baldwin Street. They housed assorted stores and fast-food joints on their lower levels, and from the torn shades hanging at an angle, Sophie could tell that the second floors were used as residences. She looked at the building number written in the letter. Young men and women who looked like students came out and went in distractedly, perhaps preoccupied with the war and their futures.

After paying the taxi driver, Sophie got out and stood

on the sidewalk, holding the suitcase she had packed for the trip with one hand and Andy with the other. She waited for a brief moment in front of the building's door, covered with antiwar graffiti, then pushed it with her back. The door was not locked. She left the luggage near the narrow landing at the bottom of the stairs and went up.

There was only one room above the stairs, and its doors were wide open. She stood there with Andy, taking in the scene. Then, with a sense of repulsion that felt like nausea and dizziness at the same time, she pulled Andy down the stairs with quick steps and was out of the building. All of a sudden, her other hand felt light, and still in a daze, she went back and collected the suitcase.

It was noon by the time they sat down for lunch at one of the Chinese eateries. She ordered a couple of chicken spring rolls for Andy and settled for chicken wontons and rice for herself. An oriental girl, probably the daughter of the old man behind the cash register, went back and forth serving the few others. Sophie tried to draw her attention, and after some time when the girl returned to their table, Sophie ordered a small Coke for her son.

"Mommy, what was Daddy doing on the floor?" Andy asked while waiting for the food. "What are the others doing there?"

"We arrived too soon. Daddy was still sleeping." Sophie felt light-headed and sick to her stomach as she answered Andy. She had tried to block his view of the room, but the little boy must have seen things before that.

"Are we going to see Daddy after we eat lunch?" Andy asked.

"No, Son. We'll be going back home after this." There was nothing for her to do in Baldwin Village. Chris wouldn't even know that she was there, because he himself was lost. She noticed the little boy's face had brightened up after she'd said this. He looked content as he sipped Coke from a plastic cup.

After lunch, they went back to the Greyhound station. She was tired from the bus ride from Long Island. It had taken them the whole night. It would take another night to go back. Luckily, she could change her return tickets to that night. She sank into a chair with heavy limbs, resting her feet on the suitcase. Andy sat in another chair still holding the plastic cup, which the girl had refilled. As Sophie tried to close her eyes, the images from that room upstairs at Baldwin Street forced themselves upon her.

There had been about six or seven half-naked men and women in that room. Actually, Sophie had seen more men than women. She hadn't been able to tell their ages, but they hadn't looked like college students. The men had worn long tunics, and unkempt hair hung to their shoulders, while the couple of women had practically nothing on them. They had all sprawled on the floor, their bodies reeking of filth and ganja even from the landing where Sophie had stood. Empty beer cans and thick butts of rolled paper filled with marijuana had been strewn all over the floor, along with paper plates with dry food sticking to them.

Chris had been splayed on his side like a dead animal, his right hand placed on top of a woman's breast. In the streaming sunlight, the woman had looked pale, and freckles had covered her face. She had looked much younger than Sophie. Somehow, the December cold hadn't seemed to bother them. In that small room, they had huddled together, gathering warmth from the sun and the weed.

For a brief moment, Sophie felt misplaced. Nevertheless, when she opened her eyes and collected herself, she was glad that she had made the trip. Chris had come full circle, from an aimless hippie to a political activist to an aimless hippie again. She sat up straight on the bench and pulled Andy toward her. It would be a while before they boarded the bus. Andy leaned against her and fell asleep to the sounds of people and buses pulling in and out.

On their way back, as the bus drove through known and unknown places in the dark, Sophie knew for sure that in a short period of time another chapter in her life had ended, but this time she didn't feel any sadness from the core of her heart.

Chapter Seven

Mohan was cooking the midday meal when he heard footsteps on the stairs. He opened his door slightly and saw Sophie climbing up with Andy. He hadn't been expecting them for another week. Instead of closing his door and retreating, he opened it all the way and stood there. Sophie looked exhausted from the travel, but he could tell that the boy was wide-awake and upbeat. Mohan waited until they reached the landing. He knew that things hadn't gone well with the visit to Chris.

"We arrived too early. Daddy was sleeping with friends . . . on the floor. Too many friends." Andy showed all the fingers of both hands when he said this. "There was no place for us. Right, Mommy?" Andy asked his mother, to validate what he understood to be the reason for their coming back.

Without saying anything, Sophie got the key out of her purse and opened the door to their apartment. She had left the suitcase downstairs and was about to go to get it when Mohan went ahead of her, saying, "I'll bring it up." The suitcase was small but heavy. Sophie had packed seven days-worth of clothing for both of them. Mohan put the luggage at the threshold of their door and retreated to his room. Sophie pulled it behind her as mother and son went in. In two days, the apartment had acquired a musty smell, and she kept the door open to air it out.

Mohan's lunch was almost ready. He dumped the boiled rice into a small colander to drain the water. As he got the plate out, he thought about Sophie—her long journey, back and forth, with a child. He wondered if they had anything to eat at home. However, he was hesitant to invite her to his apartment. He didn't want to mislead her in any way. He looked at the dishes he had made. In spite of the urge to stay away from her, he went and tapped on the half-open door to Sophie's apartment. He wanted to be sensible. He thought that any reasonable person would extend hospitality in such a situation. "I have cooked a simple meal for myself. I would like to have you both over for lunch, if it is okay with you," he said when Sophie came to the door.

"That would be too much trouble for you," Sophie said, hesitating at first. Then she agreed when she remembered that there was nothing in the refrigerator.

They sat down to a simple meal of rice, dal, and fried cauliflower with potatoes. For Andy, Mohan put a slice of American cheese on top of a toasted bread. After lunch, Sophie offered to do the dishes. Andy was pushing and pulling his red car, making "vroom, vroom" noises with his mouth.

"Did Chris tell you that Andy is not his son?" Sophie asked, facing the sink.

"Yes . . . he mentioned it," Mohan said it after keeping quiet for a while. He didn't want to tell a lie; at the same time, he didn't want to hurt her.

"I thought you must have known. He told everyone," Sophie said casually as she wiped the kitchen sink with a paper towel.

"What happened?" Mohan asked not wanting to sound intrusive but knowing well how his question would be interpreted.

"You mean with the visit, or with Andy's father?" Sophie asked without sarcasm.

"You don't have to tell me about either of them. I'm

sorry I asked." Saying this, Mohan emptied the leftover food into small containers.

"No, actually, I want to tell you," Sophie said. Then she described how they'd arrived and how, through the open door, she'd seen Chris lying there on the floor. How there had been half-naked men and women, all passed out from smoking weed. She told him about turning back as quickly as possible to protect Andy from witnessing the vulgar scene.

Mohan kept quiet, not knowing how to respond. He had never thought that there was any emotional bond between Sophie and Chris, and now Chris had deserted her, setting her free. He felt happy for her, but expressing this could have been construed as showing sympathy, so all he did was put the containers in the refrigerator and soaked the pots in water.

"And Andy . . ." Sophie started again while wiping the plates with a paper napkin. "Robert and I went to the same high school and after that to college. Soon after we got married, he was sent to Vietnam. He died in a trench, fighting the Vietcong. I found out that I was pregnant right after he left."

"Did he know you were pregnant?" Mohan asked.

"Yes," she replied shortly. She took a glance at Andy. He was busy playing with his red car, not paying any attention to the adults. "I wrote to him. He had just left, but he couldn't wait to come home," she continued, turning her face the other way, but her choked voice gave her away.

They were both quiet for a while. Mohan thought about the loss she had endured and the hardship she was going through. He wondered about Chris. He had surely inserted himself into her life to dodge the draft, but then he had run away to Canada like a coward.

Then Sophie turned around and looked at Mohan. "Chris isn't a bad person," she said, as if she could read Mohan's mind. "They were friends from elementary school. I was devastated after Robert's death, and within a few months, Chris proposed to me. It was strange, though. We hadn't gone out with each other or anything. I think he married me out of pity. For a few months, things seemed fine. He was attentive. He helped with chores. But things changed after Andy was born. Chris could never love him, and it hurt me more than anything else. Something was happening to Chris. The war got into his head."

Mohan tried to understand the irony of the way things were. Sophie had lost the man she loved, to the war. Chris had claimed her and the child to be his family out of sympathy or, more likely, to evade the war. There had been no love in it, just some self-centered calculation. Yet, instead of being thankful for what he had, he had left behind everything Robert would have wanted to have at any cost.

That day, Sophie thanked Mohan after lunch and went back to her apartment with Andy. They didn't see much of each other until after New Year's Day, only waving from a distance if they happened to cross each other's paths. Soon, the Christmas break ended and students returned to the campus. One of those days, as Mohan prepared to get ready to go to the department, it started snowing. Within an hour, the snow was blowing and piling up on streets, looking like puffed cotton. He waited, knowing that the university would open late. From his window, Mohan saw Francesca and Julia arriving together.

Then Mohan heard footsteps coming up the stairs, and his heart sank. He could hear the mother and daughter talking in Italian before they banged on Sophie's door.

"You are late, again," Mohan heard the mother saying as soon as the door opened. "We have been very accommodating."

"I'm sorry. Within two weeks I'll pay you for the whole month," Sophie said in a low voice.

"We're running a business. How many times can we make exceptions?" the daughter asked. "We need the money, now. Otherwise, you have to vacate the apartment at the end of this week," she added.

Mohan knew that Sophie was short on cash because of her trip to Canada. He thought he could help her out this one time, hoping she would be all right once she got her paycheck. Nevertheless, he didn't want to offer the money in front of the landlady. After retrieving the fifty dollars Sophie had given him in exchange for babysitting Andy, Mohan waited until the women's footsteps receded and disappeared beyond the entrance.

Then he knocked on her door. It was a while before Sophie opened it. She was surprised to see Mohan. The tension of one person's asking for a favor had given way to the awkwardness of another's offering of help. "You can pay it back to me whenever you want," Mohan said to her, as he held out the envelope containing the dollar bills.

Sophie looked into his eyes, trying to gauge the depth of his empathy. For the first time since Robert's death, she let her guard down, and tears rolled down her cheeks. She felt no shame in crying in front of a man. This man, a foreigner, was nothing to her. Yet, unlike the other men in her life, he had understood her anguish and humiliation. For more than a year, he had been a silent witness to everything that had happened in her life, and there was no hiding from this. She wiped her eyes with the back of her palm and without reservation extended her hand to accept the envelope from him.

After a fortnight, Sophie returned the money to Mohan. He put the dollars back in the same place, insurance against another difficult day in her unforeseeable future. Meanwhile, a few more months passed and one more winter was over with the promise of summer around the corner. The Vietnam War and everything else related to it dominated the news, day after day. However, soon after Walter Cronkite delivered the news on CBS, people escaped to the television sitcom, *All in the Family*, which had debuted right after the New Year.

Sometimes, after a long day's work, Mohan looked forward to the comedy show at night. He got a peek into the mind of the working middle class through Archie Bunker, the chauvinist. Mohan saw the biases that swamped the minds of ordinary people, portrayed by the boxed-in character. He was amazed by the fact that topics from rape to abortion and homosexuality were discussed so openly on the television and wondered whether different generations of families watched the show together.

In spite of the prejudices, he was presented with, Mohan found virtue in people all around him, who struggled to be righteous and embraced the vast diaspora of culture that surrounded them. He often thought about Sophie, whose weathered life had no place for bias but just infinite strength of mind.

The more Mohan thought about Sophie, the more judgmental he became of the people back at home, including his parents. They kept writing about his marriage prospects. To them, everything—caste, class, social standing, virginity—was part of a list that had to be fulfilled when a bride was chosen. Mohan wondered what would happen if he ever told his parents that he wanted to marry Sophie.

Months and seasons passed, and they remained busy with their own lives. The close proximity of their living quarters occasionally brought them together, but they lived on the periphery of each other's feelings. Nevertheless, they both drew comfort from the physical nearness of their existences. A wall separated them, but there was contentment to coming home and knowing that there was life on the other side, someone probably thinking the same thoughts.

As time passed, Mohan felt less conflicted about his interactions with Sophie and the child. If he heard a knock on the door, he opened it without hesitation and enjoyed the small ways he could help her out. He didn't mind looking after Andy. The boy had outgrown his tantrums and kept himself occupied by building houses and cars with Lego bricks, which he got as special treats from his mother for behaving well.

Sometimes, on weekends, one of them invited the other for a simple meal of pasta and salad or rice and curry. Mohan always carried a small packet of cookies for Andy when he visited them. This friendship and cordiality between them were without guilt or reproach. Yet Mohan could never bring himself to talk about Sophie and Andy to anyone. He felt safe shrouded in the veil of secrecy, even though there was nothing to hide.

Once a year, the three of them went to the city to see the Christmas tree lighting, riding the same bus but Mohan always taking a seat a couple of rows behind Sophie and Andy. After they'd reached their destination, Mohan would take Andy's hand while they walked around Rockefeller Center at night, the cold air whipping their faces. They'd get lost in the midst of countless people, no one caring to know how they were related to one another. When they got back, Mohan would carry the sleeping child from the bus and put him on his bed, then say a quick goodnight to Sophie before returning to his apartment.

It wasn't that he hadn't thought about spending the night with Sophie. He would lie in his bed imagining his hard organ inside her butter-soft body. His young virgin body would writhe with pain as he thought about the carnal pleasure he hadn't experienced yet. Then, as his body moved alone to some familiar rhythm, he would hold on to himself and feel the whole place exploding into bits and pieces within him. After that, a deep sleep would overtake him. He avoided asking himself if Sophie shared the same agony. There was no sign from her. Passion rose, then subsided, because neither of them thought it could be plausible for them to belong to the same home.

They both lived this way in their guarded enclave, trying not to tip the balance. Once in a while, Mohan went out in the evenings with friends and fellow students, but when he returned home, he looked forward to seeing the light from Sophie's apartment or to hearing her reading a story to her son. If it happened to be late, the dark and silent place would stare back at him, and with a heavy heart he would go to bed. On weekends, while he sat near the window writing his thesis, he'd see Sophie walking by the water with Andy, or mother and son returning from the store with groceries. Andy was almost seven then. Instead of holding his mother's hand, he carried a small bag of food all by himself.

Finally, four winters had passed, and it dawned on Mohan that that summer would be his last on the campus. After one more winter, by the end of the next spring semester, he would have gotten his doctorate degree and would have moved on to some other place with a job. At the thought of leaving the place, Mohan felt emptiness rising in his heart, and the future he had so eagerly awaited when he'd arrived felt distant and bleak. He couldn't imagine a new place for himself without Sophie and Andy living next to him. He realized that their presence had filled his emotional void and had sustained him all these years.

Nevertheless, he knew that he would have to think about his parents. They had been waiting patiently for him to return and fulfill their last dreams—to have a daughter-in-law and grandchildren. Where he came from, those weren't unfair expectations for his parents' generation. After all, he had known people living under the same roof generation after generation, not giving any thought to it.

At the thought of his parents, Mohan felt a tug at his heart. He hadn't seen them for more than four years. Their life without him must have been a long, continuous wait, every moment of it lived with anticipation. Their entire existence had revolved around him. They had sought very little material comfort of their own and given everything they had for his advancement in life. It was inconceivable to him to leave them alone in their old age, lonely and without hope.

***

It was a hot day in July of that last summer. The temperature wasn't that high, but humidity made it oppressive. Mohan opened the window all the way to get some fresh air. From a distance, he saw Sophie and Andy walking toward the harbor, then Andy turning back and looking toward his apartment. The next moment, the boy was knocking on Mohan's door.

"We are planning to take the ferry tomorrow evening. I want you to come." Andy said it as soon as Mohan opened the door. "My mother said you wouldn't, but I want you to. It will be so much fun," Andy continued before Mohan could answer.

"I've a lot to do, Andy. Maybe another day," Mohan replied, expecting the young boy to understand.

"We won't be going another time," Andy persisted. "You have the whole summer." After he said this, he stood there looking at Mohan, waiting for an answer.

Mohan wanted to resist the boy's invitation. He observed Andy closely. He had grown tall and thin, like a reed, in the past few years. His face still held the innocence of his childhood, but his voice had acquired a maturity that was a combination of persuasiveness and sincerity. He wasn't ready, yet, to understand why his mother thought that Mohan wouldn't be able to accompany them. It would be a while before the boy discerned the gray area, the muddled spectrum, undefined ground between black and white. What Mohan and Sophie felt for each other wasn't an absolute truth or a complete lie, but it was something in between. Andy was too young to understand that.

Mohan went back to the window and looked out. Sophie had turned around and stood facing the apartment. She must have been waiting for an answer, just like her son. Then he looked at Andy and felt caught between the mother and son. Finally, Mohan took out the dollar bills from under the clothes and told the boy, "Let's go." He insisted on buying the tickets for all three of them.

The next day was bright and clear. So was the evening. Mohan, Sophie, and Andy boarded the ship at dusk. A half-moon emerged from the sky, its reflection floating on the waves. This time, they seated themselves in the same row, Andy taking the middle seat. After the ship was loaded with cars on the lower two decks and people on the topmost one, it moved leisurely from Port Jefferson to Bridgeport, Connecticut. The seagulls, along with the landscape, receded into the background as the ship made its way across the Long Island Sound.

The three of them sat quietly, watching the ship chugging through the water and leaving swaths of waves behind. Halfway through the ride, they could see lights along the coast of Bridgeport. The distance wasn't much, about eighteen miles from shore to shore, and the ride took little more than an hour. Once the ship docked in Bridgeport, the boat emptied of passengers and cars, and new passengers and cars filed in. Mohan, Sophie, and Andy remained in their seats. It would be the last ferry back, and the little shops near the ticket office were closed. The only thing that remained open was an ice-cream stall with pictures of different kinds of ice cream and cones attached to its sides.

"Mom, can we have ice cream?" Andy asked, as the kiosk caught his attention.

"We may not have enough time," Sophie replied.

"But . . . Mom, it will take only five minutes to go and get it," Andy said, and kept looking at the stall expectantly.

"I think we can make it, if you hurry," Mohan said, and looked at his watch. They still had fifteen minutes before the ferry went back. It was one of the treats Mohan himself enjoyed. He remembered the ice cream bars of his childhood days. In the heat of summer, after school was dismissed at noon, everybody ran out to the street to buy ice cream before going home. Mohan liked the coconut-flavored bars. As he licked them slowly, the sugar and coconut flavor would get sucked out first, and it would be only ice that remained attached to the stick. Even the ice had tasted good then.

Mohan and Andy came back with three cones of single scoops. Mohan savored the ice-cold smooth cream, flavored with vanilla, as it floated over his palate and melted into his throat. It tasted so much better than the ice-cream bars of his childhood, yet he felt nostalgic at the thought of the sugary water solidified around a long stick. For a brief moment, he thought about his parents. He hadn't written to them for the past month.

On their way back, Mohan told Sophie about his getting his degree and leaving the place in less than a year. He told her about his parents, how they had been waiting eagerly for him to return. He didn't mention anything about the plans they had for his marriage.

"You won't be coming back, I presume." Mohan sensed sadness in Sophie's voice as she said it. He himself felt emptiness at the thought of leaving the place that he had called home for the last four years.

"It depends. I've applied to a few places. If I get a job, I'll be back for some more years." As he said it, he sincerely hoped to come back again to see Sophie and Andy. If he got married, he would bring his wife to meet them. She would understand his friendship with Sophie because they were nothing more than friends.

His resolve to return to India after he got his degree had diminished, by the time he was about to finish his studies. He had halfheartedly applied to a few places back at home but fervently wanted to stay for a few more years in the States. "It won't be forever," he told himself. He hoped to convince his parents to accept the idea of his staying in the States by telling them about the abundant opportunities he would have in this country to further his career. At times, though, he had doubted the honesty behind his reasoning for wanting to stay.

"Would you come and visit us?" Andy asked, as if he could read Mohan's mind.

"We don't know which place he'll be going to. It would be too much trouble for him to visit us," Sophie answered her son before Mohan could say anything. She wanted to make the break as easy as possible for everyone. No matter what she felt for him, she had never thought of holding him back for her own happiness. She could never take advantage of his generosity.

Andy didn't say anything to his mother's reply. All he knew was that Chris had disappeared from his life. This time it was different. He really liked Mohan. All three of them sat quietly, each immersed in their own impending loss. Andy and Sophie could claim no hold on Mohan and he no hold on them, yet the thought of separation ripped at the seam of their known existence. It was late when the ferry returned to Port Jefferson. The harbor was quiet except for the cars being driven from the ferry and disappearing at the bend of the street. Mohan, Sophie, and Andy walked together into the night and to their apartments, trying to comprehend the loneliness that awaited them.

They hardly saw one another during the winter months. Sophie got promoted to a supervisory position at the campus cafeteria. She worked long hours six days a week, and on Sundays, she shopped for groceries and organized her home for the upcoming week. After school, Andy hung out at the cafeteria, finishing his homework and waiting patiently to accompany his mother home.

Mohan felt busier than ever. His doctorate thesis was typed, after the graphs and equations had been checked and rechecked. He flew to a couple of places for job interviews, always thinking of visiting Sophie and Andy if he found a job. Then, at the end of March, when he got a call from one of the universities in California offering him a postdoctoral position, he kept the news to himself. He was supposed to feel happy at his own accomplishments and finally feel free to chart his own life, but this place, where he had spent the last five years, had made him feel bound to it.

He realized that the place had entwined him with Sophie and Andy, and it felt hard to extricate from them, as if he were leaving a part of himself behind. With all his hesitation and circumvention, with alternate tugs of love and denial, his heart had crumbled to pieces so many times, but it had waited patiently for him to look inside and find the truth.

Nevertheless, at the end of May of that year, Mohan packed his belongings in two suitcases and knocked on Sophie's door. It was late evening, and Sophie was home, cooking. The same subtle aroma of spice that Mohan smelled in the beginning when he'd first moved to the place, was wafting from inside the apartment. He hesitated for a moment, but waited.

"I'm sorry it took me so long," Sophie said as she opened the door and saw Mohan. A smile spread across her face, exhausted from the daily grind from morning till evening. "Come in," she said.

"No, sorry, I've to go." He pretended to be devoid of emotion. "I'll be flying back tomorrow." His demeanor was matter-of-fact, as if the parting were just after a brief meeting, not like what one would expect after two people had lived next door to each other for five years. He didn't tell her about the job. She didn't call Andy to bid him good-bye. When he shook her hand to say farewell, her hand went limply into his. Then, without saying anything, she turned around and closed the door softly. They had tried to protect each other with the utmost care.

Part Two

Chapter One

Instead of flying to California, Mohan had returned to Long Island without sending any notice to Sophie. As he got out of the taxi, from a distance, he didn't see any light coming from Sophie's apartment, and his heart sank with fear. A lot could have happened in the last month while he was in India. It was possible that she had moved to another place. In that case, he would have to wait until morning to find out her new address from Francesca. Then a new anxiety took hold of him—a dread that Francesca might refuse to divulge her whereabouts.

In his confusion, he hadn't thought to look at the apartment he had occupied for so many years. The light was pouring through the open windows on both sides of the room. A gentle breeze swayed the curtains from side to side. He had never noticed the place looking so lively from outside when he was there. He waited for a moment before proceeding. Then pulling his suitcases, he headed in that familiar direction in the hope that whoever was living there would be able to help him.

It was a balmy August evening, the same time of the year as when, five years back, he had come to America to study. The golden hue of the setting sun spread on the harbor, and the herons dipped into the water for their last fill of the day. He looked for signs, something to tell him that all wasn't lost. Not Sophie. Not Andy. The place— the street, the beauty salon, and the apartments above it—looked exactly the same. He moved fast and crossed the street to the other side. As his heart quickened with anticipation, he twisted the knob to the outside door, and the door opened.

Mohan climbed up the stairs and knocked gently on the door of his old apartment. He felt like an intruder who had no business being there. There was no response. He could hear the sound of a television in the background. This time around, he knocked a little louder. Then he heard a woman's voice, unmistakably Sophie's. "You forgot to lock the door again. Now . . . who could it be?" As he heard footsteps coming closer, Mohan recognized the sign he had been looking for—the unlocked door.

They stood at the door looking at each other, not knowing what to say, as if they had lost their ability to speak. They hadn't averted their eyes and looked elsewhere, as they had done before, but when the eyes met, they were laced with the sadness of the repressed emotions of the lost days.

"What are you doing here?" asked Sophie finally, unable to believe her eyes.

"I've come back for you," replied Mohan. There was no uncertainty in his voice.

"What do you mean?" Sophie asked, surprised. "I never thought I would see you again."

They both stood there in silence. Then, after what seemed like a long time, Sophie pushed his suitcase inside the room, as she said, "You are welcome to stay for the night, if you don't mind the cramped space."

Andy was absorbed in a cartoon show, but as soon as he saw Mohan, he jumped up from his chair. "You left without saying good-bye to me" was the first thing he said to Mohan. He stood beside his mother, his face beaming with joy. "We gave up our apartment and took yours. Mom said we would have a better view of the harbor." He said this apologetically, thinking that Mohan had nowhere to go.

"It's all right, Son. We have enough space for him." Saying this, Sophie told Andy to set the table for the three of them. After dinner was finished, Mohan helped Sophie with the dishes. Once they were done taking care of the kitchen, Sophie spread two blankets on the floor, one for Andy and one for her, and gave the bed to Mohan in spite of his protest. He fell into a deep sleep, exhausted from the long journey and finding comfort in the setting he wanted to make his own.

By the time Mohan was up, Andy had already left for school. Sophie was making toast and coffee for them. Mohan came and stood near her. The hard floor had kept her tossing and turning for the better part of the night. Not only that, she had been trying to decipher the meaning of Mohan's return and what he had said upon his arrival.

For the first time in five years, they were alone with each other. Their bodies felt the stress from the tension arising all around them. They were happy and scared at the same time. Living next to each other for so long hadn't prepared them for this moment.

"I thought you left for good," Sophie said as she poured coffee into two mugs.

"I have a postdoctoral position at Berkeley," Mohan responded with guilt. He had left Port Jefferson like a thief, trying to obliterate any familiarity with her. Now he could not ask her to be a part of his life without sounding shallow. However, the conflicts that had shrouded his life had given way to the truth he was waiting for. "Sophie, I love you. Would you marry me?" he asked, looking at her.

Sophie looked away. "I don't know," she said. In the past years, she had often thought about Mohan. Nevertheless, she had never considered marrying him. She had always been grateful for his help but could not ignore the distance they had tried to maintain with each other. There had been no room for romance or falling in love. They had both walked a measured path, strewn with limited words and subdued emotions. "I don't know how it would work," she added.

Mohan wasn't surprised by Sophie's answer. He thought about his own aloofness till the day he'd left the place after he got the degree. His relationship with his parents had ended over her, but she had neither any part in that nor any knowledge of it. She had no obligation to fulfill his dreams. Yet he knew that he was in love with her. "I'll try my best to make it work. I love you," he said as he kept looking at her.

Sophie was at a loss. Something unexpected had come hurtling her way, and she needed to collect herself to regain her balance. She had forgotten how being in love felt, and she wasn't looking for it. "I need time. It's so sudden." Sophie looked beyond the street and the harbor to the calm Long Island Sound as she said this.

"No matter. I'll wait." Saying this, Mohan hesitated for a moment, then, planted a soft kiss on her lips. There was a newfound exhilaration when their bodies brushed against each other, and the long-suppressed desires spread through their limbs like currents. However, neither one acted on it, for they would wait for Sophie's answer, free from any physical bondage.

Mohan had to leave for the train station before Andy got home. He missed the chance to say good-bye to the boy. He had to take the train to New York and, from there, catch an afternoon flight to San Francisco from the John F. Kennedy airport. "I will call you once I have a phone. If it's okay with you," Mohan told Sophie as he went down the stairs. He didn't want to impose on her in any way.

"I would like that," Sophie said as she waited on the landing.

Before Mohan closed the outer door, he turned around and glanced at her. She waved at him and went in. As he crossed the road, he looked up and saw her silhouette against the still curtain. He wondered whether he would see Sophie and Andy again. However, he decided not to feel despondent. He hoped that time would bring them together.

As Mohan walked out of her view, Sophie observed the water in the harbor from behind the sheer curtains. There were no waves, only small ripples. The same sea that crashed into its shores with great force elsewhere, lost its currents surrounded by land. Her own life felt like that restrained sea. The events in her life had changed the natural course of her existence, making her unable to feel the waves of joy waiting to carry her out to the unbound vastness. All she had to do was let time chart her course.

On his way to the airport, Mohan wondered whether he had made a mistake. Even though he understood Sophie's reluctance, he wouldn't know how to chart his life's course if she declined to marry him. The undeniable realization of his love for her, combined with his parents' rejection, made him feel weak.

He called her as soon as he got a phone in his apartment. After so many years of self-imposed silence, it felt as if they were learning to talk with each other. As the weeks passed, the small talk about the weather and their day-to-day lives began to come naturally. In the beginning, it was Mohan who initiated the calls, but after a while, Andy wanted Sophie to call so that he could talk to Mohan.

Mohan spent that time at Berkeley working on research problems and discussing them with colleagues, all the while waiting to hear from Sophie regarding her decision. During that time, he didn't write to his parents, because there was nothing to write; his life was on hold. As Christmas became nearer, Mohan thought about the trips he had taken to New York City with Sophie and Andy and wished they were in California with him. Three months had gone by since he had seen them the last time, and he missed them more than ever.

Then one day, Sophie called right after Mohan had returned from the university. After the exchange of pleasantries, she was quiet for a while, as if searching for the correct words. "Mohan, I was thinking . . ." She stopped before finishing. He waited eagerly. Could it be that she was thinking about the same thing that had occupied him every moment of every day? After a long pause, she said, "Maybe we could all go to the city during Christmas. But only if you have time."

Mohan would have waited as long as it took to hear this from Sophie. He didn't believe she was asking him to fly all the way from California to take them to the city just for the night. His instinct told him that this was the invitation of a lifetime. Yet he found no words worthy enough to respond to her. He simply said, "Thank you."

***

They were returning from New York City after the light show. Unlike on the previous trips, Mohan and Sophie were sitting next to each other. Andy sat in the row just in front of them and kept looking through the comic book

Mohan had bought for him. The bus mostly dropped people off on its route. It was late at night for anybody to get on and go somewhere. Mohan sat silently, holding Sophie's hand.

"I've thought about it," Sophie said finally. For a brief moment, her hand quivered inside his hand. She had known him for more than five years—as a neighbor and a friend— as someone amid his own struggles in a foreign country who had helped her at the worst of times. Moreover, she had seen him up close, a decent human being who had never tried to take advantage of her. Not only that, he had loved Andy all along.

"So, the answer is, yes?" Mohan said as he kissed her trembling hand in the dark. He was too shy to kiss her lips in front of other people on the bus. She leaned her head against him, and their racing hearts beat to a single rhythm. "When would you like to come?" he asked with joy.

"How long can you stay this time?" Sophie asked. "We would need at least two weeks' time to get married," she added.

"I can work it out," Mohan said, and the prospect of the three of them going back to California thrilled him.

The next couple of days they spent collecting documents in preparation for their marriage. After that, all three of them went to the county courthouse to apply for the marriage license. The clerk looked at them quizzically, as if they didn't fit into the same picture. He made them wait the better part of the morning before he could look at their papers. It wasn't as easy as Mohan had thought. Sophie had to provide a myriad of documents, including her first husband's death certificate and papers proving divorce from Chris by abandonment, along with an identification card and birth certificate for herself. That was when Mohan found out that she was his age.

The clerk was extra careful while checking Mohan's documents. He leafed through Mohan's employment papers like he was combing through his hair with a fine-tooth comb, looking for head lice. Once he was satisfied, the clerk returned the documents to Sophie instead of to Mohan. They were asked to come back after two days to collect the license.

With license in hand, they went to a nearby church to get married by the minister. It was nothing like what Mohan's parents had had in mind for him—days and days of celebration with relatives, and sweetmeats spilling from every corner of the house. The whole village would have been invited to the feast and to look at the bride while his parents basked in pride. The bride would have been covered with jewelry from head to toe, while henna adorned her fair hands.

No such celebration waited for them at the church. They exchanged the thin gold bands Mohan had picked up for both of them at the airport gift shop in India. They exchanged the customary vows of "Till death do us part" in front of witnesses from the church, and then according to the custom, Mohan planted a quick kiss on Sophie's lips after the minister had pronounced them man and wife. Mohan felt his body tense with excitement at the thought of their long-awaited union. They went to an Indian restaurant for lunch to celebrate the wedding.

They consummated their marriage after Andy left for school the next day. Once he boarded the school bus, Mohan closed the windows and moved the mattress to the floor, mindful of the customers in the beauty salon. They both stayed in bed the whole day until it was time for Andy to come home. Just before he got home, Mohan put the mattress back on the bed. During the night, they took their assigned places—one slept on the floor while the other on the bed—waiting impatiently for the next day to arrive. Later, Mohan couldn't remember leaving their small living space for the whole week. He didn't even go down to meet Francesca. With Sophie and Andy in it, the place felt complete.

It was one of the mornings that week. After breakfast, they had made love passionately and lay next to each other in total bliss. It wasn't nine o'clock yet, and Sophie had taken the whole week off. That was when she asked him about his parents and family. It wasn't that it hadn't occurred to her to ask about them before, but an unknown fear had kept her from wanting to know the truth. She had never been sure if he loved her when they'd lived side by side for the past few years, but she had no doubt about it now. She was afraid of the price he could have paid for her sake.

"I'm the only child. My father was a police constable, now retired. My mother always stayed home, like most Indian women do." Mohan said all this at a stretch, as if he had rehearsed the words for this moment. He didn't want to say anything that would take away from Sophie's happiness.

"They are not happy about this marriage, I presume." She nudged him.

"No. They wanted me to marry someone Indian, someone who could follow their customs." Mohan's gaze was fixed on the ceiling as he said it. He was quiet for a while. Then he turned toward her and continued, "They will come around. It is not your fault."

"I feel terrible. I'm so sorry, Mohan," Sophie said, as she faced him with the realization that her newfound joy had created a rift between him and his parents. It was true that she had never given any indication of how she felt toward him before she had agreed to marry him, how night after night she had wanted to be held in his arms and forget about the loneliness that encompassed her. Yet she felt like she had snatched somebody else's happiness and made it her own.

"Don't you see? I couldn't live without you. I was the one who came to you. Can you forget that we had this discussion?" Mohan moved the few strands of hair from Sophie's face and looked into her eyes as he said this. They looked calm from years and years of struggle, but they were resilient. She could not have accepted anybody's pity, even unknowingly. That was what Mohan loved about her the most. Then, to change the subject, he said, "We'll buy a secondhand car once we go to California. And you are going to teach me how to drive."

"You must be out of your mind. When did you see me driving?" Sophie replied with amusement. "I don't have a license to drive a car, let alone teach you."

"Well, you must have driven once. I'm sure you know how to drive," Mohan said good-naturedly.

"You are right. My parents gave me their old car in high school, which was a while ago."

"Are they in New York?" Mohan was curious now that Sophie had brought them up. Knowingly, he hadn't asked about her parents or if she had siblings. He had heard their landlady ask her, and she hadn't answered her. Mohan had figured she would tell him of her own accord.

"They live in New Jersey. But we are not in touch. My father was against my marriage to Robert. He didn't like him. He thought Robert was too gentle, too nice. He looked at it as a character flaw. Things got worse after his death. Then when Chris came into the picture and I married him out of despair, they told me that I was on my own."

"Have they seen Andy?" Mohan asked.

"No. They haven't," she replied.

Mohan didn't know what to think of Sophie's story. What was the probability of two people getting together and both being rejected by their parents? Quite low, he imagined, but it still seemed hilarious to him. "Any siblings?" he wanted to know.

"A sister. Two years younger. The darling of the family. She is the obedient one."

"So, what happened to the car? They took it back as punishment?" Mohan thought he knew the answer.

"No. Actually, I totaled it. It wasn't my fault, though. An old man ran the red light and hit the car on the passenger side, right at the middle. I was lucky to be alive but quite shaken up. I hadn't driven since then." Then, as an afterthought, she said, "With all these things going on in my life, driving was my last priority."

"But you need to drive once you are in California. I can help you after I've taken my driving lessons," Mohan said.

"I don't mind taking the public transportation. And in any case, I will be going to places with you," she replied.

"All right. We'll see how you feel about it later." Mohan didn't want to persist then. Once he got his license, he would try to persuade her, again. He didn't want her to go through the trouble of carrying grocery bags on the bus. Sooner or later, Andy would be involved in extracurricular activities and she would have to drive him.

At the end of two weeks, Mohan flew back to California alone to look for a place. He wanted it to be big enough for each of them to have their own private space. Sophie stayed back in Long Island to take care of things before she resigned from her job. He talked to Sophie and

Andy every day, missing them, yet reminding himself that this could not be worse than the last few months, the time he had lived in a void.

Even though the real estate market near the university town was less affected by the explosion of Silicon Valley during that period than San Francisco and the areas to its south, it took a good effort on Mohan's part to find a two-bedroom apartment at a reasonable price. He didn't wait until he had furnished the apartment before having Sophie and Andy join him. He decided that they could do it together.

The day they flew in, Mohan had made macaroni and cheese, which Andy loved. He had made the salad the way Sophie made it. They slept on the floor for the first month, until they got a full bed for their room and a twin bed for Andy. Soon after that, Mohan bought a secondhand car from a former graduate student who was moving across the country after finishing his degree.

They found the California weather to be much more pleasant than the bitter cold that persisted for months in Long Island. Moreover, he liked the campus. California had become a melting pot with people of all races and nationalities, and the campus reflected it. He saw many students from India and the subcontinent, struggling, studying hard, and trying to find the American dream, just like him.

Sophie and Andy had filled Mohan's lonely life. He woke up early in the mornings and got Andy ready for school. They walked together to the bus stop, a brown man and a white boy, but nobody noticed, as they would have on Long Island. By the time Mohan returned, Sophie was up. They had fried eggs and toast for breakfast, and sometimes they just had plain cereal with milk. Mohan prepared tea.

Sophie had tried boiling milk and water with a piece of ginger in it, then adding tea leaves and boiling the mixture some more, but it never came out the way Mohan made it. She had come to love the tea, but only when Mohan prepared it himself.

By the time Mohan came home in the evenings, Sophie had taken care of shopping and cooking. Often, she surprised him with new Indian dishes, for which she got the recipes from a cookbook at their local library. If there was still daylight, he went out with Andy and worked on teaching him how to play soccer. After supper, he helped Andy with his unfinished homework. Mohan had a simple, blissful married life, the kind of life he had witnessed his parents leading and the one he had envisioned for himself.

At the thought of his parents, Mohan's heart would become heavy. In the three months after his marriage, he had written them three letters, telling them about his marrying Sophie. He had told them about Andy, saying they would like him once they saw him. He hadn't received any reply from them. He had decided to give them space in the hope that with the passage of time, their disappointment in him would cease and forgiveness would follow. He had resolved to write a letter to them every month, regardless of whether they responded.

Meanwhile, he had applied to adopt Andy. After moving to California, Andy had wanted to know how to address Mohan, and Mohan had told him to call him by his name. He wanted Andy not to have another father but a friend. Mohan had observed the boy closely for the past few months. Day by day, he grew more thoughtful and mature, and he acted older than his age. He had known Mohan since he was three years old, and in the new household, Andy had adapted to him instantly. At the same time, he held Mohan in a reverence that was uncalled for from a boy his age.

When Mohan made him breakfast in the morning, Andy wanted him to eat with him, and when Mohan said he would wait for Andy's mother, the boy's face radiated with happiness. It was as if he had always understood his mother's suffering and was grateful to Mohan for taking care of her now. Likewise, if Sophie gave Andy something special to eat, he always asked her if she had saved any for Mohan.

Mohan knew that Sophie's resilience and the love for Andy had taught the boy to be appreciative of everything in life and not to take anything for granted. He had the wisdom to sense the change in their lives and made every effort to feel the grace of God. He did well in school. He made friends easily. He was polite and well mannered. He made Mohan proud of him. Sometimes it scared Mohan to see so much happiness in their lives, and he thanked to God for his blessings.

Months passed, and Sophie hadn't seen any letter coming from Mohan's home. At the end of every month, he wrote a letter to his parents and waited the whole month in anticipation. The letter never came. Sophie noticed the anxiety in his face when he went through the mail in the evening, and she understood his dejected feelings. For a brief moment, he would become unmindful, as if the happiness around him had lost its meaning. Then, like a floating cloud, his sadness would pass, and he'd become himself again.

In those moments, Sophie left him alone. She had lived through that experience. After Andy's birth, every time the phone rang, she had picked it up with excitement, thinking that the call was from her parents. It had been eight years since then, and her mind had accepted this reality. She hoped that it would be different with Mohan's parents. In the beginning, she had asked him to call them, but Mohan had told her that they didn't have a telephone, and no one else in their village did either.

"Maybe they will forgive me once they have a grandchild," Sophie blurted out one day, right after Mohan had gone through the mail. Mohan didn't reply. The idea stuck in her mind for some time. She stopped using contraceptive pills. After a couple of months, her body felt different. She felt sick in the morning. Then she bled until her belly expelled the life she so dearly wanted. In a few days, her body returned to its previous state. It happened again and again.

Each time Sophie miscarried, Mohan felt the pain. At times, he thought that their union was cursed, and he didn't deserve to have a child after depriving his parents of the pleasure of his company in their old age. After a while, he and Sophie gave up on having a baby. They both took this as a penance for their love for each other, which was without the blessings of their parents, and they poured all their efforts into Andy.

After his postdoctoral position, Mohan moved to the private sector, building bridges and skyscrapers while adhering to strict codes to prevent damage from earthquakes. They bought a three-bedroom house with a small yard, where Sophie grew flowers. They both drove, and Sophie had her own car. She drove Andy home after his tennis practices and violin lessons.

Amid the harmony in their life, Mohan's desire for a letter from his parents hung like fog, waiting to be lifted by fate. He wrote to them asking their permission to visit them, still they didn't write back. He wrote to his uncle asking about his parents' wellbeing and didn't hear anything from him either. In their eyes, he was an outcast, as good as dead. Yet he didn't know how to obliterate that part of his life. If five years weren't enough for his parents to forgive him, he would wait as long as they needed.

Chapter Two

Years passed as Mohan, Sophie, and Andy lived what seemed to be a happy, uneventful life. In the evenings, they sat around the dinner table and talked about their days. Often Mohan and Sophie discussed the events that dominated the news. There was a certain normalcy in the air once the Vietnam War had ended and the student unrest had subsided. Although Mohan still witnessed student movements at Berkeley, they were of a different kind—they were mostly about the cultural and social changes, like the black power movement, the gay rights movement, and the other movements started in the sixties.

The year 1981 held much news for everyone to celebrate. People all over the globe watched Prince Charles's marriage to Diana, and Sophie wasn't any exception. She sat glued to their television set, the whole day, to view the spectacular royal wedding. Mohan and Andy left her alone that morning, preparing their own breakfast. She wouldn't even let Andy flip the channels to look for advertisements about the release of his much-coveted IBM Personal Computer.

Andy watched the advertisements about IBM announcing its first PC, intently. The release made the computer a household item. Mohan had promised Andy he'd buy one, once they were in stores. The whole summer, while his school was out, he wished he had a computer, while his mother claimed the television for herself at times. However, he waited for it patiently, and when he got the wonder machine, he wasn't about to share it with anyone.

Then, when Sandra Day O'Connor was sworn in as the first woman justice on the Supreme Court, Sophie celebrated the news with great enthusiasm. During dinner that evening, she and Mohan discussed at length how India was ahead of its time. It had elected Mrs. Indira Gandhi as its prime minister, a while back.

Nevertheless, that year also found itself with the first diagnosed cases of a disease involving severe immune deficiency, which would be later known as AIDS. It would afflict the US for decades to come and change the lives of people in ways that were then unimaginable. The diagnosis of the disease was in its infancy. Even the experts didn't know much about it. However, they were certain that the virus from an affected person entered the victim's bloodstream through the mingling of blood and saliva. They knew that gay people and drug addicts who shared needles were at greater risk than the general population.

Andy had just turned fifteen that year and was in his second year of high school. He had joined the school basketball team in his freshman year. With his long arms and legs, it was easy for him to make jump shots and score. He spent his weekends playing the sport and was really getting good at it. However, in his sophomore year, Sophie was refusing to let him continue on the team. She wanted him to play tennis or something else but not basketball. Often, he asked his mother whether he could join the team again. She wouldn't hear anything of it.

To Sophie's discontent, the previous year, she had noticed Andy getting close to another player, Dylan, in the basketball team, who was a year senior to him. Andy wanted to hang out with the boy all the time. Frequently, Andy asked his mother whether he could invite Dylan to their house. If not, he wanted to ride the bus with Dylan to his house.

In the beginning, Sophie had felt relieved that Andy wasn't interested in girls at such a young age. However, as the school year progressed, she had gotten frightened at the thought that there could be something more than just friendship between the two boys. She had the nagging fear that Andy was attracted to Dylan. She thought that Andy had started to pay more attention to what he wore and how he looked. He selected his clothes with great care the night before school days and laid them out neatly for the morning. Before going to school, he would stand in front of the mirror for a long time combing his hair. First, he would make the part on the left, then on the right; then he'd try to curl the ends of his hair with a comb. Sometimes, he'd dabbed himself with Mohan's aftershave cologne before heading to the bus stop.

Sophie didn't want to mention her suspicion to Mohan. The notion that Andy could be gay would be devastating and would rock the foundation of their happiness. She felt as if she would be perceived as a deficient mother for not raising him to think straight, in case he was gay. The thought consumed her day and night and would not let her out of its grip.

Sophie feared that she was losing control over Andy. He wasn't a little boy anymore. What if he was tempted to experiment with sex with Dylan? The evening news fueled her fear. One could not escape seeing the emaciated men in hospital beds, unable to move or take care of themselves. They were young, yet their immune systems just gave up when invaded by the virus. Every day, the experts in that field discovered new findings. AT the same time, she heard that San Francisco had become the epicenter of the disease because of its gay population. Sophie became overly concerned about Andy. For any ailment he went to the doctor, she remembered to ask, "Could it be related to his immune system?"

Now Sophie wished that Andy had a girlfriend. Amid the privilege of love and assurance, her life started hoarding a multitude of what-ifs. Even though, other than her intuition, she had no proof that he was gay, she wasn't ready to admit that it could be just her imagination. In any case, once the first year of high school was over, Sophie breathed a sigh of relief. She did not let Andy invite Dylan to their house over the summer. She had made up her mind not to let him play basketball either so that he would have no reason to spend time with Dylan.

It was the beginning of Andy's second year of high school. After finishing his homework, Andy came into the kitchen. Sophie was almost done with cooking dinner. She asked him to set the table before Mohan came home.

"Can I join the basketball team?" Andy was at it again.

"No. I told you no already."

"Why can't I? What's wrong?" Andy demanded.

"You just cannot." Sophie felt irritated as she said it. She had noticed that since Andy had started high school, he challenged her about everything. In spite of her being easy and understanding about most things, they ended up arguing often.

"I don't understand. I can't play. I can't have friends. You two should put me in a cage." Andy shut his bedroom door with a loud noise after saying this.

"What did you say? We two? When did Mohan tell you anything?" Saying this, Sophie barged angrily into his room. "You are being very unfair to him."

"Maybe he should run away like Chris, if I'm unfair."

Andy realized his mistake as soon as the words were out of his mouth. Even though he had been a little boy when Chris deserted him, he still remembered the meanness with which Chris had treated him. There was no comparison between Mohan and Chris. Mohan was more than a father to him. "I'm sorry for what I said. I didn't mean it," Andy said soon after he'd spoken. He looked remorseful. His war was with his mother, not with Mohan.

Sophie was struck by Andy's insensitivity. His tongue had turned into a weapon. She felt numb from the toxic words expelled from his mouth. He was old enough to understand what she had gone through to raise him from a baby and what Mohan had given up to make them a family. Nevertheless, she decided to forget what he'd said and forgive her son this one time. She didn't want Mohan to find out about their fight and Andy's thoughtlessness.

By the time Mohan was back in the evening, the table was set. Andy had set it without any conversation with his mother and gone back to his room to finish his homework. "Where is Andy?" Mohan asked as soon as he'd changed into more comfortable clothing and was seated at the dining table. Recently he had observed tension between the mother and son for no apparent reason.

"He is in his room," Sophie replied as she brought the dishes to the dining table. The pasta had turned out too soft.

"Isn't he eating with us? Something happened at school?" Mohan seemed concerned.

"It's the same thing. Basketball. It has gotten into his head." Sophie put the pasta on the plates and was about to serve meat when Mohan got up from his chair.

"Andy, dinner is served!" he yelled from under the stairs and heard Andy's bedroom door open.

"We'll talk to him afterwards." Saying this, Mohan sat in his chair and waited for Andy.

Sophie didn't say anything. It was too hurtful to revisit the squabble she'd had with her son.

Andy came down and ate the dinner as if nothing had happened. When Mohan asked him about school, he was polite, telling him that things were fine. After dinner, Andy quietly helped his mother clear the dishes and put water in the teapot for Mohan. Andy had taken it upon himself to prepare the evening tea for Mohan because it was easy to dip a tea bag into hot water. That was how Mohan liked his tea made in the evening.

"How is your tennis going?" Mohan asked, after Andy handed him the cup of tea.

"It's okay. I'm not that interested in it," Andy replied.

"Did you talk to your mom about basketball, recently?" Mohan inquired, even though he knew well that that was what they had discussed before he arrived home; he wanted Andy to feel free to talk to him.

"Yes. She wouldn't agree. I don't understand what she is afraid of," Andy said, as he was about to go back to his room.

"Maybe I can discuss with her, later. Is everything okay with your math?" Mohan asked, because the previous year Andy hadn't done well in the subject. With Mohan's help, he had improved considerably. "Let me know when you need help," Mohan added.

"I will. Thank you." After saying this, Andy left to practice his violin. Every time, he talked to Mohan, Andy felt appreciation for him. He couldn't have been more grateful for having Mohan in their lives. Sometimes at night, just before sleep overtook him, Andy remembered Chris and his vulgar ways—his loud screaming and his loud groaning at night when he did whatever he did to his mother. It had scared him. As he grew older and realized what Chris did, he felt disgust toward him.

Mohan drank his tea alone in his study. Sophie was still occupied in the kitchen, making sandwiches for the next day. After he was done, he rinsed his cup and put it in the dishwasher. He waited for her to finish, and they sat together to watch a rerun of *All in the Family*. He could hear Andy playing Beethoven's Fifth Concerto. Midway through the show, Mohan lowered the sound and said, "Let him play basketball."

Sophie was deep into the jokes and laughter of the characters, and at first, she didn't hear what he said. When he repeated it, she shot back, "But don't you understand? I hope you are listening to the news."

"What are you afraid of? You cannot put him in a cocoon," Mohan said.

"It is strange . . . You are talking like him," she replied and got up to leave. She thought that it was impossible for him to understand anything. She had been fighting this battle with Andy for a while, and it seemed to her as if Mohan had joined forces with her son.

"They say it afflicts mostly homosexual men," Mohan said. He knew that what the news said about this new disease was confusing, but he was at a loss as to why Sophie was so scared about Andy.

Nevertheless, it was difficult to convince Sophie. She never divulged her true fear to Mohan. Every day, there was news of new cases of the mysterious immune disease and, it made her paranoid.

It was puzzling for Mohan to witness the vulnerability that surrounded her. The unknown fear, so intangible, was corroding her, and he was at a loss. Eventually, he gave up on reasoning with her. She had turned fierce in her protectiveness toward Andy, which had obscured their happiness. At times, he felt resentful toward her and her consuming obsession with her son's welfare, as if Andy were in imminent danger. At other times, he understood her paranoia. He had seen the mother and son walking hand in hand when he was a little boy. When she had been cheated by death and abandoned by luck, Andy had been the only meaning to her lonely survival. She clung to him with her life. Mohan couldn't make her feel secure.

She loved Mohan, but it was the kind of love tinged with guilt and gratitude, unlike the free and abundant love she'd had for her first husband. Every day, she went about building a family life while Mohan built skyscrapers. Then, in the evenings, when she observed his aloneness, when he opened the mailbox and searched for the long-awaited letter, she couldn't help but blame herself for that. It was a sadness he didn't want to share with anyone, particularly not with her. His gentle disposition forbade him from making her feel like an accomplice in bringing about his plight. Whereas, he went about his life compartmentalizing, keeping everything in its place, her sense of culpability was built on his momentary act of aloofness.

At times, she wrestled with emotions so alien that, it scared her. The novelty of a secure married life had slipped away with the passing years, and a dull, aching monotony had taken its place. She could not point a finger at any one thing. It was the sum total of small, as well as big, real and perceived failures that gave rise to her doubts.

It seemed to Sophie that, in his quiet, almost silent way, Mohan had moved on, but the waiting for a letter would be always there. The piling on of time just made it worse for her. The frequent thoughts of "Because of me" bounced in her head at various times. However, she didn't talk about them or know how to discard them.

She often thought about their lives, but there were things she could never discuss with Mohan. His abandonment by his parents had stabbed her like a knife. She had failed to produce a grandchild for them, the only possible way she thought she could mend their relationship with Mohan. Her body had healed from the multiple miscarriages, but little by little, depression had scarred her mind. Her resilient disposition had slowly been taken over by anxiety.

In the beginning, she had enjoyed a carefree life after moving to California. After so many years of struggle, she had been happy to stay at home and take care of Andy and Mohan. Besides taking care of the home, she spent a major part of her time taking Andy to and from school activities and extracurricular lessons. Though she exchanged quick greetings with parents she met at the school, Sophie never thought of building any deep friendships with any of the other mothers. Occasionally, she invited a few couples over for dinner, people Mohan knew through work. Sometimes, on Mohan's insistent, they visited the friends. Nevertheless, she never felt the need to discuss anything of a personal nature with them. She thought that she was content with just Andy and Mohan.

However, as Andy grew up, Sophie felt a void in her life and didn't know what to do with it. She couldn't bring herself to initiate friendships with people she had been acquainted with for years, and remained indifferent to everyone, in general, outside of her family. As time passed, she had nothing much to take care of and became obsessed with Andy's welfare.

To make matters worse, Andy became more and more

defiant of Sophie. He did it silently. After their last fight, he didn't talk about playing basketball anymore or argue with Sophie, but it became a pattern with him to withdraw, mostly from his mother. When Sophie tried to pry open the closed-up aspect of his personality, it made him more of a recluse.

To spite her, he would stay in his room until Mohan came home, then come down and engage with him about school and the news of the day, as if his mother weren't even there. Mohan realized that this was intended to torment Sophie, but he was also the recipient of inadvertent pain caused by this. At night, Mohan tried to talk to Sophie, telling her to be patient. He told her that things would pass, and Andy would revert to his own self once again. He told her that they should let him play basketball. She had made up her mind. Mohan knew that Andy's rebellion was due to her stubbornness.

Mohan recognized the anguish Sophie must have felt. He talked about Andy's childhood to give her solace. However, those years were vanishing fast, without a trace. Mohan attributed Andy's undesirable temperament to that particular time in his life. That was how teenagers behaved, he told her. He often tried to mediate between mother and son, but his neutrality was doubted on both sides. Andy didn't part with his troubled innermost feelings with Mohan either. Frustrated, Mohan retreated to his study and let them be.

The year that followed Sophie's fight with Andy over basketball was the precursor to what life would bring for each one of them. It was Andy's junior year in high school. As part of the community service part of his school curriculum, he had signed up to deliver food to homeless shelters. On Sundays, all the volunteers gathered in a kitchen run by the city, and filled Styrofoam boxes with turkey or ham sandwiches and warmed-up canned vegetables. They would carefully tape a chocolate chip cookie packet to the top of each box. Then the students were driven to various shelters by their parents.

Mohan volunteered to take Andy to their assigned homeless shelter. That way, he could spend time with Andy and feel useful. Once they arrived at the shelter, Mohan would stay in the car, and Andy would go out with the huge basket of sandwich boxes with Mark, another student from school who rode with them. From a distance, Mohan would see the men and women in tattered clothes forming a line in anticipation of their lunch, which was more likely the staple of their sustenance for the whole day. The two boys, one carrying the basket while the other delivered the boxes from it, would go through the line.

It didn't take them too long to finish the job. Andy always looked happy after that, and Mohan was glad for him. On their way back, he would take the boys to a McDonald's for burgers and fries, or to the Pizza Hut for pizza, so that Sophie could have the time to herself. Mark usually wanted to be dropped off at the library near the school where Mohan picked him up in the mornings. He wanted to walk home from there.

That year, Mohan felt a sense of relief. Andy was less resentful toward his mother and took up tennis once more. He got really good at playing violin. His grades were much better than the previous year. He became good friends with Mark. Everything looked promising, the way it should have been. No one, Mohan included, saw the undercurrent beneath the calm surface.

***

It was the junior prom night. Andy was taking Emily, one of the girls in his class, to the prom. Sophie had seen to everything—renting a tuxedo for him and buying a corsage for her. She had sent a check in advance to his school for the limousine ride and the dinner.

Sophie dropped Andy at Emily's house in the evening. As he got out of the car and walked away, Sophie could not help but notice how tall he had grown lately. His arms hung loosely from his square shoulders. He was almost a man. For a brief moment, instead of fearful, she felt proud of him.

From her car, she saw Emily open the door to Andy, and her mother came out and waved at Sophie. Sophie waved back and drove away as the limousine pulled in. She felt happy for her son. Her old fear had given way to new hopes. She thought that this was how things started. He just had to go out and experience the life that awaited him. That was how, one day, he would fall in love, just as she had fallen in love with his father.

To Sophie's astonishment, Andy called her around midnight to come and pick him up from the hotel where the dinner and dance were being held. He was supposed to go to Emily's house with a group of boys and girls and spend the night there. Without waking Mohan up, Sophie drove to the hotel. The roads were almost empty. Foreboding thoughts occupied her mind over the ten miles from her house to the hotel. Once she reached the place, the other students and the limousines were nowhere in sight. The party was over, and everybody had left.

She was relieved to see Andy from a distance, standing with another boy near the entrance to the hotel. At least he was safe. He was with someone. They were together. Although she was baffled as to why he wasn't with Emily or the group of kids he had planned to hang out with, in that moment, she was happy to know that nothing bad had happened to her son.

Andy and the boy approached her car as she pulled in front of the hotel. She recognized the boy, Mark, Andy's new friend, with whom he had been spending a lot of his free time recently. Their volunteer work at the shelter had ended, but they still hung out together. She felt weird seeing them together at the hotel on the prom night. A fear nudged her mind, displacing the relief she had felt a moment before, as if her motherly intuition told her that the boy had replaced Emily. She remembered her anxiety about Dylan all over again.

"What happened?" she asked.

"We were just talking. We noticed they were all gone after they'd left." Andy sounded awkward as he said it and got into the car with Mark.

"But I thought you both had a partner to take care of," Sophie said as she started to drive. Other than saying "Hello" to her, Mark hadn't uttered a word.

"I didn't have a date," Mark said finally.

"Where is Emily?" Sophie asked, turning toward Andy.

"She must have gone home with the others, I assume." As Andy answered her, Sophie could feel the buried tension creeping around them, but she decided to leave the matter alone until they reached home.

"Where should I drop you, Mark?" she asked her passenger in the back, trying to get a glimpse of him in the rearview mirror. She could see the silhouette of his head in the faint light emitted from the lampposts on both sides of the street.

"Could he stay with us?" Andy asked. "His parents aren't home."

Anger churned inside Sophie, twisting her thoughts. She wasn't able to say anything, and she wouldn't be able to confront Andy until Mark left in the morning. It must have been Mark who had persuaded her son to leave the party, for his sake. Moreover, he must have been seventeen, like Andy. He didn't need his parents to be home. Yet she couldn't say no to him. "Yes, sure," she muttered.

Mohan was up when they arrived home. He followed Andy as he carried a pillow and blanket to the basement and opened the sofa bed for Mark. Mark was already downstairs leafing through an art book they kept on a small wooden table.

"Hi, nice seeing you," Mohan said to Mark. Mark stood out of respect to greet Mohan. Mohan knew him to be always polite, almost to a fault, as if he was trying to compensate some inadequacy in himself by diverting attention from it and letting the attention rest on the surface. "How was the prom?" Mohan asked, not knowing what had happened.

Mark didn't say anything and looked at Andy. Then Andy replied, "It was all right." He was afraid that Mohan was going to ask the same questions Sophie had asked in the car. To his relief, Mohan left them, wishing them good night, and went up the stairs.

"Where is Andy?" Sophie sounded agitated when Mohan came into the bedroom. She had gone straight to bed after driving Andy and Mark home, but was wide-awake.

"They were still talking when I left," Mohan replied. He thought that driving in the middle of the night must have upset her.

"After skipping out on the prom, don't you think he should be in bed now?" She turned toward him as she asked this. "To tell you the truth, I don't like this boy, Mark. Something tells me this is not normal."

"Just relax. What's not normal about two friends talking? At least Andy is home . . . not getting drunk with the others," Mohan said as he climbed into the bed with her. "You are too worried. First, he couldn't play sports. Now he cannot have friends. Let him be, for God's sake," Mohan said as he switched off the light, sounding annoyed. Then they both heard Andy coming up the stairs and closing his bedroom door.

"You don't understand. He left Emily at the prom and was hanging out with Mark," Sophie continued. "And where are his parents? Surely Andy can't be his only friend."

"Well, why not? Mark is Andy's only friend. Thanks to you." Mohan suddenly came to his senses as he heard his own accusation against Sophie. Nevertheless, he felt that the words had come to him naturally, the result of an overbearing suffocation on Sophie's part. Lately he felt that the more he tried to help Andy, the more she tried to smother him.

Sophie was livid. Even though, for a change, Mohan had agreed that Andy was safer at home, just as she had thought all this time, his words sounded twisted to her, as if they were growing tentacles. She had to protect herself from the long-reaching arms of his words. All of a sudden she sat up in the bed and said, "You are not Andy's father. Mark is a faggot. What is it to you?" After delivering the blow, she rested her head on the headboard and remained awake for a long time.

Mohan lay in bed, silent, limp from the shock. What was he expected to do? His own father had abandoned him for falling in love, as if it was the worst crime he could have committed. If anything, this had taught him to be more perceptive about Andy's struggles. Mohan had forsaken his parents and everything else that had once been familiar to him. For whom? For what? A bitterness rose to his throat like bile.

Sophie barely slept that night. She kept thinking about finding an inconspicuous spot to park the car when she dropped Andy off at school that Monday. She did not want to run into Emily or, worse, into her mother. In the morning, Sophie hardly talked to anyone. She dreaded making conversation for fear that her thoughts might turn into spiked words and hurt someone, just as she had hurt Mohan.

Both the boys ate heartily the omelet and toasts she offered them without making any inquiry about their wellbeing. Other than greeting Sophie when he came upstairs, Mark had pretty much kept to himself. After breakfast, she offered to take him home, but he declined politely. He said he liked to walk.

Even though it was a Sunday, Mohan had left for the office before anybody was up. As he drove, the past had presented itself from under the layers of drifting fog slowly melting with the advancing morning. His thoughts were not about his parents this time. They were about the time when he had first heard Andy playing in the next apartment, and a barrage of abusive words had hit the walls from a man who was not the boy's father.

It was true that Mohan had felt pity for Andy when he was a child. It was also true that that pity had led Mohan to fall in love with Sophie and to marry her, and she knew that. Andy was not his son, not his flesh and blood, but his love for the boy went beyond any bonds held within the imprints of mere DNA. Mohan told himself that he wasn't about to be caught between Sophie's paranoia and his own positivity about Andy. By the time he returned home in the evening, he had put the previous night behind him, but he could sense their lives veering from their smooth trajectory and heading toward upheaval.

Mohan often noticed Sophie's mood swings when he returned home from work. Around that time of day, she became agitated about everything. If he was a little late, she was anxious that he could have been in an accident. Of course, her concern for Andy was constant. At night, after she fell asleep, Mohan remained awake and worried for her.

What he could not understand was Sophie's feeling of uncertainty about the life they had built together. Her confidence and resilience were giving way to self-doubt. He could not pinpoint any reason for this other than the fact that Andy was growing up and getting more independent and she was losing control. At times, it seemed as if her son was her worst enemy.

"Maybe you should consult a doctor," Mohan had suggested to her. He wanted to help her in any way he could. She had replied that she was fine and there was nothing wrong with her.

Then, just like that, she asked him one day, "Have you ever thought of leaving all this behind and going back to your own people?"

The question hurt him immensely, because she had mistrusted the depth of his love for her and Andy. He had tried to make them his own at any cost. He simply asked her back, "What do you think?" to which she didn't answer.

Chapter Three

Andy never went to Mark's house, because Sophie would never allow him to. Every day, she dropped him off at school and picked him up. After the prom, whenever Mark came to their house after school, Sophie stayed in the living room, pretending to read a book, and watched the boys' every movement out of the corner of her eye, as if they were little toddlers. They did their homework together and, sometime, just sat and chatted, always Andy's door wide open.

Sophie would sit there, her eyes glued on the same page but her ears trying to catch their every spoken word and pick up on the unspoken words floating between them. Sometimes she would get up and walk toward Andy's room to offer them a snack or some juice. Mark always turned down the offer politely, and Andy wouldn't respond. Before returning to her chair, she would sniff around like a dog, looking for some smell that would make her suspicion real.

"Won't you stay for dinner?" Sophie would ask Mark halfheartedly when it was time for him to go home. She always felt a sense of relief when he declined. He never accepted her offer to drive him home. He would walk to his house, which none of them had seen. After he left, everything became normal for her again. She felt free from the danger she thought she faced or, more precisely, Andy faced from Mark.

She did not want to discuss any of these feelings

with Mohan for fear that he would dismiss her concerns as baseless. Moreover, what proof did she have that Mark was gay? Even if he was gay, it was not an airborne disease that would afflict Andy. Yet every time she switched on the news, she heard about AIDS spreading in the gay community in San Francisco like forest fire, and her already weak mind felt shaky from the threat. She did not have any proof of Andy being a homosexual either. However, she thought that Mark, like Dylan before, was a bad influence on him.

She very much wanted to find out about Mark, but she didn't even know his last name. She couldn't ask Andy. Once again, her communication with him had broken down for reasons quite obvious to her. On one occasion, she had followed Mark on his way to his home. It was a small, unkempt apartment complex not too far from the school and the grocery store where she shopped. Sophie saw Mark open the door to the ground-floor apartment and close it behind him. As she was about to turn around, she saw a bulky bearded man enter the same apartment. She assumed that it was Mark's father.

Sophie decided to wait patiently for one more year for Andy to finish high school. She had succeeded in keeping Dylan and Andy apart. She would make sure that Mark and Andy did not end up at the same university. She didn't have to wait long for her wish to come true.

One day, Mark came home with Andy. Grudgingly, Sophie had picked them up from school. After Mark left, there was the usual tension between her and Andy. Mohan had just arrived home from work, and they were about to sit down to dinner when she heard two loud knocks on the door. Through the sheer curtains on the window, she could see the revolving blue and red flashing lights from a police cruiser. When she opened the door, the officers asked for Andy. He needed to go to the hospital to identify Mark.

That evening, as Mark had tried to cross an intersection to catch the bus after leaving Andy's house, he had been hit by a car and died instantly. It was raining, and fog had shrouded the streets like cobweb. He had refused Sophie's offer to drive him and said That he would like to walk. Once the police arrived at the scene of the accident, they found two addresses in his backpack. Andy's was one of them.

When Sophie arrived in the hospital with Mohan and Andy, accompanied by the policemen, she didn't see anyone near Mark's stretcher. It rested outside the emergency room, out of view from other patients. A white sheet covered his body from head to toe. As the doctor lifted the covering from the head, she took one look and felt sick to her stomach. Then she heard Andy identify "Mark Thomas" for the police to jot the name down. She ran to the nearest restroom and vomited into the sink.

As the three of them turned to leave, from a distance, they saw two figures advancing in their direction. Both looked dazed and the air reeked of marijuana as they approached. When they crossed paths with Sophie, Mohan, and Andy, the man squinted toward them for a brief moment and walked on.

The man had shoulder-length hair that was flowing freely, covering half of his face. It was the same man Sophie had seen near the apartment. He wore baggy pants and a short-sleeve shirt covering his big, protruding belly. His arms were covered with tattoos of Christ on the cross.

The woman had cropped hair, and little strands were hanging on both sides of her neck. She looked much older than the man. She wore an ankle-length skirt with a loose blouse. Her head was wrapped in a red bandana. Sophie assumed that the woman was Mark's mother because of the similarity in their facial features.

Instead of proceeding with her son and Mohan, Sophie turned around and walked toward the dead body. She stood at a distance while the woman identified herself as "Ellen Thomas, mother" to the attending doctor. Sophie was about to turn, when she heard the man say in a loud voice, "Harry Woods, stepfather."

All of a sudden, the man reminded her of Chris. Harry must have done the same thing to Mark that Chris had done to Andy years back—abandoned his duty to take care of him. It was obvious that the woman must have met Harry when Mark was already a young boy. Sophie could not comprehend how the woman was so blind as to not have cared for her own son. She thought that the fact that Mark was so reluctant to go home after school proved her point. She turned around and walked away, feeling dizzy.

Sophie was overtaken by her own guilt. She realized that Mark visited Andy because he had nowhere else to go. He must have felt like an orphan in his own home. He hadn't wanted anyone to know where he lived or how he lived. His mother and stepfather could have been with him in the same apartment but in a world of their own. She wondered if they were passed out from drugs and sex when Mark returned from school.

Yet she knew that her guilt had nothing to do with them. She herself had judged Mark for not having friends, for hanging out at her house like a homeless person. Not only that, she had taken him for a homosexual trying to corrupt her son and give him the dreaded disease, when the only thing Mark had wanted in her house had been a little affection and empathy.

On her way back home, she couldn't help thinking that, somehow, she was responsible for Mark's death. She sat quietly the entire ride, oblivious of the fact that Mohan and Andy were with her. She felt the pain of aloneness spreading inside her like fire, yet she couldn't tell where it came from. It burnt her limb by limb. Then she stopped feeling anything. Once she reached home, she went straight to bed. Mohan was calling her to come and have dinner, but she only heard his voice ricocheting from wall to wall.

As the days passed, Sophie withdrew more and more, creating a shell around herself, which neither Mohan nor Andy could penetrate. The rip she had created in the fabric of her family life made her feel like a total failure as a mother. During the daytime, alone at home, she reflected on her life up to then. It seemed without purpose. She felt abandoned by everyone, even by the unborn fetuses she had so much wished for not so long ago

For a change, the house became quiet. Sophie didn't have the energy to worry about Andy contracting AIDS or Mohan not getting any letter from his parents. Even Mark wasn't there to annoy her; he must have been in a better place. She felt happy for him. She slept whenever she felt like. In fact, she wished to fall asleep and never wake up. She had cleaned, cooked, and taken care of everything for so long. It hadn't done anything for her.

All the same, Sophie took care of the chores around the house like a zombie. Mohan often took Andy to school. Sometimes she forgot to pick him up and he walked home. She was relieved that Andy was taking driving lessons. She wouldn't have to take him around anymore. She cooked but her heart wasn't in it. The things she had enjoyed in the past had become tedious.

At that point, Mohan insisted on her seeing a mental

health professional. "Please, please, see a doctor," he pleaded. "I'll take the day off and come with you, if you want," he added. It hurt him to see her falling apart in front of his eyes, and he felt helpless.

Finally, Sophie agreed. It took a couple of weeks to get the appointment with a psychologist. She looked upbeat that morning as Mohan drove her to the doctor. On their way back, Mohan asked how things had gone. "Hope you discussed everything," he said.

Sophie remained silent for a while, then replied, "I didn't know where to start."

"What do you mean?" Mohan asked.

"It has been such a long stretch of time. Who has time to listen to that?" As she said it, she thought about her life, a jumble of unhappy convergences of events. The only time she had felt whole was when she was with Robert, but that had been short-lived. She couldn't even love Andy, their son, like before.

"That is what the doctor is for." Mohan sounded concerned and touched her hand. He had come to understand that her paranoia about Andy and AIDS was a manifestation of cumulative insecurities she had to deal with all the time.

"Six months have passed since Mark's death," Sophie said as she looked out the window. "I told the doctor that I didn't want him anywhere near Andy, but I did not want him dead."

"That wasn't your fault. It was an accident," Mohan said, trying to console her.

"It was my fault. If you only knew," Sophie shot back at Mohan with visible irritation. "I feel so sorry. I cannot make it right for him." Sophie started sobbing into her hands as she said this.

"Not everything is lost. You can make it right for Andy. You have to think about him," Mohan said.

They had reached home by that time. The jacaranda tree in their yard was laden with flowers. Sophie passed by it without paying any attention. After she had moved to California, she had fallen in love with the majestic tree with its purple flowers, adorning gardens and the sides of the roads. Mohan had bought her a sapling from a nursery when they moved to the house. In a few years, it had grown big and occupied almost half of the yard. "Andy doesn't need me." Saying this, Sophie went in.

Mohan accompanied Sophie to see the doctor on a regular basis. He could see that she still struggled with herself. Sometimes he thought that he got a glimpse of her old self, but that never lasted for long. Like a pendulum, her mood swung. The doctor had prescribed her antidepressants. She assured Mohan that she took them diligently.

***

It was a few weeks before Christmas. Mohan brought down the small artificial tree and the ornament boxes from the attic. With help from Andy, he set up the tree in its usual place in the living room. Sophie always looked forward to decorating the tree with trinkets collected over the years. However, that Christmas, she showed no inclination to decorate it. "Maybe all three of us can work on it this weekend," Mohan said, trying to coax her by offering help, knowing very well that Andy wouldn't participate. He was too busy applying to colleges. Not only that, since Mark's death, he couldn't stand to be in the same room with his mother.

That Friday, Mohan returned home early. It was not yet five o'clock, but dusk was about to set in. In the evening, he had planned to take Sophie and Andy out to dinner. As Mohan left the main road and took the turn onto a side road leading toward his neighborhood, an ambulance whizzed passed him. He thought about the old man, his neighbor's father, who often ended up in the hospital because of recurring pneumonia.

However, as Mohan got closer to his house, he could see the police car, its lights flashing, parked in his driveway. The ambulance had also stopped right there. His heart started pounding. It reminded him of the day, not too far in the past, when they had to identify Mark. As he parked his car near the curb and walked toward home, a police officer stopped him. "Do you live here?" he demanded.

"I'm . . . I'm . . . Mohan Samanta. This is my home. What's wrong, officer?" Mohan looked toward the door with vacant eyes as he asked. He wondered why Andy or Sophie wasn't coming to the door. They surely knew he was there. Could it be that they'd had a bad fight and Andy had called the police on his mother? But what was the ambulance doing there? Mohan thought his heart was about to jump out of his chest.

The police officer looked at him from head to toe. "Are you the husband?" he inquired.

"What is wrong with Sophie?" Mohan asked, and sat down on the spot, his legs buckling from the fear that something terrible had happened to her.

"We don't know yet. We'll find out." The officer said it as a matter of fact.

"May I go in?" Mohan asked. He held his head in both hands and kept looking toward his house. Then he saw the silhouette of the paramedics near his bedroom window. He got up and ran to the door before the officer could stop him. He was crying. The officer ran after him.

Andy sat on the living room floor, his back toward the Christmas tree. He made no effort to get up when he saw Mohan, as if he were stuck to the ground.

"What happened? Where is your mom?" Mohan asked, sounding like a madman. The police prevented him from going to the bedroom.

"She took all the pills," Andy replied. After coming home from school, he had heard some strange noise coming from Sophie and Mohan's room. The door had been closed but not locked. When he opened it, he saw his mother on the floor, stiff and shaking, froth coming out of her mouth. That was when he called 911. It couldn't be more than fifteen minutes back.

After a while, the paramedics came out of the room carrying Sophie on a stretcher. As they headed toward the ambulance, Mohan took a brief look at her, and it didn't seem good. Her face was pale like a sheet of paper. Vomit covered her long hair. Her eyes were half-open, as though she was taking everything in, one last time. He couldn't tell whether she was breathing or not.

Mohan, with Andy in the car, followed the police and the ambulance to the same hospital where they had gone to identify Mark. While in the emergency room a doctor tried to flush the antidepressants out Sophie's stomach, in a corner of the lobby the police officer asked Mohan a barrage of personal questions. He answered them like a machine as if they didn't pertain to him. When the police officer asked him if there had been any domestic violence, Mohan looked up at him like he didn't understand the question. Then he started sobbing, saying, *"No. No.* I love her," shaking his head.

After what felt like a long time, the doctor asked to talk to Mohan and gave him the dreaded news that he could not save his wife. She had taken way too much medicine. Her system had shut down.

After the police report ruled her death a suicide, Sophie's body, crusted with vomit, was taken to the morgue. It was almost morning when Andy and Mohan arrived home. Mohan could not comprehend the turn his life had taken. Everything seemed so unreal.

***

The rest of Mohan's memory related to the incident was hazy. At some point, he had called a funeral home to arrange the service for Sophie. She had been taken to a cemetery not too far from their house. After her casket was lowered to the ground, he and Andy had each put a handful of soil on it. Mohan had laid a bouquet of jacaranda flowers next to the grave. Days later, when he tried to relive those moments, things felt jumbled and he could not recall the sequence of events.

He took the whole month off to sort out the reality of his life. Once the funeral service and the burial were done, he wanted to be home with Andy. He lived in a stupor during the day, thinking that Sophie had gone to run errands, and missed her at night when he got to the empty bed. He cooked and cleaned. After a month, he went back to work.

Nevertheless, Mohan's broken world was not supposed to be mended. The local newspapers had published the news about the suicide, and he was haunted by the fact that he had failed her, no matter how inadvertently. He tried to make sense of the whole thing — specifically, the absurdness of Sophie's taking her own life. She was gone from him, having disappeared in front of his eyes, yet he felt dissociated from the loss. His mind had adjusted to her irrationality about Andy's contracting AIDS and Mark's inflicting it upon him. Soon it got accustomed to her absence, as if he had no other choice but to feel that way. He construed the impassiveness of his own consciousness after Sophie's death as his biggest character deficit, but he accepted it, as he thought that fate had to find its own way.

After so many years, Mohan thought about his parents and longed to see them. He wondered who was looking after them or if both of them were still alive. However, he could not bring himself to write to them after the path his life had taken. All his attempts at contacting them had been futile in the past. His father's stubbornness had made Mohan bitter and proud in the face of defeat, and he vowed not to go and knock on their door, uninvited.

Chapter Four

As Mohan was losing himself to indifference, Andy became reclusive and distant. They hardly spoke to each other. Just like before, when Sophie was there, he went to his room after he got home from school and stayed there the whole night. He didn't offer to help Mohan with the cooking or the cleaning. If Mohan asked about his day, Andy simply said, "It was all right." It was hard to say whether he mourned the death of his mother and of his only friend, because he showed no sign of mourning. The only thing he waited for was to bury the past deep inside his heart, so that even he wouldn't be able to access it.

Emotionally, for a while now, Andy had felt abandoned by his mother. As they settled down in California, he had noticed a gradual change in her. His mother's natural sweetness towards him was replaced by sudden anxiety and irritability. Whereas, Andy felt happy for her, she had found fault with everything he did, and he could not comprehend the reason for it.

As Andy grew older, he tried to understand if Mohan's being different, being an Indian, could be the reason for Sophie's unhappiness. In the beginning, when Mohan took him to school, his friends looked at him quizzically. Sometimes, they had even asked, "Is that your dad?" To which he had simply replied, "Yes." To him, Mohan looked different, but he had always been different since the day he knew him. If anything, Andy thought that Mohan had given them so much happiness. He was always kind and generous to them. At times, when bits and pieces of his childhood memory floated in his mind— the screams of a man, banging on the walls, the man lying naked with a bunch of women—Andy felt gratefulness towards Mohan.

However, Andy often remembered the evenings right after they moved to California. He was perplexed by Mohan's dejected looks when he searched through the mails after coming from work. He went through them intently, then dropped them on the dining table without opening any. "What are you looking for?" Andy asked him once. His mother was standing at a distance, her face seemed pale in the evening light.

"No, it's nothing. It's a letter." Mohan replied.

"It must be important. You are looking for it every day." Andy said good-naturedly. "Is it from your dad?" he asked. His mother left for the kitchen, at that moment.

"It is. You know India is so far away. It takes so long." Mohan replied. He had regained his cheeriness by that time.

"Maybe we can go and visit your parents. I would like to see them." Andy said hopefully. Once, during the geography class, his teacher had discussed about India— different people with varieties of costumes, many different languages, varying temperature—all encompassed in a place one fourth the size of the United States. As the teacher pointed at various cities on the map and put the pointer on Calcutta, Andy was all excited and said, "My father comes from a place just below that." All the kids laughed. His mother had told him about Bhubaneswar, but he never remembered the name. "They would be happy to see me. Don't you think so, dad?" He asked.

"We'll think about it," Mohan replied and left to change his clothes.

"Put the placemats on the table, please. Dinner is ready," Andy heard his mother say. As he left for the kitchen, the idea of visiting India to meet the only set of grandparents he would have thrilled him.

"Have you thought about it?" Andy asked the next day and the day after.

"About what? Oh…I forgot." Mohan said this unmindfully as he wrote a letter. "I've to see if they are free when we plan to come." Andy even read that part of the letter, Mohan asking permission to visit his parents.

"Do I need your permission to visit you and mom once I grow up and go away?" Andy asked innocently. He thought this was his house also. He was sure he could come back anytime he felt like.

To this, Mohan didn't reply for a while. Then he slowly said, "No. You don't need our permission."

After a fortnight, Andy asked Mohan if he had received any answer from his parents. "It won't be so soon. It takes almost a month for the letter to travel back and forth," Andy heard Mohan reply.

That night, Andy could hear Sophie and Mohan arguing in the bedroom. "You should tell him the truth. What's the point of covering it up?" his mother asked.

"What am I going to tell him? That they have disown me for marrying you?" he heard Mohan reply.

Andy was ten by then. He thought he saw an ugly glimpse of their happy life. Mohan's parents had rejected not only their son but Andy and his mother, as well. Otherwise, they had Mohan's address. They could have written to Andy. He never mentioned about the letter any more.

Then Andy thought about his mother getting sick, again and again. She remained in bed for a few days, but

Mohan nourished her back. When Mohan left for work, he told Andy to look after her after school. "You are not dying, mom? are you?" he asked once. His mother looked really ashen, and without energy. "I'm scared for you. Can't the doctor do anything?" he had asked.

"No, I'm ok, son. I want a brother or sister for you. It is just that my body won't let it happen." After saying this, his mother told him to go and finish his homework. Andy was probably too young to understand how a woman's body works. Why she could have him, but not another baby, was beyond him.

"I don't want a brother or sister. I want you, mom." Andy had lingered at her bedside as he said this. Sophie had kept quiet. After a while, Andy left her to do his homework. His mother was content with him for so long. He felt as if that was not enough for her. Sometimes, he wondered whether Mohan was the one who wanted a baby, risking his mother's health.

Nevertheless, Andy could not blame Mohan. It seemed to him that his mother had lost interest in everything. He knew Mohan had pushed her to get the driver's license, but she hardly wanted to drive. They didn't go to anyone's house and people rarely visited them. When he was younger, just him and Sophie, they did things together as mother and son. She looked sad at times then, but she was happy also. She was happy for a while after they moved to California. Andy felt that everything was changing.

When Andy was in Highschool, Sophie stopped having those episodes of getting sick. He was relieved that his mother wasn't preoccupied about having a sibling for him. Nevertheless, to his dislike, she had focused all her energy on him. He felt like he was being watched by her at all times. She told him that he was too young to have girlfriends, but she found fault with his male friends, also. He felt like he was smothered by her own insecurity.

"What's wrong with mom, nowadays?" he had asked Mohan one day after Sophie told him not to bring Mark home. She had told him that Mark was a bad influence on him. He had argued with her, telling her that she was sick in the mind. "You should take her to a shrink." Andy had said this when Mohan asked him to have patience with Sophie.

However, Andy eventually lost patience with both Sophie and Mohan—Sophie, for her overbearing presence, and Mohan, for his eagerness to please her. To Andy, the home felt like a war zone and, Mohan a constant peacekeeper. In his effort to bring accord between mother and son, Mohan tried to remain neutral. Andy took his impartiality as ignoring the issue rather than solving it. He would have liked Mohan to tell Sophie, "For god's sake, let him be like others." It took Andy a while to realize that Mohan felt as helpless as him when it came to Sophie. It hurt him to see his mother descending on a downward spiral.

Finally, Mark's death had defined Andy's relationship regarding his mother. He thought about his own childhood. The renewed knowledge that Chris, his own step-father, hated him when he was a little boy, broke his heart for Mark. Andy could not get over the fact that in spite of being abused emotionally by his mother and the step-father, Mark always had a gentle disposition. That was what drew Andy to him. If Mark ever sensed Sophie's displeasure towards him, he didn't let Andy know about it. They were just friends. Sophie had sullied their friendship. After Mark's death, Andy often wondered whether his friend had any inkling that Sophie had branded him as a fagot. He wondered if his death was deliberate.

After Mark was gone, Andy couldn't care less about Sophie's feeling guilty. His pity for his mother had taken over any empathy. He could see that they were a broken family at the core. Mohan tried to keep up with everything. However, he had seemed impersonal in his daily life. He cooked and cleaned after he came home, took Andy to his practices, while Sophie stayed in the dark corner within herself.

Andy wasn't shocked over his mother's death. Death had hovered over her for a while now. To him, the loss of her happy self could be considered as death, also. In that process, the impending death had altered Andy's perspective about life, love, and the relationship to each other in the family. If anything, he felt angry. He felt being deprived of his own happiness and felt cheated.

Therefore, by the end of Highschool, it felt natural to Andy that the trajectory of his life would search for an escape. The gentle, loving, Mohan of his childhood was nowhere to be found. He was immerged in his own sorrow, and Andy was being forgotten. So, one day, in the year 1984, Andy announced that instead of going to Berkeley, he had accepted an offer of admission from a small university in New York City. He felt free from his bondage to Mohan.

However, Andy's heart ached as he thought about the separation. He thought about the irony of it. He thought of what would become of Mohan. The people for whom Mohan had thrown his life away were leaving him, First Sophie, then him. In any case, Andy tried to tell himself that Mohan was not his father.

Chapter Five

After Andy left for college, Mohan would come home late. He'd stay at work until nightfall to finalize deals and to meet clients. On his way back, he'd drop by at a temple he'd often frequented after Sophie's death. The temple was full of Hindu gods and goddesses, the kind he used to visit with his mother when he was a little boy. On most evenings, the discourse on Bhagavad Gita kept him there until the gates to the temple were shut and everyone, including the temple priests, left for the night.

Nevertheless, Mohan waited for Andy's phone calls every day, just as he had waited for letters from his parents. When Andy called, it was brief. He said he was fine, and Mohan pretended to believe him. In any case, he always asked Andy whether he needed extra cash. Mohan paid Andy's room and board, as well as his tuition like a dutiful father who was hanging on to the last thing he had on earth. Sometimes sadness overwhelmed him when he thought about his aloneness. The ten years of his married life had come to an end.

Loneliness had driven Mohan to the temple, in the first place. He hardly spoke to anyone in the audience, but the presence of others, who resembled him and had come from India leaving everything behind, like him, was a source of comfort to him. While listening to the discussion of Gita, his eyes sometimes wandered from face to face as he tried to figure out the secrets hidden behind the facades. Surely, he wasn't the only one who had been dealt with a bad hand.

The evenings always started with devotional songs to the deities. Then the priest chanted in Sanskrit while offering flowers and *prasad*—vegetarian dishes cooked without onion or garlic—to the gods and goddesses. After that, *prasad* was distributed, free, to whoever came to the temple. The staple was simple—plain rice with sweet dal and some kind of mixed vegetable curry. It was strictly vegetarian. Mohan ate the *prasad* eagerly, and whatever was given was always enough for him. After he finished the food, he would walk conspicuously to the donation box and drop a dollar or two into it.

Even though he was tired to his bones by that time, he would hang out with the other devotees to participate in the discussion of Gita, which lay at the core of the Mahabharata. His mother had told him the story of Mahabharata—the war between the Pandavas and the Kauravas—the good and the evil. As a child, he had listened to the stories without any particular liking. The characters had been too dark and too complicated for him.

As he grew up, he had made efforts to read Gita, which encompassed the just and moral advice given to one of the Pandava brothers, Arjuna, by his charioteer, Lord Krishna. However, Mohan had been too young to take the advice to heart. It was too demanding and religious for him. He'd had no time for it then, but now it took on new meanings.

There were three or four swamis who came from the various ashrams in the nearby states and discussed Gita. They wore long hair and saffron robes. One of the swamis, Saralananda, came once a week from near Eugene, Oregon. He was skinny and tall for an Indian, almost six feet in height. He had soft yet piercing eyes that looked as if they could bore into someone's soul and extract thoughts without any effort.

After eating *prasad*, the devotees would sit down on the carpeted floor in a circle in front of the deity Lord Krishna. Except for Saralananda, the swami usually took the place in the circle directly facing the God and always had a slightly elevated seat, which separated him from his disciples, as if the long hair and saffron robe alone could not do the job.

However, Swami Saralananda always sat on the floor, just like the devotees, and never in the same place. He sat erect, towering over the people around him, and looked distinguished. He wore his long hair tied into a ponytail, and his beard touched his chest. By the time everyone assembled after *prasad*, he had come out of meditation and motioned them to take their places.

"Where were we last time?" he asked no one in particular, one night. Usually, that evening's teacher took over the Gita discussion where the previous one had left off. That day, everybody had a different opinion as to what should be read. Swami Saralananda scanned the audience, and his eyes rested on Mohan. The swami had noticed him before. He never talked to anyone. Sadness covered his face like a shadow that originated from somewhere deep inside his heart.

Mohan felt the swami's eyes on him. Instead of averting his gaze, he looked straight at Saralananda. "Do you remember the last reading?" the swami asked.

"No, Swami. I'm new to this. Can we start from the beginning?" Mohan replied without hesitation. Then he looked around to see if anyone minded. He heard a murmur from the crowd and understood that they wouldn't mind hearing the whole thing again.

"From the very beginning?" Swami Saralananda wanted to confirm.

"Yes, Swami. If it is all right with you," Mohan replied, looking animated.

"You all know about Mahabharata, the epic story of the Pandavas and the Kauravas, the descendants of King Bharata," the swami said, looking briefly at Mohan as he started at the very beginning. "Pandavas were the five sons of Pandu, the younger brother of Dhrutarastra. Pandu ruled the kingdom because Dhrutarastra was blind. Dhrutarastra had a hundred sons, and they were called Kauravas. After Pandu's death, the Kauravas wanted the kingdom for themselves. The eldest of the Kaurava brothers, Duryodhana, was malicious and jealous of the righteous Pandava brothers and had tried to kill them many times. Worst of all, they had tried to disrobe Draupadi, the wife of the Pandava brothers, in an assembly of elders and kings. In an unfair gambling match, the Pandavas lost the kingdom and were exiled for thirteen years. After thirteen years, when they came back and claimed the kingdom, Duryodhana wouldn't give them even five villages. Hence, the battle at Kurukshetra began.

"But, as you all know, there is much more to it than that." The swami closed his eyes and reflected as he said this. "Everybody who took part in the war was related to one of the two parties and sometimes to both. The war brought much pain and heartache to the Pandava brothers from seeing their dear ones being killed. That was when Lord Krishna, who had taken the side of the five brothers and was the charioteer of the famous warrior brother Arjuna, presented himself as the speaker of the Gita, which represents the philosophy and ultimate truth about life."

The swami paused after laying the background for Gita and surveyed his audience. They waited eagerly for him to continue. "You must have known this much?" he asked Mohan.

"Yes, Swamiji." Mohan replied. He knew the simple story behind Mahabharata, but what he could not fathom were the innumerable characters related in some way to one another and the way they betrayed and were betrayed in return. He greatly disliked the conniving Kauravas, and that stole the pleasant aspect of listening to the story. After a while, he had told his mother that he was sleepy whenever she started telling him about such and such characters in the tale.

"Even though Mahabharata is the backdrop for Gita, Bhagavad Gita is not about winning or losing the war but about righteousness and justice and giving yourself up to the supreme god, Lord Krishna. To be whole and to find moksha from this material world, we need to have a direct relationship to God." As the swami gave this simple introduction to Gita, he gazed from face to face and found Mohan listening to him intently.

At the end of the discussion, the swami asked the devotees if they wanted to discuss what he had said further. Mohan raised his hand like a small child who was lost and was eager to find himself.

"We can talk more after class, if you prefer," the swami said as he waved his hands and dismissed everyone else. It was almost ten by then. "Tell me what ails you," he said to Mohan and came closer to sit next to him.

"Sorry?" Mohan looked up at the swami abruptly. Even though Mohan knew that the new lines on his face mapped the ruins of his heart, he seemed healthy in every other way. He wasn't ready to talk to a stranger about his troubled soul. The swami might have been right in his perception, but he had no right to inquire about Mohan's life. Nevertheless, Mohan tried to reason with himself. The fact that he was still there after everybody had left could mean only one thing—he needed to know how to cope with the loss of Sophie and the separation from Andy. Before Mohan had started coming here, he had thought that his mind was lost as well. He looked at Swami Saralananda and saw a shadow of compassion in his probing eyes. "My wife died," Mohan replied.

"You want to talk about it?" the swami asked Mohan with a concerned expression on his face. He didn't ask how long ago or what happened. He would leave it up to Mohan to tell as much or as little he wanted to tell him.

Mohan assumed that the swami had heard these stories over and over. He hesitated for a moment and then said, "She killed herself." That was the first time he had brought up Sophie's death with a stranger. He was afraid that the associations with suicide would present him in an unfavorable light to the swami. Tears gathered in Mohan's eyes, but he blinked them away.

"Did you love her?" The swami asked this without sounding judgmental. "How about kids?" he added.

"Yes, I loved her. Very much." Mohan looked up at the swami as he said this. After Sophie was gone, he had realized that he had loved her more than he'd thought. "And the kid . . . well . . . my wife's son just left for college." Mohan said this haltingly, and shame overtook him because, after raising Andy for so many years, he still couldn't call him his son.

"And now?" the swami asked, looking at Mohan intently. "How do you feel? What do you think should happen?" the swami asked at a stretch.

"I feel that my life is in ruins, Swami. I see only darkness," Mohan replied, as he looked straight at the deities, avoiding the swami's gaze.

"Tell me more."

"You mean about my past, where I came from? My parents disowned me after I married an American." Mohan felt rage toward his parents as he said it, and he waited for more inquiries from the swami.

Swami Saralananda got up and paced in front of Lord Krishna and then came back and sat with Mohan once again. The swami had heard from many devotees who had gone through worse situations, but something told him that Mohan was totally lost. Before his scab had healed, he had been wounded again and was in great pain. "You are saying that your life is in ruins. Do you hear any echoes from deep down?" Saralananda moved closer to Mohan and put his hand on his back as he asked.

"No, Swami. All I hear is voiceless despair. It comes in waves, sweeping but silent. They pull me back with them. I get sucked into a narrow passage and into what looks like a dark chamber. As I try to climb out of it, I feel hands pulling me down." Mohan said all this as he felt the warmth from the touch of the swami's hand spreading to his heart and lessening his grief.

"Have you ever thought that the dark chamber is your own life, and the hands are those of the people you love, trying to hold you down to this mortal world? You have to break yourself free from it, in order to hear the beautiful, eternal song in the ruins within yourself." The swami looked at Mohan, observed his face reduced to anguish, and continued, "What humans think of love, I mean all kinds of love, is just illusion. In this worldly journey, someone always leaves the other person behind. The relationships one cries over are a sleight of hand, the hand of what one calls fate." Saralananda got up again and stood in front of Lord Krishna. "What do you see on his face?" he asked Mohan, pointing at Lord Krishna.

"His face, Swami, has no emotion. But he is the Almighty, God. He is supposed to be that way, I guess."

"You are wrong. He was as much of flesh and blood as you and me when he was the charioteer of Arjuna in the Kurukshetra war," the swami answered. "The whole universe revolves inside him, I agree, but the Gita, the practical way to view life, was recounted from his earthly form. When everything was destroyed in the ruins of Kurukshetra, what sustained the Pandavas was the wisdom that had poured forth from Krishna in the form of Bhagavad Gita and had entered their souls like songs of divine blessings, to guide them to their ultimate abode, heaven."

"But, Swami, my pain is too much for me to think about the songs of God. All I see is the dark abyss, littered with soundless figures floating around. If I try to reach them, they pull my hand before crumbling to dust." Mohan thought that he had explained himself as much as he could, exposing his inner turmoil to someone he hardly knew. However, he found the swami to be comforting.

"The only way you can leave the sorrow behind is by giving yourself to God completely." The swami said this as he collected his books and stood. "I hope to see you next week." He cradled the books of Bhagavad Gita and texts on Vedanta philosophies in his left arm and was about to climb down the few steps when he turned around abruptly and saw Mohan watching him closely. He came back and handed the copy of the Bhagavad Gita to Mohan, saying, "You can read this. I have one more."

Mohan accepted the book with both hands while bending from his waist to touch the swami's feet. The last time Mohan had touched someone's feet, they had been his parents', and it seemed as if it had been in another life. "But, Swami, I'm not a religious person," he said as Swami Saralananda put his hand on his head and blessed him.

"To believe in God, you don't have to be religious. Gita is about the philosophies of life, which show us the right path to travel through this mortal world. It will teach you ways to mend your heart." The swami descended the steps after he'd said this.

Mohan waited until the swami left the premises and then walked toward his own car. Somehow, he liked the silence and the quiet of the night. His heart didn't flutter as it had before. By the time he reached home it was almost midnight. He kept the Gita next to his bed and tried to sleep. However, the empty house resonated with the memory of Sophie, and he remained awake for a long time.

When he woke up in the morning, he looked at the Gita and remembered his discussion from the night before. Before starting the day, he decided to read from the Gita and read aloud to himself: "The mind is restless and difficult to restrain, but it is subdued by practice."

He cried like a little child after reading this. He wondered how long it would take him to lessen the immense pain he was suffering. He thought about Sophie. He flipped to a different page and read: "Whatever you do, make it an offering to me—the food you eat, the sacrifices you make, the help you give, even, your suffering."

The second quote seemed meaningless to Mohan. He opened the closet doors and looked at Sophie's belongings. Then he went to Andy's room. He hadn't taken his violin to college. Mohan sat down on Andy's bed and touched the strings, but they felt fragile in his hands, and he put the instrument down. He thought that nobody could take his suffering, not even God.

That evening, when Mohan arrived at the temple on his way home from work, Swami Saralananda had already left for the week. Mohan searched for him. Instead, Mohan saw another swami seated in the spot where the rest of the swamis usually sat. With great disappointment, Mohan took his place. He listened to the discussion of Gita but couldn't take it to heart. He kept thinking about Swami Saralananda's interaction with him the previous night—how it had been full of empathy. His pain had lessened a bit after he had talked to him.

The following week, when Swami Saralananda visited, the devotees ate their *prasad* and sat in a circle to listen to him. He came and sat next to Mohan. Throughout the evening, Saralananda often interacted with the devotees and asked what they thought about a given passage from the Gita. As usual, Mohan remained quiet. It made him feel comfortable that the swami left him alone.

"Did you get a chance to go over the book?" the swami asked Mohan after the discussion was over and the others had left.

"Yes, Swami. I tried. But it made me think of Sophie and Andy even more," Mohan replied. He could not comprehend the expectation that, the book could make him forget the people in his life whom he had loved so much.

Swami Saralananda opened the Gita and held a page in front of Mohan. "Read it to me, what it says," he told Mohan as he pointed his index finger to one particular quote.

Mohan wavered, then read, "Little by little, through patience and repeated effort, the mind will become stilled in the Self."

"Do you think it makes sense?" the swami asked. Then without waiting to hear the answer, he said, "You have to believe in what you just read. Death is the ultimate blow a heart has to deal with. However, there is no escape from it. So, what do you do? How do you forget?" He looked straight at Mohan and continued, "You have to make a conscious effort not to dwell on it but to accept it." It was getting late. The swami collected the Gita and got up to leave. "Go home and get some sleep," he told Mohan in a fatherly tone.

Thereafter, before going to work in the morning, Mohan made an effort to read a few pages from the Bhagavad Gita. If he read quietly, he heard Sophie's voice. When he read aloud, the words got lost in the emptiness of the house and his mind drifted along, thinking about his parents, Sophie, and Andy. Sometimes he closed the book and sat still, trying to create a vacuum around himself, pretending that nothing else had existed before this. However, his mind failed to conform to his self-imposed amnesia, and at times, he cried like a child in desperation. During those times, he waited eagerly for Swami Saralananda. His presence felt comforting and made Mohan feel less alone.

On one of the nights when Saralananda was at the temple, after the swami had finished teaching he asked Mohan, "Tell me how reading the Gita has helped you, so far."

Six months had passed since Mohan had come in contact with Swami Saralananda. What had drawn Mohan to the swami was the compassion he had shown toward him. He read Gita because the swami wanted him to read it, but it didn't touch him. "Not much, Swami," Mohan replied, after reflecting for a while.

"It will take time for you to heal. You have to learn to let go of your mind in order to ease the pain. Then little by little, you'll tell it what to do," the swami said. "It didn't happen with me overnight either," he said and got up from the floor. Then he sat down again and said, "My life was pretty much like yours. I wouldn't say 'worse,' because everything is relative."

Mohan had thought about the swami's life before. Had he chosen the ascetic life since a young age, or had something propelled him toward it? Now that the swami himself brought this up, Mohan waited eagerly to hear about it.

"I was in England, studying law. My wife and our little son, along with my parents and my younger sister, were burned to death during the Brahmin massacre in Maharashtra. It was 1948. You were probably a toddler. Where you are now, regarding your loss—I was stuck at that point for a long time." Swami Saralananda remained silent for a while, as if trying to shake the memory off, all over again. "You see. The memories will be always there. But you learn not to dwell on them."

It was getting late. They both got up and descended the few steps as the swami said, "See you next week."

On his way home, shivers ran through Mohan when he thought about the swami's whole family being killed in such a gruesome way, particularly the young child. Somehow, Mohan's pain felt a little less that night. The swami must have been really young to renounce everything of this world at that time. Mohan felt a kinship with him through their loss.

Indian history after independence was fraught with Hindu and Muslim uprisings. However, Mohan had no knowledge about the specific violence against the Brahmins of Maharashtra. The next day, he made a point of leaving work on time rather than working late so he could go to the local library to read about it. Once there, he searched chronologically, year after year, and found articles describing the atrocities.

Mohan knew that Nathuram Godse had assassinated Mahatma Gandhi, the Father of the Nation, in 1948. What Mohan didn't know was that Godse had been a Brahmin from Maharashtra. The oppressed lower caste Hindus had found a reason to turn against the Brahmins of that region. What surprised Mohan more was that people from the Congress Party had actively taken part in the killings and burnings. They had raped and tortured women before setting them on fire.

Mohan felt that it wasn't essential for him to know what had happened to the swami after that or how he had chosen an ascetic life. The fact that he had survived the worst possible pain a heart could endure and was still there, trying to help people like Mohan, made Saralananda larger than life. Mohan believed that with his guidance, one day, he would arrive at the place the swami was now.

Chapter Six

In the beginning, it wasn't easy for Mohan to follow the swami's teaching. He still visited the ruins in the voids of his life. He constantly thought about his parents, about Sophie, and of course, about Andy. Andy visited him at first. That stopped when Mohan went through the metamorphosis, growing long hair and donning long saffron robes at home. Andy felt ashamed around Mohan. Regardless, Mohan took care of Andy's college expenses, writing him checks throughout the years.

Mohan had received a letter from Andy just before his graduation, telling him that there was no need for Mohan to come to the commencement. He didn't want Mohan to fly so far to the East Coast. He didn't tell him whether he had a job after he got the degree, which was fine with Mohan. By that time, he was slowly drifting away from the material world and donned the saffron robe day and night.

Mohan had stopped working even before Andy graduated from college. For a while, he had visited the work sites wearing his regular work apparel. However, he felt imprisoned in it, as if the pants and shirts and the neckties, like his life, were squeezing him from all angles. The moment he arrived home, he would change into his long robe and leave for the temple. Sometimes, he wouldn't go to the office at all for fear of changing into the normal attire. After a while, he left the job he'd loved so much, building the skyscrapers and bridges. He felt intimidated and threatened by the lifeless, monstrous, brick and mortar structures.

At home, after reading Gita for half of the night, he would get up before dawn and cleanse himself with a cold shower. With an old blender he didn't even know existed, he'd make himself a breakfast of fruit and yogurt smoothie. Then he'd walk the two miles to the temple because he had given away his car to a local charity.

At the same time, Mohan had to take care of his worldly possessions before he could retire from them. He left his home to the temple and his bank balance to Andy. He no longer had an address on this earth. However, it would take him a while to dispose of the memories of an unfulfilled life that made him restless, and he read the Bhagavad Gita to find the way. He remembered that he had to have patience.

After that, the temple became a sanctuary to him. He spent his days at the temple under a banyan tree. In one corner, under the tree, he would spread a small saffron-colored cloth and remain there reading the Bhagavad Gita and the Vedanta philosophies, skipping his meals until evening. At times, he closed his eyes and tried not to think of anything, his mind blank as a clean slate, while trying to purge unclean thoughts from it. Devotees came to the temple at all hours of the day, and before leaving, they'd leave a dollar or two near the tree as alms for him. In the evening, when he went into the temple to have *prasad* and listen to the swami, Mohan would deposit the offerings in the temple's donation box.

Sometimes Mohan cried while reading Gita or listening to the discourse of Vedanta. At first, he didn't know whether the tears were of joy because of a new beginning in his life or whether they were of sadness because he was leaving behind everything in the past. One thing he knew for sure was there was nothing left for him in this world.

The world had left him, by design or by accident. In either case, he had to find his way into another world, the spiritual world that transcended the mortal existence, where his soul would be free. His body would feel no pain of hunger or lust. He was eager to hear the eternal song that would ensue from deep within him and vibrate with each breath he took as it traveled upward, arising out of the world he knew and traveling beyond the ether.

Mohan waited eagerly for the weekly return of Swami Saralananda. Since the temple had become Mohan's home, he spent as much time as possible with the swami, who taught him the different kinds of meditation. "You try to sit straight, in lotus position. Keep your palms upward on your folded knees," the swami instructed him. He taught Mohan how to break down the syllable "Om." "Say, 'Ooo . . .' as you breath in, and say, 'Mmm . . .' as you breath out." The swami watched Mohan's posture as he tried hard to acquire the lotus position. "Just crossing your legs would be fine for now. It should get easier as you practice more," the swami encouraged him.

Mohan practiced meditation dutifully every day. He noticed that his mind wasn't indulging in sad memories as often. When he missed Sophie, he sat down and tried to concentrate on his breathing, saying, "Om." His thoughts and the sound of "Om" became one. So, when he read in Gita that "When meditation is mastered, the mind is unwavering, like the flame of a lamp in a windless place," he found truth in it and was eager to learn more.

A year had passed by since Mohan had moved out of his home. Along with the meditation, the swami taught him simple yoga. He bent and stretched his body and asked Mohan to follow him. He told Mohan to be careful, lest he hurt himself.

Then one day, Mohan asked, "Swami, the Gita says, 'Yoga is a journey of the self, through the self, to the self,' and I don't get it." By this time, Mohan was reading the Gita regularly and discussing it with the swami.

"I've been waiting for you to ask me that. That is what real yoga is about. What you did until now was to make your body flexible," the swami said. "The real yoga, simply stated, is a journey of the soul through different levels of our consciousness to find our spiritual self. Yoga helps you detach yourself from the material thoughts. When you practice it until it is flawless, that stage is called 'trance.' While you are in trance, you can see your 'self,' or the soul, through a pure and divine mind. It frees you from material bonds," Swami Saralananda said, explaining it as plainly as he could to Mohan.

"Do you think I'm ready for that, Swami?" Mohan asked readily.

"You…tell me. Only you know when you are ready to make that journey," the swami replied.

From then on, under the swami's guidance, Mohan practiced various types of yoga, meditation, and other ways to attain spirituality. He worked at becoming versed in all kinds of books to gain knowledge about the "self."

After two years of reading the scriptures and living an austere life, he was finally considered worthy to be the swami's disciple.

Mohan started his days with morning prayers and devotional songs. He slept under the banyan tree, and before sunrise, he offered his prayers and went into meditation. If he was hungry, he tried not to feel it. He'd fill a jug with the tap water from the temple to quench his thirst but never broke his meditation to drink it. He sat in the sun, meditating from morning till noon, trying to control all his senses. When he woke up from the concentration, he let himself drink from the jug and spent the afternoon reading scriptures. The only meal he allowed himself in the evening was the *prasad* from the temple.

In the evening, after *prasad*, he sat in the circle with others, like before, and listened to various swamis as they discussed the sacred books on religion and God. He saw devotees who were still living in that outside world, but Mohan had no need to stay in touch with it. He even tried to forget that a world existed beyond the temple premises and the banyan tree. If ever the thought of his parents, or Sophie, or Andy came to his mind, he punished himself by skipping the only meal of the day or meditated more under the hot sun to cleanse his soul.

For a while, as his body became weaker from lack of food and material comfort, his whole being, an existence he could comprehend and what he presumed to be his soul, became more aware to the moksha he was seeking. This search took over his mortal body and made it stronger and pliable. He could sit in the lotus position while concentrating and chanting "Om" for hours at a time. He felt neither hunger nor pain. "Om," the cosmic sound, the sound of Brahman, liberated him from his body and made him recognize his true self.

At the end of four years, when Swami Saralananda was convinced that his disciple was ready to serve the God, the swami initiated him, giving him a new beginning and giving him the name "Sukhatma," the happy soul. "Sukhatma" also aligned more with his own name, "Saralananda," which meant "simple happiness."

Within a year of Mohan's initiation, his guru, Swami Saralananda, started visiting the temple intermittently instead of every week. "My work is done at this place," he told Sukhatma. "Pretty soon I'll stop coming," the swami revealed. Then one evening, after the discourse on Gita, he mentioned to Sukhatma that it would be his last time at the temple. "You will be teaching in my place," he said to him. "Don't waver from finding your true self," the swami said, as Sukhatma touched his feet for blessings.

Sukhatma missed the swami's teaching and felt his absence to a great extent. He felt as if he were a child and the swami had let go of his hand. By that time, the memory of his parents, Sophie, and Andy had moved farther back into Sukhatma's consciousness. However, this new void threw him off his course temporarily, and he felt as if he was failing the guru by veering from his designated path. As a penance, he punished his body for these conscious reactions by not sleeping the whole week and not thinking about his guru either. As Sukhatma became less and less aware of his body, through meditation and yoga, his mind regained its true self once more.

It was at the end of his fifth year at the temple that Sukhatma was ordered to come to Oregon by Swami Saralananda. Sukhatma had heard from the other swamis that his guru was about to shed his mortal body. Sukhatma stepped out of the temple for the first time in five years. In his saffron robe and a long saffron bag which extended from his shoulder and held his books, he boarded a bus to Oregon. He didn't wonder whether he would be back or not. It took him the whole night to reach Eugene. He sat still in the bus, meditating the whole time and asking God to guide him in the absence of his guru.

When Sukhatma arrived at the bus station in Eugene, he was received by a much younger disciple of Swami Saralananda, who touched his feet and said, "Harihara at your service, Swami," and walked with him to the parking lot of the station. It was apparent from Harihara's name that he wasn't initiated as a swami, and Sukhatma would find out later that he wasn't initiated as a priest either. As he opened the passenger side door of an old Volkswagen Beetle, he realized that Sukhatma was not as tall as Swami Saralananda. He then went around to slide the seat forward so that his passenger wouldn't be too far back.

Harihara drove through the town of Eugene before heading toward the guru's ashram. As Sukhatma looked out, he could not help but notice the serenity of the place — miles and miles of green, rolling valley, surrounded by the Calapooya Mountains. The sun was just breaking through the fog, and he could see the Willamette River running through the valley like a snake. In the calm and quiet of the morning, he heard songs from the valley echoing back from the mountains.

Sukhatma moved his head in the direction the songs were coming from. A bunch of Buddhist monks were chanting as they walked closer to the water.

"*Buddham Saranam Gacchami.*" *I take refuge in Buddha.*

"*Dhamam Saranam Gacchami.*" *I take refuge in the cosmic law and order.*

"*Sangham Saranam Gacchami.*" *I take refuge in the company of the enlightened ones.*

All of them had shaved heads, and their faces glowed in the morning sun. They were young, perhaps too young to give up worldly possessions and become monks. Their songs floated in the morning air and filled the place with pulsating energy. They had donned saffron robes, just like Sukhatma and Harihara. They repeated the lines again and again.

"There is a Buddhist temple nearby," Harihara volunteered. Though Sukhatma didn't reply, the happy and solemn song reverberated in his heart until they were way past the monks and reached the ashram. Then he said, "*Om Tat Sat,*" the words resounding throughout the place. He repeated the words with a force that traveled with each breath from his navel through his heart to his forehead and back again.

Swami Saralananda lay on the floor on a mat. A soft pillow supported his head. His body looked emaciated, but his face and eyes shone as they had before. He was awake. The devotees, young and old, surrounded him, and they read from Bhagavad Gita, taking turns. As Sukhatma entered the room and touched his guru's feet, the reading continued. Sukhatma stayed near the feet and waited for his turn and read from the scripture: "As a person puts on new garments, giving up old ones, the soul similarly accepts new material bodies, giving up old and useless ones." After he'd read, the swami motioned him to come and sit closer to his mouth.

"I'll be leaving this body soon," said the swami with a weak and raspy voice. "Once I'm gone, you will be Swami Sukhatma and guru of this ashram." After waiting for a while, as if he was reflecting on something, he continued. "You have mastered your mortal body, but to conquer your soul and find moksha, you have to come face-to-face, once again, with what you have run away from." His voice became a whisper when he said, "I'll still be guiding you. I'll tell you when the time is right to start your next journey." Those were Swami Saralananda's last words, spoken as he drew his final breath.

The guru's command to Swami Sukhatma that he had to deal with his past reverberated in his mind and he felt unsettled. With the guru's direction, he had achieved the difficult task of leaving the past, as well as all memories of it, behind. He was shaken by the thought that any connection with the world he had renounced would derail his progress. Yet he thought that he had to follow the guru's wish to hear the song he sought.

After Swami Saralananda's body was cremated, Swami Sukhatma looked at all his disciples and saw their sadness at the departure of their beloved guru. He gathered them around him and read from the Gita: "Death is as sure for that which is born, as birth is for that which is dead. Therefore, grieve not for what is inevitable." He told them to find the strength to go on and manage the ashram.

***

The ashram was situated in the foothills of Calapooya Mountains, at a bend in the Willamette River. There was hardly any traffic of any kind. Unlike at the temple in Berkeley, where devotees visited the place all the time, no one came to the ashram. Instead, the devotees from the ashram went to the nearby temples when they finished practicing yoga and reading the scriptures for the day.

The disciples, all five of them, were in various stages of their spiritual development, Harihara being the youngest and the latest to be brought to the place. Regardless of their places in the ashram life, they all shared the chores to maintain the ashram. They grew a vegetable garden. The Mediterranean climate, where the summers were dry and warm and the winters were wet and cool, helped them grow a variety of vegetables. They grew every kind of vegetable that one could find in the supermarket, from beets to cauliflower. They had some fruit trees as well. With buckets, they got water from the river and poured it on their garden. Whatever produce they could not eat, they took to the farmers' market and sold there. In fact, they always got a big crowd around their stall.

Everybody, including Swami Sukhatma, took turns with different jobs, keeping the ashram clean. In the morning, they washed the cement floor with water and swept the veranda with a broom. Every day, they cleaned the only latrine as many times as it needed to be cleaned. They washed their saffron robes and cooked simple meals of rice, dal, and vegetables. The rest of the time, they meditated and read various religious books. After the evening prayer, they sat down in a circle with Swami Sukhatma in front of the gods and goddesses and participated in a discussion of Vedanta and Bhagavad Gita.

Harihara was the only one who drove the car. He had bought it while he was a graduate student at the University of Oregon. He came from a religious family back in India. The first thing he had looked for after he arrived in America was a temple. After listening to Swami Saralananda at one of the temples, Harihara had never missed his discourses. Eventually, much to his parents' chagrin, he left his studies and followed the swami to the ashram.

The disciples would pile into the small car and go to the farmers' market to sell vegetables or visit temples. Occasionally, Swami Sukhatma went to the local temples to discuss and meet other devotees. Since Harihara could take only five people including him, someone had to volunteer to stay back when Sukhatma went along. With that, they took turns, also. Usually, Jibatma, the senior most devotee among the five, wanted to stay back. He had a history of going into what they called trance while listening to Swami Saralananda's discussions. It would become difficult to revive him and bring him back to the ashram. He was afraid that the same thing would happen to him while listening to Swami Sukhatma.

The other four had been priests at different Hindu

temples in Oregon and had trailed Swami Saralananda to gain more spiritual knowledge. They simply got tired of the temple life, worshiping the deities throughout the day. People came to the temples to offer their gratitude in exchange for whatever they asked of the deities. The priests worshiped on behalf of these people, chanting the same Sanskrit *shlokas* they had learned at the time of their initiation into the priesthood.

They liked the quiet, solitary ashram life, shunning life's material needs. As far as spirituality was concerned, they proceeded at their own pace. They were a bunch of happy souls who sang devotional songs while tilling the vegetable garden or washing their saffron robes. They did yoga and meditated and read the scriptures, but to a degree that it felt as if they were following a duty rather than a calling. Swami Saralananda's spiritual discourse had held them to the place, but they fell short of becoming swamis themselves. It felt as if they were substituting one way of life for another.

None of them knew how Swami Saralananda had come to be there or anything about his life before he came. They had accepted him as their guru, and he had left them pretty much alone. He was too busy traveling and giving religious lectures all over the West Coast to get too involved with their day-to-day lives. He liked to travel by plane because he thought that it was a waste of God's time to take the bus or train. Harihara drove him back and forth to the Eugene Airport in his beaten up auto. The swami went to places like Denver, Seattle, Chicago, Oakland, Berkeley, and San Francisco, wherever there were temples and devotees.

While Harihara drove, Swami Saralananda prepared his lectures in the back seat of the car. He hardly spoke, which was fine with Harihara because he was always afraid that the guru might ask him about his spiritual progress or ask him to explain some difficult philosophy from one of the holy books. After a while, he was assured that there was no such danger; the guru knew the answers without asking him. After the swami left on such a trip, the five of them would devote their time to taking care of the garden, which wasn't a small chore. They looked forward to going to the market and selling their produce so that they could buy some essential stuff, such as soap, tea, and sugar. Nevertheless, they adhered to their routine of meditation and reading to justify their living in the ashram.

All that changed when Swami Sukhatma arrived there and became the guru. He hardly traveled anywhere outside the Eugene area, and his days were spent at the ashram meditating and reading. He went to the local temples to impart his knowledge of Bhagavad Gita and Vedanta only when one of the assigned swamis could not make it. His disciples at the ashram became his main audience and hence were required not only to listen to him but to discuss with him, as well.

Not only that, Swami Sukhatma had less need for food than Swami Saralananda. Sukhatma went on fasting for days at a time, sustaining himself with only water. The devotees tried to follow his example whenever they could. After a while, they realized that instead of three meals a day, they could live on one. In those times of fasting, they followed the Swami and engaged in self-development.

However, they could not get used to the fact that Swami Sukhatma spent a good deal of time near the Willamette River, sometimes, in the water. Often, he was found meditating in the edge of the river, where the water was shallow and crystal clear. They couldn't water the vegetable garden while he was there, for fear that they would disturb him. If they tried to beat him to the river early in the morning, to their surprise, they would find him in the water, waist-deep, chanting, *"Om Tat Sat."* The time of the year and the weather didn't matter to him.

***

Seventeen years had passed since Sukhatma had heard the Mahabharata from the beginning to the end from Swami Saralananda and begun his life as a hermit. During that time, what went on in this world had been immaterial to him. He was aware that the earth revolved around the sun. At night, the moonlight showed him the way to the river, but when there was no moon, there were the stars to guide him. As he walked from the ashram at night, he chanted, *"Om Tat Sat,"* at the top of his lungs, and the whole place stood still as it made those magical words its own.

The milestones in Sukhatma's life had not only fallen away but were completely gone. He didn't know or keep a record of the fact that in New York, where he had first stepped down from a plane in this country, more than twenty-six hundred people had died in a terrorist attack. It happened seventeen years after Andy had left for college. It had taken Sukhatma nearly two decades to obliterate the faces and voices from his past, along with the stories that went with them. There would be no ruins to look at, because he had left everything far behind. His life as a sage did not seek anything or wait for anybody.

Nevertheless, all the while, Swami Sukhatma was waiting to hear the eternal song he had been promised by his guru. Sukhatma waited patiently to hear from him that it was time to begin his next journey. The guru had said explicitly that Sukhatma had to come face-to-face with his past, which he took to literally mean he had to go back to the place he came from. It meant that he had to step out of the solitary life in the ashram and mingle with the world again. If the thought disturbed him in any way, he punished his body by submerging in the cold water of the river to discipline his mind.

Then, finally, Sukhatma heard from his guru one day while meditating on the riverbank. He had sat there in the lotus position since the dawn without any food or drink. The night was about to fall when he saw a bright light descending from above and heard his guru's voice asking, "Are you ready?" The place brightened up with the light, as if the sun were about to rise.

At first, Sukhatma was confused. He had been waiting for the last twelve years for this. The swami must know that he was ready. In his confusion, he remained silent.

"Are you ready to leave this place and go?" Swami Saralananda asked.

"Yes, Swami," Sukhatma answered him without wasting another moment, out of fear that his guru might leave before hearing him and not come back for a while.

"Then go back to the river you came from, and find your true self." The light disappeared soon after the voice finished speaking, leaving Sukhatma alone. As he came out of his meditation, Sukhatma looked all around, but was greeted by only the dark of the night. He knew that the guru was there and had instructed him to start his journey to the faraway land. If, decades ago, his initiation into his present being had required of him that he discard his old self, including the name given to him by his parents, he was now being asked by his guru to delve once again into the past to prove that the past didn't own him.

When Sukhatma returned to the ashram that night, he found his disciples waiting for him to have the *prasad* they had cooked. He had been fasting for the last four days. Every day, they had waited for him to break his fast, but he had retreated to his room without eating anything. That day, he joined them for supper.

"I've orders from Swamiji," he told them after they had eaten the *prasad*. They looked at him, horrified, thinking that he was going to abandon them at the ashram. "But it will take a while to get my papers ready," he added. They knew that none of them was fit to be called swami yet. But after so many years in the ashram, they couldn't return to the priesthood in the temples.

"We would like to come with you, Swamiji," Harihara volunteered. He thought that wherever Swami Sukhatma was going, there must have been an ashram like the one they were living in. Certainly, he would need Harihara to drive him to various places. Then, to his disappointment, he remembered that the guru didn't travel much. He would definitely need them to grow the food and maintain the ashram, Harihara reasoned. Most of all, Swami Sukhatma needed his disciples, for without disciples, there would be no need for a guru. The other four sat quietly, thinking like Harihara.

"It is the guru's order that I go alone," Sukhatma replied. "But, in my absence, strive for your spiritual growth as much as you can. By now, you should know how close you are to your goals." He looked at all of his five disciples' faces as he said this. Outside of discussions of Bhagavad Gita and Vedanta, it was the most Sukhatma had spoken in the twelve years of his ashram life.

On behalf of the swami, Harihara inquired at various places as to how to prepare his travel documents. It was solely his responsibility. Sukhatma had given him a small saffron pouch, which held an old Indian passport in the name of "Mohan Samanta."

Tucked inside the passport, Harihara found the swami's Permanent Residence Card for the United States. Those were the only mementos from the swami's past, which he was required to keep because his mortal body was still bound to the laws of this world.

Harihara had to drive with the swami to San Francisco, the location of the nearest Indian consulate, where the swami had to appear to get a new passport. Before that, it had taken Harihara a while to collect the application forms and to convince the swami to accompany him to a studio for passport pictures. After many long drives in the old car and persuading the clerks at the consulate that Mohan Samanta and Swami Sukhatma were the same person, Harihara secured an interview for the swami at the consul general in San Francisco.

As Harihara drove untiringly for nine hours, taking breaks only when nature called, Swami Sukhatma remained in the narrow back seat in lotus position the whole time. While passing through the valley in the morning, Sukhatma heard the chanting of the Buddhist monks and kept repeating, *"Om Tat Sat."* He had blessed each disciple before leaving the ashram because he had decided to leave from San Francisco if his passport could be secured. His guru would be putting him to the ultimate test at the end of his journey, and Sukhatma didn't know if he would be retracing his path back to the ashram.

By nightfall, they arrived at the temple in Berkeley, where Sukhatma had met Swami Saralananda more than seventeen years back. The place under the banyan tree had remained empty since the time Sukhatma had been called by his guru. He walked into the temple to pray to the deities, and Harihara followed him. No one there recognized the swami, who had left his house to the temple. After *prasad,*

Sukhatma went to the banyan tree, where he spent the night, and Harihara spread his mat on the temple floor.

Next morning, they left for San Francisco before the rush hour had started, and they were at the consulate on time for their ten o'clock appointment. The consul general was there, curious to meet a swami who had forsaken the material world for all practical purposes after coming to this country of plenty. He ushered Sukhatma into his office and offered him a chair opposite to him. Instead, Sukhatma sat on the floor with his legs crossed in lotus position and his long hair hanging over his shoulder. He closed his eyes and concentrated on Swami Saralananda, on whose order he was undertaking this journey.

The official sat in his designated chair, holding the old passport with Mohan's picture in his left hand and, in his right hand, holding the new unstamped passport with the newly minted photo of Swami Sukhatma. He glanced at the swami to try to find any resemblance with the old picture. When the consul took his eyes off of him, to his surprise, he saw the ghost of a young man in the chair, his face looking exactly like Mohan's. The official blinked his eyes in disbelief. He raised himself from his chair and walked around the room. He kept seeing the face from wherever he looked.

This was the first time the official had witnessed a miracle. He had seen more trickery than he would have liked to remember in his twenty years as consul general in various places. However, there was no doubt in his mind that Mohan and Sukhatma were the same person. The consul stamped the new passport with the consulate seal and sat down on the floor after touching the swami's feet. The swami opened his eyes slowly and blessed the official with a raised hand and walked out of the room.

All this time, Harihara had waited outside the office, not sure of what to expect. He didn't hear the official's voice asking questions or the swami's voice answering any. He heard footsteps pacing the room but didn't know whom they belonged to. Finally, the official escorted the swami out and came and shook Harihara's hand. That was when Harihara realized that everything had gone well with the interview.

From there, Harihara took the swami to the Air India office to buy a ticket. Harihara had dipped into the savings they had accumulated from selling produce throughout the years. He got a ticket for the next day. After they spent the night at the temple in Berkeley, Harihara drove Swami Sukhatma to the San Francisco airport with a heavy heart, unsure of whether he would meet the swami again. As he touched his guru's feet, the guru blessed him, saying, "*Om Tat Sat*," then disappeared behind the security checkpoint.

After losing everything on either side of the earth, Sukhatma had given himself to the spiritual life, driven by the philosophies of Bhagavad Gita and Vedanta. He had punished his mortal body through hunger and deprivation of earthly pleasures and had practiced meditation for years and years to find moksha, to forget everything that belonged to the past. However, he had to face the world once again.

Chapter Seven

It was the month of September, in the year 1991, seventeen years since Andy left home for the Queens College in New York. As he sat in his office on the 102nd floor of the World Trade center, he reflected on his childhood, his friendship with Mark, his mother's death, and above all, Mohan. He had decided to leave California to get away from the past, but There were no going around the memory. It had taken him years and years to work through it.

The skyscrapers stood in unison, stretching in front of him for miles and miles, as if a single giant mural had been painted on top of the city. From where he was, everything looked like a speck on space. The glass windows of the buildings, tall and not so tall, reflected the morning sun in every-each way. He could see the clear blue sky above, and the Hudson River below at a distance. The boats with their white sails looked like flocks of swans gliding on the water.

Andy loved the scenery, particularly in the morning. He was one of the few to arrive first in the office. His own rhythm of life had gotten accustomed to the heartbeat of the city. Even, so far up there, he felt the soul of the city slowly waking up and getting ready for a new day. There would be traffic jams, accidents, robbery, deaths and numerous other things taking place somewhere in the city, throughout the day. After a while, tourists would flow through the city's every vein, including the North Tower, just to feel alive, to make sure that they were part of it; not outsiders. All that would happen later, but the morning belonged to Andy.

As Andy sipped the coffee, he had picked on his way up, he looked at the single picture he kept on his desk. The picture was taken at a Sear's portrait studio right after his mother and Mohan got married. They were sitting close, Andy in the middle and leaning more towards Mohan. Mohan's hand touched Sophie's. They looked happy, but knowing what Andy knew later, he could now see the glimpse of sadness in Mohan's eyes.

He had taken Mohan's permission to bring that picture with him when he first left for college. Without saying anything, Mohan had carefully wrapped it with newspapers and handed it to him. There was no indication that Mohan was going to miss the picture. By all accounts, Andy knew by then that Mohan was far from missing anybody or anything. Andy himself hadn't unwrapped the picture for years. His mother was gone, in a bitter way. The only person Andy could lean on had given up living. His own picture of the happy childhood could not console him.

College years had been an uphill battle for him. He remained aloof, so as not to expose his wounded self. He was always busy, studying. Within the perimeters of his dormitory, classes, cafeteria and library, life held no love or promises of escape. The past sneaked upon him at every opportunity. Mohan remained the only link to his past. Yet, Andy felt that he was beyond Andy's approach. Now he realized more than ever that what Mohan felt for him was a sense of duty, devoid of affection. Seeing a mental counselor at his college was part of Andy's survival mechanism.

It was true that Andy didn't have to worry about money. Mohan covered all the expenses. However, he forgot the little things. He didn't wish Andy a happy birthday, or told him to have a nice meal to celebrate it. Andy tried hard to remember whether Mohan had ever enquired about his happiness after he left home. On the few trips he took home, it felt as if he lived in a monastery for that duration. Ha was appalled to see Mohan in those long saffron robes. There were no traces of the life he once lived in that house.

So, When Andy returned to campus, he had to see the mental counselor more times than he would have cared to, to ease back to a semi-normal life. Every return to that so called home made more fissures in his already broken spirit. Finally, when the counselor told him that he would have to see an off-campus therapist, he had no desire to visit Mohan again. To put an end to that chapter of his life, he wrote to Mohan not to travel to his graduation. He thanked him for his generosity and putting him through college, and wrote that he didn't need the money anymore.

After his graduation, he had struggled with two parttime jobs to support his Master's program in Finance. At that point, money from Mohan had stopped coming and Andy was glad for it. However, after about a year, he received a package from a lawyer in California. His heart skipped a bit. When he opened the manila envelope, he found a trust Mohan had created on his behalf. Inside the big envelope, there was a smaller one which was sealed. When Andy opened it, there was a small piece of paper inside. There was just one sentence from Mohan, "One day, in the ruins of your heart, you will find the song to carry you through your life." At that moment, it had sounded to Andy like a sermon from a holy man.

It would take some more time for Andy to realized that along with the Trust, that piece of paper was the last earthly parting gift from Mohan who had tried to love him selflessly, always. He came to understand that Mohan felt his pain, but Mohan's own hurt overshadowed everything else. It was pointless to hold grudge against a man who had given up this world rather than trying to find a new life. That knowledge hadn't come to him naturally. It was Clara who showed him the insight into his past.

Andy often thought about Clara—happy, and wise beyond her age—the only person he knew who lessened his affliction. If it wasn't for her, he would not have known how to heal from his gnawing wound. Her being there in the same city made him aware of his own beating heart. He could not even get lost in that enormous place because of the one person who knew exactly where to find him, infuse hope into him.

He thought about that bitter cold morning in January, almost ten years back. The wind was howling from all directions. Andy got down from the bus that shuttled between his apartment and the campus. As he started walking towards the Math building, from a distance, he saw Clara waiting in front of it. All of a sudden, he remembered that the night before he was supposed to meet her in the campus cafeteria for dinner.

"I'm so sorry, I forgot," Andy volunteered. Their statistics class was another hour away. "We still have enough time for a cup of coffee." He said it and held the door open for her. It was their second year in the Master's program and they both remained preoccupied with their projects.

"No big deal," Clara replied, shortly. Her gentle voice had an edge to it. "This isn't the first time or the second time, after all."

"I understand you must be upset. I just forgot we're supposed to meet," Andy replied. He had met Clara in graduate school. After years of counselling, he still felt vulnerable. He felt different around Clara, though. She was unassuming and Andy felt at ease with her. They exchanged lecture notes and often studied together. Slowly, he had opened up to her and, by this time, she knew enough about him.

What ensued was a big argument between them. "If you forget things this easily, why can't you forgive your mom and stepdad?" Clara said in a raised voice. "Had your therapist ever asked you what pain they went through?" Clara continued. She looked exited.

"Let's not talk about it." Andy seemed angry.

"Why not? The problem is in you. Have you ever thought of visiting the place where your mom struggled alone? How far is it from here? Your stepdad had left everything for you. Is he alive? Is he dead? Do you know?" Clara asked all this in one breath. "Have some empathy for them. That's the only thing that would heal you."

"I'm not asking for empathy from you. For god's sake, what is this all about, right in the morning? I said I forgot." Andy said it and looked around to see if anyone was listening to them. Students were coming in from the cold and heading towards their lecture halls. No one paid any attention.

"No, you don't forget. You're self-absorbed. You look for sympathy, not empathy. You see me every day. Have you ever thought of asking how things are with me? You think, I'm some rich girl from Long Island. I don't have problems? My mother drinks. My father carries on affairs with women half his age. I don't hold the pain like a badge to pity myself. I wish my father could be like your stepdad, giving up everything for the woman he married." After saying this, Clara had walked towards the lecture hall. Andy stood there for a while, speechless, then followed.

Andy could not concentrate in class. Clara's words were going back and forth in his head. He wondered what made her so resilient in the face of constant unhappiness at home. He was sure that neither parent was emotionally available to her as she was growing up. However, instead of falling apart, she had put that behind and marched on. He waited for Clara in the hall. "I'm sorry. Please forgive me," he said when Clara came out.

"That's alright. I'm okay," saying this, Clara looked at the watch. They had another class in the afternoon. "Maybe I'll have something before I go to the library. You want to join?"

"Thank you," Andy said, and they walked to the cafeteria together. "I'm sorry to hear about your parents," he said halfway.

"I don't feel sorry for myself," Clara replied. "Everybody has to live their lives, including my parents. We all go through loss, different kinds, I guess."

That was what Andy liked about Clara. She said things without pretense. The truth, she so effortlessly presented, healed instead of creating deeper wounds. In fact, after they finished the graduate school and went their separate ways, he missed seeing her every day and her wise words. He was at a loss when they graduated.

Before they parted, they went out together to eat at a descent Italian restaurant in Queens, not far from the campus, to celebrate their graduation. It was a breezy summer evening in May and the place was crowded. They asked to be seated outside. The crowd was mostly young college kids, still trying to maneuver life away from home. "So, what are your plans before you start?" Andy asked. He had landed a job as a Financial Analyst with the Wall Street. He felt apprehensive about the whole thing. The impersonal name itself scared him.

"I don't know. I have a month before I join." Clara

felt silent for a while after she said it. Andy knew that she was going as a Financial Adviser to a big Non-profit Organization treating alcohol addicts. "I've been looking for a studio apartment in Manhattan, closer to the Headquarter, but everything is so expensive," Clara said. "I might visit mom for a week or so before I start," she added as an afterthought. "How about you?" she asked him.

"You know, I've been thinking the same thing since our last argument. I'm thinking of flying to California to see how my stepdad is doing. I'll probably move to an apartment in Queens after I'm back and commute from there." Andy looked at Clara through the dim evening lights as he said this, then added, "I'm going to miss you."

"Oh, come on. You make me sentimental now." Clara said this good naturedly. "We would be a phone call away in the same city. I can still get mad at you, depending on how many dinner appointments you forget." They both laughed after she said this. They were just friends. They had no inclination to get involved romantically. At times, Andy had reflected on their friendship and was grateful for what he had. If it ever developed to anything more than that, Andy knew that he would be the luckiest person on earth.

Andy had traveled to California to visit Mohan. He knew from the trust that the house was given to the temple and he stayed in a nearby hotel. Next morning, he had walked a mile to the home. Everything looked the same from outside except a little fence in one corner of the backyard. His mother's favorite jacaranda was in full bloom.

When he rang the doorbell, it sounded hollow as if it carried the vibe of the whole house. He waited for ten minutes and still no one came to greet him. He then walked to the back and sat on the grass under the jacaranda.

Through the chain linked fence, he could see a patch of vegetable garden.

As he sat there, Andy felt the old days washing over him—Mohan, Sophie and him—happy and sad days. He remembered his closeness towards Mohan and how much Mohan had loved Sophie. Amidst the sad things that happened in the house, he found the happy memories buried beneath it. He lay down on the grass and fell asleep.

It was mid-morning when Andy opened his eyes. The sun had changed direction and he felt the direct rays on him. There was no sign of Mohan yet. Andy broke a small branch from the jacaranda, laden with flowers, and walked towards the cemetery. It wasn't that far.

It took him some time to find his mother's grave. The headstone, bearing her name, was simple. There were no fresh flowers or, for that matter wilted ones on the stone. He wondered if Mohan ever visited her. As he lay the jacaranda on the base of the stone, for the first time in years, he missed her. He remembered his happy childhood, holding his mother's hand and walking near the sea in Port Jefferson. He stood there under the sun, its hot rays beating on his head. The wind gently rustled through the weeping willows. It sounded like his mother's lullaby she sang to him when he was little. Then slowly, he walked towards the hotel.

The next morning, instead of going to the house, Andy went straight to the temple. He wore a saffron colored tee shirt with jeans. He remembered how Mohan had worn long saffron robes all the time when they last saw each other and how much Andy hated him for that. He just wanted Mohan to know that it didn't matter what he wore, he loved him, nevertheless. During his long journey to find himself, he had missed Mohan's warmth.

Andy took his slippers off, like the other devotees, as he entered the temple. It was still early in the morning. The priests, in saffron robes, were getting ready for the day. Someone washed the deities with milk and honey and someone made garlands from fresh flowers. Andy kept looking at their faces, searching for Mohan. "How can I help you?" asked one of them.

"I'm looking for Mohan Samanta." Andy said the whole name to be more specific.

"There is no one named Mohan Samanta here." The person looked at Andy from head to toe as he answered. He wondered what a young white guy was doing in the temple so early in the morning. "Maybe he has another name?" he asked.

"No, it is Mohan, the person who has given his home to the temple." Andy said this and a fear took over him that Mohan could have gone to another temple, somewhere.

"Oh, you are talking about Swami Sukhatma. I asked you if Mohan has another name. I'll take you there. Does he know you?" Before Andy could answer, the man went ahead through the narrow corridor to the back of the temple. Lots of people come to see the Swamiji. They all couldn't know him, he thought to himself. "Here is the Swami. After the *darsan*, you can come back the same way and go out," saying this the man left.

From a distance, Andy saw Mohan under a huge banyan tree, its pilar like roots hanging down from branches and entering the earth. Mohan sat in a lotus position with closed eyes. The saffron robe covered his entire body. His hairs had grown long and looked disheveled. His body looked like a thin reed.

However, what struck Andy the most was Mohan's face. It was awash with the soft morning light and exuded an air of tranquility. As he kept repeating "Om," over and over, his emaciated body remained still and his face lit up with an inner joy. It seemed to Andy as if Mohan had never lived any other life before. He wondered whether Mohan would recognize him.

Andy sat down on the steps and waited for Mohan to wake up from his meditation. Hours passed, but Mohan remained in that position, chanting "Om" continuously. The sun hit hard on his face now. Yet, Andy could not notice any inclination on Mohan's part to shift his position. He stayed grounded like the banyan tree.

"Are you still here?" Andy heard. As he turned around, he saw the same person who showed him there. "No one stayed so long for the *darshan*."

"When is he going to finish?" Andy asked. "I can stay a little longer, if it's okay with you," Andy said it and thought that Mohan must be done with his meditation and soon would be getting up to eat or relieve himself.

"You can wait as long as you wish. Is there something you want?" The man asked abruptly. When he saw Andy searching for words, he said, "This swami doesn't look at hands and tell fortune, if that's what you are waiting for."

"It's nothing like that," Andy replied. He didn't see any need to divulge that he was related to Mohan. "I'm waiting to seek his blessings," Andy said finally.

"The Swami has been sitting like this for the past four days. We don't know when he would get up. Sometimes, it can be weeks." The person said this and was about to go back, then said, "There is *Prasad* being distributed, if you're interested."

"I should be going. Thank you for your kind offer," Andy replied, but wasn't sure whether the man heard him. He had already started walking towards the temple door.

Andy stood there for a few more minutes. Something told him that, even if Mohan saw him face to face, he wouldn't know that it was Andy. Mohan seemed to be in another world. Andy remembered the writing on the little piece of paper Mohan had left for him with the trust. He sincerely hoped that Mohan had found his song. He seemed at peace.

The first thing Andy did after arriving in Queens was unwrap the framed photograph of Sophie, Mohan and him. The photo had turned yellow around the edges. however, the picture was the only reminder that all three of them once belonged to each other. He inspected each face from different angles and saw how time had imposed on them and robbed the reality of what could have been. He then moved the hooks to open the frame and gently put the little piece of paper behind the picture and closed the glass.

Ten years had passed since then. Andy looked at the picture intently, thinking of the happy days. He pulled out the handkerchief from his pants-pocket and wiped the dust from the photograph. He thought about the little piece of paper behind it. He wondered if Mohan was still in California and how he was doing.

The phone was ringing, and Andy came back to the present again. It was Clara. They were still in touch, still friends. She was always ready to help him with her wise words. She called to tell him about her upcoming business trip to Atlanta. She sounded happy. After he hung up the phone, Andy thought that he himself hadn't done so bad, after all.

Andy looked at his watch after he finished the coffee. It was just 8:45. Other employees were still coming. His first appointment with a client was in half an hour and he had plenty of time. He sent a graph with the financial analysis to the printer, and it spit out the hard copy with the date 9/11/2001 printed on it. As he picked up the papers, something hit the building. The immense tower shook and swayed violently. For a brief moment, his gaze shifted to the photograph again, and he saw the numerous little waves of the Long Island Sound from the ferry he once took with his mother and Mohan. He could not tell whether he was falling into the waves or flying through the clouds. The universe around him exploded and then everything became still.

Part Three

Chapter One

"Mohan, you are back?" he thought he heard someone asking him. "It is good to come back and find your roots, isn't it?" he heard a voice say, carried over time from another world. The voice was soft and fleeting. He knew who Mohan was, and he knew the voice. But it was beyond him to answer to any of that knowledge. Swami Sukhatma's world was supposed to be devoid of any earthly wisdom.

It had all happened so long ago that the memory eluded Sukhatma. All that had happened in another life, a life that should have been erased from memory by then. He had no part in it. His parents hadn't died of broken hearts, at least not because of him. What he remembered was like a story he had read somewhere in some books and had forgotten in its entirety. He opened his eyes and pulled himself up to a sitting position, sand clinging to his body. He held a fistful of it in his right hand and squeezed hard to cleanse himself of thoughts not pertaining to his world. As the raw sand slipped through his fingers, he replenished it quickly and squeezed it hard against his palm and fingers until his hand was red and almost bleeding. Doing so was his penance for dueling with forbidden thoughts. His past memories about his parents and the village he was coming back to, slipped with the river sand between his fingers.

Then slowly he got up and stepped into the water. The Murudi River with its narrow stream of crystal-clear water, the parched lands surrounding it, the gulmohar some distance away—they were all real. They couldn't tell him from which end of the earth he had traveled, but they knew that it was in their midst he had grown up and that his life's journey had begun from here. *"Om Tat Sat, Om!"* It *is truth*. This place would be his testing ground. He would prove to himself that he had conquered his own desires and thoughts and had become a real sannyasi.

Evening was fast approaching. Before the dusk turned into night, he had to reach the village or, if not, at least the bridge. He got out of the water and walked slowly toward the gulmohar.

After retrieving the bag from under the tree, he walked on the dirt road alongside the river. The warm air around him collected the moisture from his wet robe, and his long, matted hair blew over his gentle face, half covering his eyes. It was a moonless dusk. He had to be careful about not stepping on any living creatures for fear that he might trample them to death. The village, Anantpur, wasn't that far. In a while, about a quarter of a mile upstream, he would cross the narrow bridge to reach his destination.

Once he crossed the bridge, Anantpur came into view. From a distance, faint lights from various rooms of the houses signaled the flow of electricity. He tried to spot one particular house, but it was too dark, and he hadn't been to the village in almost thirty years. Moreover, in the dark, the village didn't look the same. He saw lights coming from clusters of houses he had no memory of. As he made his way in the semidarkness, he heard an owl hooting from high above on a branch. From a nearby tree, bats flapped their wings. A bunch of stray dogs came running toward him, barking all the while.

After going a few yards past the bridge, Sukhatma heard footsteps from behind. He knew that somebody else was going to the same village. He slowed down his own stride to let the other person pass as the approaching footsteps came closer and overtook him. Then suddenly, the ground was illuminated with a flashlight, and the figure turned around. Swami Sukhatma's saffron robe and walking stick had drawn the man's attention when he went past him.

"Let me have your stick, Baba." Before Sukhatma could respond, the young man grabbed his walking stick and started hitting a snake that lay on their path. As the snake raised its hood and came crawling toward them, the man gave its head a final blow.

The snake, a long ugly leathery creature, writhed for a short while, giving the impression of a rope being pulled from either end. Then it became still and finally died. The young man looked at the walking stick splattered with the snake's blood.

"There was no need to kill it." Sukhatma's voice was gentle and unperturbed. "The snake had not harmed us."

"I'll go and wash the stick in the river. If it was not for my flashlight, the snake would have certainly bitten one of us." Saying this, the young man threw the snake into the bushes with the end of the stick. Then he ran toward the water, bursts of light from his flashlight illuminating the surroundings.

Sukhatma sat down on the same spot where the young man had left him and waited. He took out the beads and started chanting again, "*Om Tat Sat, Om!*" as the beads rolled between his fingers. *It is reality. Only the God is unchanging. Only the God is everlasting.*

After a while, he saw the dance of light and shadows as the young man ran back from the river. He had wiped the wet stick with dry leaves and now handed it back to Sukhatma.

"Where are you going to, Baba?" the young man asked, touching the swami's feet. He had forgotten to do that in the act of killing the snake. "I can take you there," the man said and started walking. Sadhus, on their pilgrimages to various parts of India, often passed through this place. They never stayed at anybody's house, but at a reasonable distance from the dwellings. In the evenings, they accepted offerings of food from the villagers, and by the next morning, they were gone.

"Please let me know just before we enter the village," the swami said.

They walked in the dark, the young man leading the way by a few steps. Every now and then, a thin stream of light surged from the flashlight. By this time, the stray dogs had stopped barking and ran alongside the two of them. The narrow dirt road was difficult to negotiate in the dark. Sukhatma could feel thick shrubs extending from either side of the path and thorns from them brushing and piercing his thin rob. It did not bother him. What he was afraid of was hurting or, worse, killing something inadvertently in the dark. He kept repeating, "*Om Tat Sat, Om!*" now silently.

As they got closer to the village, Sukhatma saw a patch of land with tall bamboo plants and walked toward it. The young man followed him.

"This is where I will remain. You go on now," he said to the young man. In the dark, he opened the saffron bag hanging from his shoulder and pulled out a small blanket. All around him it was dark. The air was filled with a continuous stream of clamor from the crickets. One could hear a fox howling in the distance. The night breeze was still warm, and overhead, the bamboo leaves rustled gently.

"But, Baba . . . it's too dark and too dangerous," the young man said. "There are jackals and wild dogs and of course, snakes." Then he said hesitantly, "Maybe . . . you should come a little closer to the village."

Without answering, Sukhatma spread the blanket on

the ground and sat, crossing his legs in a yoga position, his walking stick and a book next to him. Then, his hands on his lap, he started chanting, *"Om Tat Sat, Om!" God is good. God is reality*.

It seemed to the young man that slowly the sadhu was losing awareness of his surroundings. The air around him hummed with his chanting. The young man left Sukhatma praying and walked toward home. Once again, the stray dogs followed him, all the way to the village. He decided to come back early next morning with food for the sadhu.

***

The young man, Gopal, opened the gate to the modest house and walked through the yard, dimly lit by a bulb hanging from a bare socket on the veranda. As he opened the door to the outer room of the house, he saw the man's figure—old and frail—hunched over a newspaper. The old man must have been waiting for him so they could have dinner together.

"You are late. Did you miss the bus?" the old man said, raising his eyes from the paper.

"Yes, Baba. Today, I met a sannyasi on my way home," replied Gopal. He then narrated the encounter with the snake and the sannyasi to his father. His mother had already retreated to her bedroom.

"Wash your hands, Son. Dinner is getting cold," the old man said without saying anything about the sannyasi or the snake. He got up from his chair and seated himself near the dining table. They both ate silently, the old man taking small bites, mostly tasting the food, as if it was a chore he was performing. If his son asked him, he answered he wasn't that hungry, that he'd had a snack of puffed rice with peanuts in the evening.

Chapter Two

Gopal got up early the next morning, before daybreak, and collected the basket in which he had placed some food for the sannyasi. The night before, as usual, his mother had gotten the dinner ready for them and retreated to her bedroom. After he had finished eating, he had taken both his and his father's plate to the kitchen sink and poured water on them to let them soak. Then he had warmed the milk in a clay pot and emptied it into two glasses—one for his father and one for himself.

After he served the milk to the old man, instead of going to bed, Gopal went back to the kitchen and looked for food. He saved his share of milk in a glass jar and took a piece of the rice cake his mother had made for breakfast. He didn't think that it would be enough for the swami. He looked into the cupboards and found bananas his mother had kept as offering for the deities, and took one from the bunch. He organized the milk jar, cake, and banana neatly in a little bamboo basket and hid it under his bed till morning.

When he arrived at the outskirts of the village, he could see a small fire from a distance. The early morning was cold. With the basket, Gopal proceeded toward the fire. The swami was nowhere to be seen. For a brief moment, Gopal panicked that the sadhu had left their village. He went around to look for the cloth bag and found it nearby, under a cluster of bamboos, the blanket folded neatly and placed on top of it.

As Gopal started walking toward the river, the basket

in hand, he could hear the chanting of "Om," rising from the river and spreading in the silent morning air, rejuvenating the whole place. He walked slowly, his mind half-alert, mesmerized by the power of one simple word repeated in a continuous stream, as if the word had no beginning and no end. From a distance, he saw the swami standing, half of his body submerged in the cold water, his hands folded together in prayer.

Gopal sat down on the bank of the river, carefully keeping the basket to one side of him. He felt like an interloper. It felt as if he was secretly listening to the most intimate of conversations the swami was having with someone, which was not meant for anybody else. He was offering his deepest love, pouring from the innermost corner of his heart, and he alone was privy to the knowledge of who was listening on the other end. Gopal could observe this only from a distance. The moment held a kind of sanctity, which an ordinary human being dared not mar by their presence.

The sun hadn't risen yet, but the distant horizon was slowly waking up with a hint of light spreading upward, dividing the mortal earth below and the eternal space above. Gopal sat there motionless, trying to calm his restless mind. He had felt all kinds of different emotions in his twenty years of life. He understood the love he felt for his aged parents and the hatred for them that ensued when neither of them reciprocated. He had known the feeling of sadness and disappointment when Hena's parents married her off, and she didn't even tell him that she was getting married. At least, that was the minimum he thought he deserved from her.

He had heard about his brother from others. Even though his brother had left the place long before he was born, Gopal often felt a longing for him. He understood that his own existence was unable to fill the void created by his brother. Unlike others, though, Gopal could never blame his brother for that. Gopal had an over-powering desire to meet him someday, if for nothing else but to tell him that they were both misfits—one for leaving the place and one for not being able to leave. They occupied the same void.

Yet what Gopal felt that day was none of the emotions he had ever sensed before. His mind did not pull him down with the weight of his being, and he felt a lightness enveloping him at that moment. The chants from the swami rose from the crystal-clear water, enclosing Gopal's consciousness, as if giving a new life to him. He closed his eyes. The sound of "Om," the sound that touched eternity, creation itself, filled his heart. He stayed there on the grass soaked with the morning dew and let the chant lift him upward to another state of being.

After a while, the sun broke through the horizon, and fog surrounding the Murudi River slowly dissipated. Gopal saw a flock of herons descending toward the water in search of food. Not far from the riverbed, a cluster of *kia* flowers stretched their long necks from between their large thorny leaves. A light breeze carried their sweet smell, making their presence known. Gopal had forgotten all about them since Hena's departure. As a child, she was the one who had challenged him to venture into the formidable growth and break a stem for her. All of a sudden, he returned to the real world, and wondered what Hena was doing.

***

As the sun rose, Sukhatma folded his hands and offered his prayers to the Sun god and slowly came out of the water. He changed from the wet saffron robe that clung to his body to one he'd left on the riverbank. Then he went back to the water to wash and rinse the one he'd worn before. As he climbed the riverbank, he saw the figure sitting at a distance. Gopal stood with the basket as Sukhatma approached him. "*Pranam, Baba*," he said to the swami and bent down to touch his feet.

The swami put his hand over Gopal's head, and said, "*Om, shanti, shanti, shanti*, peace be with you," and was on his way to the bamboo grove. Gopal followed him silently, at a distance. He wondered if the sadhu remembered him or the snake from the night before. Somehow, he felt that the previous night's boldness had left him, and he felt quiet in front of the sadhu.

Once they reached the grove, Sukhatma let his long, tangled hair down, water dripping from it. He took the blanket from on top of the saffron bag and spread it on the grass. Before Gopal could offer him the basket of food, he pulled out a book and started reading it silently as his hands worked the beads he was holding. Gopal stood there waiting for him to finish reading whatever it was. He worried about his parents wondering about his whereabouts. Yet he just couldn't leave while a crow flew from one of the bamboo branches every now and then, and circled near the basket.

After what seemed like a long time, the swami closed the book and repeated, "*Om Tat Sat*" three times and got up. For the first time that morning, he became fully aware of Gopal's presence. The sun was moving up from the horizon. Sukhatma did not need to fear the heat. The deep shade from the tall bamboo plants would provide him shelter during the day, but he needed to build a little hut for the cold night. "You must have waited for a while now," he told Gopal.

"Baba, I have got some food for you." Gopal put the basket down as he said this and took out the milk jar and the rice cake. He put the banana at the swami's feet. Gopal thought that it was the right way to do it, because whenever a sadhu came to their village, the villagers treated him as if he were on his way to become one of the reincarnations of the endless deities they worshipped.

Sukhatma bent down and picked up the banana. Then he opened the jar of milk and poured some on the ground. He crumbled half of the rice cake and scattered the crumbs around him. He peeled the banana and dropped a few pieces on the grass.

"But, Baba, I brought them for you. You must be hungry since last night." Gopal looked disappointed as he said this. A long line of ants formed near the pieces of banana. The crows came flying from the treetops and snatched the crumbs from the ground.

"I just offered it first to God. There is more than enough for both of us." Saying this, Sukhatma motioned Gopal to sit down.

"I have to go, Baba. My parents . . ." Gopal stood there without completing the sentence and not showing any inclination to leave the place. He looked at the glass jar and at the basket. From what he knew, the sadhu would be on his way soon, and Gopal didn't want the stray dogs to lick the jar left behind or the crows to pull the delicate twigs from the basket with their beaks. Moreover, he didn't want the sadhu to leave the place while he was home.

"Go on then. Bring me a saw when you come next." Sukhatma had already emptied the milk into his drinking cup, made out of a round, dried, half coconut. He took the rest of the rice cake from the basket and placed it on a little cloth the size of a handkerchief. He sat down with the book open in front of him and started eating the other half of the banana while turning the pages.

It was almost midmorning by the time Gopal walked toward home. The sun was way up, and it was getting hotter by the minute. He thought about the sadhu. He seemed so much different than the other ones who had passed through the village. They eagerly accepted everything that was given to them. None of them had ever declared that there was God inside the crows, and ants, and probably dogs. They themselves would have liked to be treated like gods. For some reason, he wanted the sadhu to stay on. The fact that he had been asked to bring a saw made him hopeful, even though he didn't know what it was for.

The old man waited for him, pacing back and forth on the veranda. His son's college would not start for another couple of months. It was unusual for him to go anywhere so early. Then he remembered about the sadhu, but he couldn't imagine Gopal going to him. A couple of times, he went into the kitchen with some pretext to figure out his wife's mood, but she went on doing chores, as if she didn't miss her son's presence.

Gopal saw the old man from a distance, and his pace slowed. He knew that his father always waited for him, even though they talked little, and it annoyed him. He was sure to ask Gopal where he had been, but the old man was happy just to hear anything, not really delving into the details. Gopal's mother was no different. Her only concern was to make sure she got all the meals cooked, and she did it quietly, mainly out of duty rather than any visible love for anyone. This nonchalant manner of his parents made Gopal feel like a guest in his own home.

"You must have been out on a long walk," said the old man as soon as he saw Gopal. Then without waiting for an answer, he went and sat down in a chair at the dining table. His wife had already put the breakfast on the table. "You were gone by the time I woke up," he said.

"You should not have waited for me," said Gopal, as he washed his hands. He sat down opposite his father. They both poured hot milk from a jug into bowls and took a piece of rice cake each. As he dipped the rice cake into the milk, Gopal wondered whether his mother had noticed the missing cake and milk. She must have noticed the banana having disappeared from the bunch. He wished that she would bring up the subject and ask what had happened to these items so that they could all have a conversation. To his disappointment, no such discussion took place.

The father and son both ate silently, while Gopal's mother remained in the kitchen grinding spices. The *dhuk, dhuk* noise from the iron pestle hitting spices in the mortar was the only sound that broke the monotony in the house. After they were done eating, Gopal took the plates and put them in the kitchen sink. He saw his mother sitting on the floor, bent over, her right hand going up and down into the iron bowl. "Let me help you with that," he said and sat down on the floor next to her.

She handed the pestle to him without saying anything and got up to tend the curry on the stove. The kitchen had a small window and no fan, and Gopal was already sweating from the heat. He kept pounding until the spices turned into a coarse powder and a pungent smell wafted from them. He felt sad for his mother, old and frail, but unwilling to employ someone to do the cooking.

Gopal knew that his father had often mentioned having someone to help around the house the whole day, but his mother had stubbornly refused. A maid came in the morning to do the dishes and clean the house. Occasionally, she helped with doing the laundry. Nonetheless, Madhuri did not let anyone enter her kitchen to cook for them. She had always fancied a daughter-in-law lending her a helping hand.

However, she had a tacit appreciation for Gopal's help, even though she thought it to be wrong to depend on him. She couldn't take him for granted after what her older son had done. Often, she was afraid that her hopes would sprout from nowhere to be dashed again. So, she tried hard not to show any emotion and not to have any expectations.

Gopal lifted the heavy mortar with both hands and put it on the kitchen counter. His mother took a spoonful of the ground spice and put it in the curry. He decided to hang around the house until after lunch. He could take the saw to the sadhu before the meal, but if he waited, he could take some food for him, also. His mother surely wouldn't miss a morsel of this and that. "Lunch should be ready soon," he heard his mother saying.

When he came out of the kitchen, his father was on the veranda, leafing through a newspaper. Soon he would dab himself with coconut oil from a small bowl and head to the well in their backyard. He never liked to take a bath indoors during the summer months. The metal pipes became hot, and the water flowing from them felt warm to the skin, whereas, the water from the deep well felt cool to the touch.

Gopal headed to the well and pulled up a few buckets of water for his father's bath. He eyed the banana plants. One of the clumps hanging from them looked almost ripe. They would be ready in another day or two. He hoped the sadhu didn't leave before that. Then he went into the straw-thatched shed in one corner of the garden where his father stored miscellaneous things. He looked for a saw and found one hanging from a nail on the mud wall.

Once his father came out to take a bath, Gopal headed

in. He filled the bucket in the bathroom with water flowing from the pipe, warm from the midday sun. As he poured jugs of water on his head, he murmured, *"Om Tat Sat"* a few times and felt a kind of exhilaration at the utterance of the words. It was still a couple of months before his college opened, and he wished the sadhu to stay on. Not only did the sadhu's presence lessened the boredom in Gopal's life, but also it made him feel happy and less resentful of his parents' indifference.

After lunch, his father retired to his room for his afternoon nap and Gopal sat down at the table as his mother ate hers. She was close to seventy years old but looked much older than her age. Her face had a perennial expressionless look, as if she didn't know how to explain her life and living, anymore. The son on whom she should have bestowed her love, if anything remained after the heartbreak, sat in front of her, but she didn't take any notice.

Gopal observed the serving bowls containing food for the evening supper. His mother cooked just once for lunch and the evening meal, but more than enough for both. "Won't you have some more of this?" he asked his mother, pointing at one of the pots holding curry. She just nodded. He knew that his mother never took a second helping of anything, but he asked her anyway. Sometimes, for no reason, he felt guilty about his mother's disposition and tried to hang around her as much as possible. As his mother finished eating and got up, Gopal took the pots of food one by one and stored them on the kitchen counter. Then he got a wet cloth and wiped the table clean.

His mother did not rest during the afternoon. After lunch, usually she collected the clothes drying in the sun and prepared something for the next morning's breakfast. She rinsed the few plates they'd used and put them aside for the maid to clean them in the morning. Often, she swept the veranda a second time, just before she lit the lamp for the deities in the evening.

It was past noon. The sun was way up in the sky. Gopal got the saw from the shed and cut a leaf from the banana plant. As he washed the dust from it, he kept wondering how to take the food without informing his mother. She worked hard every day, chopping vegetables, grinding spices, and cooking dishes. He didn't feel comfortable asking her to spare food for the sadhu. However, the sadhu might stay for a while, and Gopal didn't want to steal food for him, day after day. At the same time, after saving him once from the snake, Gopal felt that it was his sole responsibility to take care of the sadhu until he left their village.

His mother was wiping the kitchen counter when Gopal came in with the banana leaf. She kept on wiping, pretending not to see him. He placed the leaf on the dining table and waited for her to finish. Finally, when she was done and was about to put the leftover dishes in the refrigerator, Gopal came and took the pot containing the rice from her hand. "There is a sadhu who is passing through," he told her.

"Did he eat the breakfast you took for him?" she simply asked. She had no desire for an answer, yet she felt that something must be different about this sadhu for her son to get so involved in his comfort. Sadhus came to their village for a day and left without notice. She could not remember food ever going missing from the kitchen on their behalf.

"Yes," Gopal replied, relieved. She knew; she noticed, he thought. At least she had the knowledge that the missing food was for a sadhu and not for Gopal. She must have known about the sadhu from the maid. He was glad he had decided against taking food this time without telling her.

"What would the sadhu like?" she asked, leaving the dishes on the counter. She had cooked a vegetarian meal that day—rice, dal, fried eggplant, and curried cauliflower.

"Maybe a little bit of everything," Gopal replied. Then he got the banana leaf and laid it on the counter top. His mother put a small heap of rice topped with dal and vegetables on the leaf. Then she folded it from all sides and made it into a square parcel. After she was done, he poured some cold water from an earthen pot into a glass jar and put everything in a basket. She noticed the saw next to the basket but didn't say anything.

The swami was still engrossed in his book when Gopal arrived with the basket and the saw. The milk and the rice cake were gone. Gopal could not tell whether the sadhu was reading or meditating. The place was really quiet during the afternoon. Even at other times, not too many people took that path from the river to the village. The path zigzagged along the bamboo grove, making it more isolated and longer. Those who lived in the village, walked downstream along the river after crossing the bridge, and took a shortcut to the village. When someone wandered this way, it was because they knew the place well, and loved its tranquility.

Sukhatma put the book down when he realized that Gopal was standing at a distance. He got up and pulled his blanket more into the shade. The bamboo trees rustled in the hot breeze. There wasn't enough water in the river to make the air cool. He had walked to a spring located on one side of the slope and fetched some water with the coconut cup, and the water was already hot.

"Baba, I have some food for you." Saying this, Gopal put the basket down and unfolded the banana leaf on all sides. He carefully placed the jar of cold water to one side.

"And here is the saw you told me to bring," he added. He then walked toward the bamboo grove to give some privacy to the sadhu while he ate.

Sukhatma took some water from the glass jar and drizzled it on top of the food, offering it to God before eating, while chanting, "*Om Tat Sat.*" The crows came flying down from the bamboo branches, and he spread some rice on the ground for them. Then he mixed everything on the banana leaf and put a handful in his mouth. A sudden taste and the smell of the food overwhelmed him. As he took a sip of water from the jar, his whole body started to quiver.

He sat motionless, and for a fleeting moment, he was deluged by thoughts he could not ignore. Slowly, he calmed his mind, and his body followed. It could not be. It was so long ago. He had returned to this place anew. What he remembered had no consequences for him. He ate as if eating were also a meditation for him, focusing on every bit of food he swallowed.

After walking around the bamboo groves for a while, Gopal went down to the riverbank, where the *kia* clusters were in full bloom. He could smell them from a distance, their fragrance mingled with the afternoon heat. He thought that he could smell Hena's presence all over the place. He hadn't seen her for the last five months, since her marriage, and he had tried hard not to think about her. Somehow, the sadhu's arrival had kept his thoughts occupied and he felt relieved. He looked toward the river. The sun's rays reflected like ribbons of silver rising from the water.

After a while, Gopal heard the noise of a saw grating against wood. As he climbed up the slope, the sadhu was nowhere to be seen. The sound came from inside the grove, and Gopal followed it. As he walked in between the bamboo, he noticed clay deities and clay horses of various sizes scattered along the way. He was sure that nobody visited or worshiped them anymore, but he wondered who had put them there and when. He decided to ask the old man once he returned home.

The sadhu had made a small clearing within the dense bamboo grove, not too far from the open space where he had previously settled. The clearing was big enough for a tall person to stretch out in all directions. He had chopped down some of the bamboo shoots to create the space. Gopal was filled with anticipation. Even if he couldn't figure out the intended outcome, he knew that the sadhu wasn't leaving in a day or two.

It felt cool under the canopy of the tall bamboo branches. The sun wouldn't be setting for a while. The crows were jumping from one branch to another, probably waiting for the sadhu to provide them their next meal. "Baba, maybe I can help you," Gopal said when he saw the sadhu trying to pull a long vine that had grown around a big tree. Without saying anything, the sadhu moved his hands up the vine a little to let Gopal place his hands where his own had been. They both tugged and twisted the live vine, and finally a long piece came dislodged from around the tree. Gopal helped him gather some more vines, even though he could not fathom their use.

Finally, Sukhatma hoisted a bamboo branch over his head and tied one end of it to a bamboo plant with a twig. Then he tied the other end to another bamboo plant standing parallel to the first one. He kept tying the ends of branches to plants, with twigs, as Gopal handed him the materials. At last, Gopal saw a thatched roof in the midst of the small clearing, and his heart skipped with joy. It would protect the sadhu from the scorching sun, and it confirmed that the sadhu would be there for some time.

Nevertheless, Gopal worried about the snakes and the foxes—the king cobra with its poisonous fangs and the rabid fox with its bushy tail—out to seek prey at night. He felt compelled to keep the sadhu from harm's way. The sannyasi had already put his blanket under the small roof and sat cross-legged in meditation, his belongings neatly arranged around him.

Gopal deliberated for a moment and then went home to get a spade and some rope. When he got back, the sadhu was still meditating. The rays from the sun had become softer, announcing the evening. He had to work fast to build a hut around the sitting figure. By the time he'd cut a few more tall bamboo shoots and divided them into equal lengths, the sun was about to set. With the spade, he tried to dig as many deep holes as possible. He would have to secure a bamboo shoot in each hole. They would serve as poles. Then he would have to tie some bamboo vertically to make walls. Of course, he would have to take care of a little door. The task seemed to him impossible before nightfall.

Gopal looked around as despair overtook him. He could not ask anyone for help. Probably not too many people in the village knew about the sannyasi, and Gopal decided to keep it that way. He was afraid that they would bring chaos to the peaceful surroundings and to the sadhu.

As darkness gathered, Gopal buried the bamboo shoots in the holes and leveled the soil around them. Then he tied the other bamboo shoots to the poles vertically with ropes. When the walls were knee-high, he had to stop. He needed more bamboo, and it would be impossible to cut it in the dark. Far off, he could hear the screeching bark of a fox. Around him, hundreds of lights twinkled as the fireflies went about the night sky.

Gopal remained outside the wall, not thinking that

the old man at home must be expecting him. The eerie calmness of the location made him forget that there was another world beyond this place. Before he knew it, a deep sleep overtook him.

***

Sukhatma sat in a trance, his legs crossed and his open palms facing upward. A bright white light, brighter than hundreds of suns, entered through his palms and traveled to every part of his body, illuminating his core, deep down to the smallest atoms. As the energy traveled from his head to his toes, dissipating into open space, his whole body trembled momentarily. As the shaking stopped, he felt a subterranean calmness, and slowly his subconscious-self took over his consciousness.

First, he heard the noise of digging and cutting wood, but the noise disappeared into the air and into the intense energy flowing around him. His body was anchored to the ground, but the light rising from within him and around him moved over the place, over the bamboo walls.

Then the light turned into a soft glow and Sukhatma followed it, his energy floating like a feather in the wind.

Chapter Three

"Where are we going?" asked Sukhatma. He saw the young man sleeping on the ground, but he followed the shapeless light and soared higher and higher, above the bamboo groves. He could see the river from there, flowing with crystal-clear water. He could even see a school of fish swimming upstream.

"You tell me." replied the glowing light. "First, tell me who you are."

"I'm Sukhatma. You taught me to be who I am, Swami."

"And, where are you?" Sukhatma heard the swami's voice asking him.

"I'm here. I'm following you." Soon after answering, Sukhatma lost sight of the glow, but it appeared again.

"Tell me where the 'here' is," prodded the voice.

"You sent me here, Swami. You should know." Sukhatma felt confused. "I don't know where I am. I'm drifting."

"Who are you?" asked the voice again.

"I'm Sukhatma. . . Su . . . kha . . . tma."

"Do you know Mohan?" asked the voice.

"I don't . . . remember."

"Think hard," said the voice.

"I'm thinking. Yes . . . a long time back . . ." Sukhatma replied.

"You are visiting Mohan. That is why you are here." This time the voice sounded nearer, as if it was coming from Sukhatma.

"It was your order to come here, Swami," Sukhatma replied, but to his disappointment, the light had disappeared. Slowly, he was leaving the blue sky and descending. Sukhatma woke up from the trance and saw that it was dark all around him. He stretched himself on the ground and fell asleep from the meditation and the exhaustion of talking to his guru.

Next morning, Sukhatma woke up early to do penance for losing control of his thoughts during meditation. He believed that the swami had reminded him about Mohan, but his response had defied his own command not to remember the past.

It was still pitch dark, and other than the howling of dogs, everything was quiet. As he tried to feel the surroundings with his outstretched hands, he felt the bamboo barrier around him. Slowly, his eyes got accustomed to the dark, and he could see the knee-high wall on all sides. With a small jump, he went outside and saw Gopal sleeping on the ground.

In the dark, Sukhatma walked down to the river and submerged into the water. Even in the month of May, the water was cold, and he took a dip to purify himself of his thoughts of the previous night. He kept repeating, "*Om Tat Sat, Om.*" *God is good and only God is the truth.* He crossed his legs and remained seated in the water, trying to cleanse his mind. He let his mind flow with the water. It could go in only one direction now. His awareness had come a long way to change the path. What he had experienced the night before was just rough terrain. He would make his mind settle down, not roam the place, even if his swami ordered it.

He sat in the cold water, meditating. The water in the river flew by him, gently bouncing his body back and forth.

A water snake coiled around his right hand, then unwrapped itself and swam away. A school of fish played about his toes, searching for food. The sand sifted under his weight, and Sukhatma sank a little deeper when small currents scattered them around. Nevertheless, he concentrated on the river, flowing gently, with no beginning and no end. He stayed in the water till the sun came up and warmed him with its rays. His body kept bouncing in the water like a buoy.

The shallow water in the river heated up as the sun's journey continued in the sky. Farther away, upstream, people and bullock carts crossed the river. A few people stopped and stared at the sight of the saffron clad sadhu doing meditation in the water. Then they went their way, not paying too much attention to another new sadhu in their midst.

***

When Gopal woke up the place was still shrouded in darkness, and he felt disoriented. His whole body ached from sleeping on the ground and from the hard work the day before. In the midst of the bamboo grove, lying on his back, he remembered that he had come there to protect the sannyasi. As he was about to turn to his side, he felt a slimy belly slithering over his legs, and he held his breath to remain still. After it was gone, he jumped up to check on the sadhu, but he wasn't there. He took it as a sign that the snake hadn't bitten either of them.

He left for home to get food for the sadhu and more rope to finish the bamboo hut. He thought that his parents might have worried about him in the night. They were still asleep when he arrived in the dark. After collecting the rope from the backyard, he tiptoed to the kitchen, and to his surprise, he saw a jar of milk and some food wrapped in a banana leaf. Instantly, he knew that his mother had saved it for the sadhu. He felt delighted to see this sign of his mother coming to life and showing some emotion, which he'd thought was impossible.

When Gopal got back with the food, the sadhu hadn't returned. He hid the bundle carefully so that crows and stray dogs wouldn't rip it apart. Then he proceeded to finish the little hut with more bamboo. After he covered all sides, he tied some canes vertically and horizontally to make a door, and attached it to one corner of the hut. Now the sadhu would be safe at night from stray dogs, foxes, and other night creatures. The next day, Gopal would plant some marigolds around the frame to deter snakes.

Then Gopal sat down in the shade, the food safely inside the hut, and waited for the sadhu. The sun reached its zenith and kept moving downward, but there was no sign of him. Panic-stricken, Gopal ran toward the river, and from a distance, he saw the sadhu's upper body rocking back and forth in the middle of the river. The sight made him wonder about the sannyasi. Gopal had never seen anyone punishing the body to such extent. He wondered what sins the sannyasi had committed in this life, or in his previous one, to make him go to such extremes to get moksha.

The sannyasi's long hair, all tangled, ran down his shoulders and his back, the ends of it floating in the water. The sun beat on him. For a moment, Gopal took him to be dead, but then realized that he couldn't be sitting if he had no life in him. As Gopal stood there and watched, the sannyasi cupped his hands, offered water to the sun, and drank some of it. Afterward, he gathered himself and walked up the riverbank. Like a shadow, Gopal followed him to the bamboo grove.

That evening, Sukhatma did not open the food, packed in the banana leaf. He looked at the glass jar. The milk had turned into curds in the heat. It had the same smell he'd noticed day before, even though that day there had been no milk or curds brought for him. He kept the banana leaf and the jar outside his little hut, by the door.

"Something wrong, Baba?" Gopal asked and realized that the milk had gone bad. As he approached the little door, anxiety took hold of him because the sadhu hadn't touched the food. Gopal stood looking at the food, then asked, "Should I bring some other food, Baba?" thinking that the food was not to the sadhu's liking. He knew very well that the sadhu probably wasn't going to reply.

"I will be fasting for a week," replied Sukhatma. He felt grateful to God for the little bamboo hut. He knew who had toiled to make it, but it was all God's wish. It was not his place to praise the young man. The young man earned good karma for his actions, which he did out of the kindness of his heart, and that was his offering to God. "No need to come or bring anything now." Saying this, Sukhatma retreated into the hut.

Gopal collected the food and started walking toward home. He felt a sense of dejection about the sadhu. The past two days, Gopal had tried to save him from snakebite, he had stolen food for him, he had labored under the sun to build the cottage, and he had guarded him while sleeping on the raw earth and escaping snakebite himself. What for? The sadhu was nothing to him. He hadn't spoken a word of gratitude to Gopal. He had taken everything for granted just because he was a holy man.

Nevertheless, as Gopal came closer to the village, he tried to think rationally. All these acts of kindness he offered the swami were of his own choosing. The swami hadn't asked for anything other than a saw to cut the bamboo. Gopal had felt the sadhu's divine power touching him the day before, and he thought he should feel lucky for that. It was he who had been the fortunate one among all the villagers to accompany the sadhu to the village. It was from his home that the sadhu had food and nourishment. The sadhu was his guest. As long as the sadhu was there, it would be Gopal's sole responsibility to look after him.

***

Sukhatma sat in the meditating position, his open palms facing skyward. He pictured two bright pillars of light entering his palms and the energy from them spreading all over his body. The energy spread outward and pushed the darkness farther and farther out. His mind sank deeper and deeper until he was floating like a leaf in the river. The water was still, like the ground he was meditating on. There was calmness, except for the voice emerging from somewhere, his guru's voice.

"Who are you?" asked the voice.

"I'm Sukhatma, Swami," he replied. He felt confused because the swami should have known who he was.

"You didn't eat anything today," said his guru.

"No, Swami. That was for Mohan."

"So you remember Mohan?" Sukhatma heard his guru asking. "Take me there," ordered his guru.

The guru's voice transformed into a speck of light and Sukhatma followed it. He was out of his own body and consciousness and became as light as a feather. He drifted over the bamboo grove and could see a village from up there. He was slowly descending as he kept moving and lost sight of the guiding light. To his dismay, he looked around and the light was nowhere to be seen. Then he heard a voice: "I can come only this far, Mohan."

Sukhatma tried to sink deeper into his meditation, but the disturbing image and voice of his guru broke his concentration. His mind trailed Mohan. Sukhatma, Mohan—they seemed as if they were one and the same. That couldn't be. Sukhatma was trying to push Mohan away, but like a shadow Mohan clung to him.

Mohan walked toward the village, alone. He didn't know which way to go or which house to go to. The whole place was surreal. He wondered what he was doing there. He walked as if he were flying. No, he was walking. Following someone. They both walked without saying a word. Mohan felt lost.

"Wait, wait for me," Mohan heard himself saying to someone in front of him.

"You need help?" the person asked Mohan as he turned around.

After thinking for a while, Mohan replied, "I am going to the . . . Samanta house." He didn't want to say he was visiting, because he was not exactly a visitor in his own home. Yet he couldn't say that he had come back home. Home was everywhere and nowhere for him.

"The Samantas? . . . We are the only family with that surname in this village. Well . . . there are two, but my grandfather's older brother and his wife and their son . . . that's another story." Having said this, the man walked on silently, as if he had divulged some secrets to a stranger. His voice had been muffled, but Mohan could understand everything. By this time, they were getting closer to the village, and they walked side by side.

Mohan tried to decipher the meaning of what the young man had just said. His grandfather's older brother and his wife—that would be Mohan's parents; yes, Mohan had an uncle. The man had also said something about their son; it must have been about Mohan himself. Mohan felt afraid of the young man, afraid of his knowledge.

He hoped that the man was young enough not to have known anything about him or that, if he was old enough, he would have at least given some independent thought to the rumors he would have heard while growing up in the village—that Mohan was the worst kind of son to have, that he had deserted his parents in their old age. He wanted the young man not to judge him for having a dream or for falling in love with a foreigner.

Sukhatma drifted in the breeze like a feather, following Mohan like a shadow.

"Who are you?" Mohan asked the young man.

"I'm Neel, the younger brother's grandson . . . I told you," replied the young man.

Then the young man turned around abruptly, as if he'd suddenly remembered that they were going to the same house, and said, "I don't think I've seen you in our house before. From your voice, I would have recognized you even in the dark."

Sukhatma woke up from the spiritual state, and his meditation became distracted. Yet again he heard his guru's command: "Go deeper and deeper into yourself, and tell me where you are."

"I'm returning from America," Mohan replied to Neel.

"Uncle Mohan . . .?" There was a long pause as the young man stopped in his tracks and turned around. His voice seemed confused. Mohan thought that the young man had disappeared into the dark. When he reappeared, he was saying something incomprehensible, as if he was afraid, as if he saw a ghost in the midst of the burning ghat, where all the dead bodies were cremated.

"Why didn't you tell us that you were coming?" Neel asked.

"I did not know that I was coming," replied Mohan.

"We are almost there," Neel said as he opened the iron-gate to his parents' house.

Mohan stood outside the gate while examining the surroundings in the dark. A two-story brick house stood inside the compound. He wondered as to when the other floor was added to the one-story house where he had visited his parents. Through the open windows, he could see the interiors of various rooms lit by electricity. The big house confused him and he thought that his uncle and his son must have done well, to have transformed their mud house into a brick-and-mortar one. He strained his eyes to get a glimpse of his parents' house, but he couldn't see anything in the dark. He remembered the last time he was there when he returned from America.

Mohan didn't see many people throughout the month while he was visiting his parents. When, a week after his arrival, he had gone to see his uncle's family, they had pretended that they did not know about his visit and were surprised to see him. "I hope you have come back for good," his uncle had said. His aunt had poured tea in small cups, made of fine bone China, and had waited for Mohan to reply.

"I will be going back to America at the end of the month," Mohan had said. "I have a job waiting for me."

"Somebody has to take care of your parents, one day," his uncle had said, looking at Mohan intently. "They have been looking for a suitable bride for you for a while now."

"Now you can marry anyone you like, and with a big dowry," his aunt said. He sensed a bit of sarcasm in her voice. She had flaunted all the nice things in her drawing room, many of which she had mentioned had been gifts, and had drawn special attention to a teapot and mugs from her daughter-in-law's parents.

He waited for a while in the hope that his aunt would introduce her daughter-in-law to him, but there was no sign of her or his cousin. "I don't see Murari?" he said.

"He has gone to the market. His wife can never plan for the whole week." Saying this, his aunt got up to go. "I've chores to do now. One of these days, you should have lunch with us before you leave," she said. Mohan touched her feet and went home. The invitation for lunch never came. His cousin didn't come to see him.

Now Mohan kept looking at the open windows. His parents were nowhere to be seen. It must have been the wrong house. Shadows drifted from window to window. In the faint electric light, Mohan saw his uncle and aunt. Other than his uncle, aunt, and cousin, there were his cousin's wife and their other two grown children, the ones he was seeing for the first time. The whole extended family lived under the same roof.

"Are you coming?" Neel asked, as he closed the gate behind them.

"What took you so long?" his uncle asked him accusingly. "Your parents cried their hearts out. Where have you been all these years?" Everybody's eyes were focused on Mohan.

"What is the point of bringing up the old stuff now? It has been a while. He has come a long way. He must be tired," Mohan heard his aunt saying. Then she told her daughter-in-law to set places for supper and asked Mohan to follow her.

As Mohan stepped inside the house, he took on the appearance of his former self. He realized that he had been to the house once before, when his parents were living there. It was a one-story house then. He remembered that, standing on the same veranda he had just walked over, his mother had once wiped his face with the end of her saree, welcoming him and hoping that he would fulfill her long-awaited dreams by living somewhere in India, not returning to that foreign land called America.

When he passed the drawing room and came to the long interior veranda, his aunt showed him the bathroom so he could wash up. This time around, the water pipe was somewhat lower on the wall than he remembered. He opened the water faucet and splashed a handful of water on his face. Then he pulled up the ends of his pants and ran the warm water on his feet. When he came out, his aunt was standing there holding a small towel for him to wipe himself.

Again, he searched for his parents. He looked at every corner of the house, and they weren't there. Are they dead? He wondered. But no one had informed him. Who had brought him to this house? Where were his parents? He wanted to ask his relatives, but what if they asked him the same question? He was their son. He was supposed to know their whereabouts.

His uncle and his cousin sat at the dining table and asked him to take one of the two remaining chairs. It still had the same four chairs. He remembered being astonished at the workmanship and staring at them for quite some time when he'd visited his parents, decades before. He couldn't imagine that a local carpenter could have created such masterful work. They looked bold and extravagant in front of the plain rectangular table, now greasy from a mixture of dust, and oil residue from food.

The dinner—he couldn't see clearly what they were

eating—tasted like chapatti and some kind of curry. Mohan ate quietly as his aunt (or was it his mother?) stood next to him.

"Where are my parents?" he asked them finally.

The people around him transformed into shadows and shuffled about, whispering among themselves.

"We don't know," they said in unison and melted into the background.

Mohan got up to leave. He wasn't welcome in this house, certainly not if his parents were still living in it.

On his way out, he passed by a room on the main floor. He remembered that, for a month, this room had once been his, the room in which he'd slept on his first visit from America to see his parents. So many of his parents' desires must have gone into this room when they built the house. In their hopes and dreams, they would have imagined him in this room, newlywed, his bride's presence filling up every corner of the empty space. In their sleep, they must have heard little footsteps running out of the room and knocking on their bedroom door. He tried to trace his memories back to his last visit with his parents. It was too painful to remember his father's last words to him, but his parents were nowhere to be seen. Slowly, Mohan drifted back toward the river as Sukhatma woke up from his meditation.

Chapter Four

The next day, Gopal returned with a bunch of marigold plants from his garden to plant around the sadhu's hut. He had heard that they were good at repelling snakes. When he arrived, the little door to the cottage was closed. Quietly, he dug holes around the bamboo walls and carefully placed a plant in each hole. A pungent smell came off the broken plants and flowers when he crushed them by accident while planting. Then with a small bucket, he carried water from the nearby spring and poured it onto the newly planted flowers.

Gopal didn't know what else to do after that. The swami would be fasting for a whole week. Gopal sat on the edge of the bamboo grove under the shade and looked at the river. Water flew in small streams in between the sandbars. It was knee deep at most places, but crystal clear, like glass. The whole place felt deserted. The crows had taken shelter on the tall branches. The stray dogs were probably searching for food in the village.

He thought about the river—the story it carried in its heart. All the people, young and old, in the towns and villages it ran past, must have told her some of their secrets, and in return, the river must have whispered, "Don't worry. I will be here for you, always." He wondered what his brother had said to her when he left the place for the last time. When Hena got married and left for her in-laws' house and crossed the river, as everybody had to cross it one way or another, Gopal had stood at the same spot he was sitting in now. Did Hena ask the river to be the witness to their childhood friendship, as Gopal had asked it once?

Gopal had heard that Hena would be back to visit her parents next month. In any case, he would be away at college. Then, Gopal thought about the sadhu. No other swami had stayed in the village for so long. What if he stayed longer than Gopal's summer break? On the pretext of bringing food, the villagers would crowd around him and ask him about their futures. They would want to know if someone would marry that year, if so-and-so would pass their exams, or if their daughter-in-law would ever give birth to a boy. Gopal presumed that the sadhu knew the answers to all of this, but unlike the other sadhus who visited the village, he wasn't going to forecast anything.

To Gopal, it seemed that the sadhu was talking less and less. Neither hunger nor thirst woke him from his meditation. Day and night he meditated, and at times it felt as if he punished his own body, and Gopal didn't know what for. What was it that the swami was searching for? Was he looking for moksha, just as Gautama Buddha had once done?

At the thought of the Buddha, Gopal remembered a story he had read as a child. As a young prince, Gautama had left his kingdom in search of enlightenment, leaving his wife and their newborn son in the palace. He had longed for moksha from rebirth and suffering, and he had deprived his body of nourishment until he reached Nirvana.

Gopal's focus shifted from the river to the bamboo hut. He wanted to know so much about the sadhu—who he was, where he came from, what had made him renounce his world. Why here? One day, the sadhu might teach his wisdom to his disciples, as Buddha had once done, but probably nobody could answer the questions Gopal asked himself.

After a while, Gopal left for home. For the last few days, he had been living in a state of euphoria. The sadhu had become the focal point of his existence. He had derived a kind of joy from serving him in his own way. He felt elated when he carried food and water from the earthen pot. The sadhu probably didn't care for any of that, but Gopal didn't mind, as long as he was in close proximity to the swami. He wanted to catch the aura of calmness exuding from the sadhu and spreading throughout the bamboo grove, all the way to the river. For the next few days, the sadhu would be fasting. Nevertheless, Gopal decided to come back and see for himself that no harm had come to him and that the villagers weren't disturbing the peace and harmony of the place.

By the time he got home, his mother had finished cooking lunch. She had a banana leaf spread on the counter top and was about to set aside a little bit of everything on it.

"There is no need to send anything for a week," Gopal said. "He will be fasting." He noticed disappointment spread on her face for a brief moment; then she collected herself.

"How long will the sadhu be staying?" she asked Gopal while removing the leaf from the counter.

"I don't know," he replied. He had noticed a change in his mother since the sadhu's arrival. She paid more attention to what she cooked and asked him if the food tasted good. She cleaned the house thoroughly, twice a day, as if the swami would arrive unannounced any time. She retreated to her bedroom early, as usual, but read the religious books she had until past midnight.

"Is he an old man? How old is he?" she asked him, without hesitation. She didn't think for a moment about her undue attention to the stranger. She wondered if the sadhu was young, like her son had been, whom she hadn't seen for nearly thirty years.

"Hard to tell . . . with his long hair graying. But he is not old; I can tell." Gopal looked around to see if his father had finished his bath as he answered her. The sadhu's arrival had had no impact on the old man. He waited for Gopal to eat his lunch and supper with him. He hardly ever asked about the whereabouts of Gopal or the food he took from home. "You can come with me next time and get his blessings," he told his mother while setting the table for lunch.

She'd had a dream the night before. Her son had returned from America. She had known it was her son but couldn't see him clearly. He was asking someone about her and her husband. She screamed at the top of her lungs to get his attention, to tell him that she was standing right there. Nevertheless, he couldn't hear or see her. She tried to run to him, but her legs were planted on the ground. She woke up in a sweat and started to cry, holding her stomach with both hands, as if her lost son had left her womb at that moment.

She felt strange that the dream had coincided with the sadhu's arrival. Maybe he could tell her about her son's whereabouts. He would know if her son would ever return to them. They hadn't written to him for almost twenty years, after he had returned to America. Mohan hadn't responded to them since his father had started writing to him ten years back. What if he believed they were dead? Remorse filled her heart at the notion that they were the ones who had abandoned their son.

Then she worried about her son's wellbeing. He must have been in his mid-fifties. His hair must have grayed. She didn't know how many children he had or whether his American wife had preferred not to have any. At the thought of her son, she felt her knees giving away and her whole body disintegrating into the earth with piercing pain. She held on to the counter top and pondered Gopal's suggestion. "I would like to ask him about your brother," she said as she started putting rice and curry on two plates.

Gopal didn't reply to this for a while. For the first time, his mother had acknowledged the existence of her other son and, in a way, had validated his presence by connecting the two of them as brothers. He did not know what to say at the mention of a brother he knew nothing about. It pained him to think that his parents never took notice of him because he would always be there; he existed like one of the fixtures in the house.

He wanted to know how it felt to be a son who was desired and welcomed. He wanted to be burdened by the hopes of his parents, just as they'd had hopes for their other son. Moreover, he wanted to be loved by them. Like acid, their indifference had etched itself into his life, corroding it, and at times making his resolve difficult to love them unconditionally.

"I will ask him after his fasting is done," he said finally, to which she didn't answer.

Nevertheless, she prepared herself to meet the sadhu by cleaning everything in the house from top to bottom. She mopped the floors and dusted the walls. She wrung a cloth in a bucket of water and wiped the doors and the windows clean. Then she washed the bedding on every bed. After that, she scrubbed the kitchen utensils until they shone in the afternoon sun. After all those chores were accomplished, she washed everyone's clothes and hung them out to dry. The formal garments, which were hardly worn and kept in tin trunks, were hauled to the veranda and aired out.

She remembered that that was how she used to prepare the house before she visited the gods in the temple, which she hadn't done since her older son had left. When she thought of visiting the sadhu, it felt like going to the temple again. In order to welcome the sadhu into her heart, even if he wouldn't be stepping into the house, everything, including her inner self and outer surroundings had to be purified. After cleansing the house, she wanted to get rid of the anger that had been sticking to her mind like wet clay, for years. However, she knew that it wasn't a small feat to be completed in a few days' time, and just like the all-knowing God, the sadhu would certainly figure out her resentment toward life, and forgive her.

While she cleaned the house bit by bit every day, she cooked the lunch just like before, although she was less careful about how she cooked since the sadhu wouldn't be eating for a while. Her husband noticed the sudden surge in energy in her but didn't know what to make of it. Only Gopal knew that his mother had come alive for the first time in decades, in the hope of getting news about her lost son.

During the whole week of the sadhu's fasting, Gopal went and made sure that no creatures, whether human or animal, disturbed the peace of the bamboo grove. It was quiet inside the hut. At times, he was worried that the sadhu might have died from the hunger or could have been bitten by a snake. Gopal tiptoed around the hut in the hope of finding a crack so that he could take a glimpse of the sadhu, but to no avail. He himself had placed the bamboo shoots too close to one another when he built it. At least he took solace in the fact that a snake couldn't wiggle through the walls. However, what troubled him the most the whole time was how to bring his mother to see the sadhu.

"You are going to ask him, aren't you?" she asked

Gopal the day after the sadhu broke his fasting, as she put a little bit of everything on a banana leaf for him. The sadhu had been there for over a week and had never visited the village for alms or to read the villagers' horoscopes. She was afraid that he might just get up one day and leave.

"I'll try to ask him," Gopal replied, briefly. He thought that it had been a bad idea on his part to offer his mother to accompany him without the sadhu's permission. It was apparent that the sadhu did not want to see anyone, let alone talk to anyone. Also, it seemed as if Gopal would be asking for a favor in exchange for the food he got from home for the sadhu. If word reached the villagers that Gopal's mother had been to see the holy man, then what would prevent them from wanting to see him?

Nevertheless, Gopal felt empathy for his mother. He understood that her whole life was spent waiting for a son who most probably would never return, but her thoughts of finding him had been ignited by the arrival of the sadhu. Like the depleted Murudi River overflowing its banks in the monsoon rain, his mother's life had leapt out of its sorrow in search of her son. The least Gopal could do to fulfill his mother's wish, as a dutiful son, was to ask the sadhu, which he didn't know how to do.

After eating lunch with his father, Gopal collected the packet of food tied in the banana leaf and headed out. Before he had gone far, he turned around impulsively. At home, the old man was getting ready for his afternoon nap. Gopal waited until his father closed the bedroom door halfway. Then he sneaked into the kitchen, where his mother was still cleaning the dishes. On the table, she had set aside a small plate of food for herself.

"You haven't gone?" she asked him.

"Why don't you come with me, now?" Gopal asked

his mother, not knowing whether she would take his offer on such a short notice. She hadn't been out of the house in as long as he remembered. "At least you can see the place, even if you cannot talk to him."

"Okay. Let me just change to a clean saree. This smells of spice," she said with excitement. Then she covered her lunch and left it on the table, and before he knew it, she was ready. Her husband would be sleeping for a while, and they should be back before he got up.

Mother and son walked in the brutal midday sun, Gopal leading the way. The last time she had walked this path was after her older son had left for good. She remembered standing at the house as he walked away. She had stood at the door, hoping for him to turn around so that she could see his face one last time. Just as he'd reached the bend in the road, he had stopped for a moment and looked back. Then, instead of turning to the left to take the usual path to cross the river, he had gone to the right, through the bamboo groves.

Once he was out of sight, she had left the house and walked after him, afflicted with sorrow. She didn't care if the villagers saw her alone acting like a madwoman, or took pleasure in her misfortune out of jealousy. She didn't see anyone on the way, as if fate had held that moment only for her to witness. By the time she had crossed the grove and arrived at the Murudi River, her son was on the other side. From there, she could see the trail of dust as the bus roared into view and her son climbed into it.

Now the path to the river had grown narrow and difficult. She could tell that the thorny bushes on either side had been freshly cut to make the way. The bamboo had grown taller and denser than she remembered, forming a canopy overhead and creating calm and quiet solitude below. However, after they'd arrived at the clearing, the bright sun hit her face again. As she squinted her eyes to escape the harsh rays, she saw the little hut nestled inside the grove and, at a distance, the river flowing like before. All of a sudden, she heard the sound of *"Om, Om . . . Om"* breaking the solitude, arising from the water and filling the empty space.

"Maybe we can wait under the shade until the swami finishes his meditation." Gopal took his mother under a cluster of bamboo, farther from the hut, as he said this. She sat there looking at the water, trying to get a clear glimpse of the sannyasi, but all she could see from that distance was his head, its long hair submerged in water. She closed her eyes and concentrated on his voice.

The voice was powerful and rich. It felt as if it were coming from somewhere deep inside the earth, penetrating the riverbed and coming through the sadhu's voice. She remembered her young son practicing the scales on his harmonium, singing along to them in his baby voice, *"Sa . . . re . . . ga . . . ma."* As he grew older, when he practiced the scales, his voice burst out with a rich and powerful tone. His otherwise gentle and passive voice had woken up to the ragas.

The "Om" resonated in her shattered heart, and she felt tormented with the thought that the voice so much resembled her son's. However, she dismissed the idea that it could belong to her son; it was wishful thinking on her part. Her son had deserted them to marry someone he loved, and for sure, lived an earthly life. It wasn't possible that the owner of this voice could be her son. Moreover, as a mother, she could never see her son as a sannyasi, begging for food and traveling with bare feet from place to place.

As she listened to his chanting of *"Om Tat Sat,"* her

fluttering heart settled down to the beautiful sounds, and she remained still the whole time. The gentle rustling of the bamboo branches in the wind, the harsh cawing songs of the crows, the barking of the dogs, got pulled into the chanted songs, which rose and fell like waterfalls. She closed her eyes and waited for the sannyasi to finish his meditation.

After a while, the cascading sound ebbed, and she saw the sannyasi rise and get out of the river. As he walked toward the bamboo grove in his saffron robe, she could not study his face from a distance. With their long hair and unshaven faces, all the sannyasis looked the same when they came to her house for alms, but the way this holy man walked was different. His long torso remained erect as he focused his eyes on the ground. She remembered how her own son had always looked down while walking, discouraging the girls in the village from thinking that he fancied them.

By the time the sannyasi reached the hut, Gopal had walked toward him with the food and a jug of cold water from the earthen pot. His mother sat in the same spot, waiting with anticipation to hear from the swami as to when he could see her and tell her about her son. Gopal put the food on the small blanket on the floor and touched the swami's feet with both hands. As Sukhatma put his hand on Gopal's head to bless him, the sannyasi's hands shook for a brief moment, and he stood motionless without uttering a word.

"What did he say?" Gopal's mother asked eagerly as soon as he came back.

"The swami is going to observe silence for a week," he answered his mother. He had been unable to bring himself to ask the swami about seeing his mother and had left. "We can come back another time," he added.

When they arrived home, the old man was still taking his nap. After eating her lunch, she went to her room and sat down in front of the deities to pray for a meeting with the sannyasi. She had been praying for so many years to keep her son safe and give him a long life. Suddenly, she felt that the sannyasi was the medium between her and the God and he would be able to tell her what God already knew. She waited for the holy man to break his silence.

***

After Gopal left the hut, Sukhatma set the food aside and opened the *Varaha Upanishad*: "That which is consciousness alone, which is all-pervading, which is eternal, which is all-full, which is of the form of bliss and which is indestructible, is the only true Brahman." He stopped to analyze what he had read and knew that after arriving at this place, he had lost touch with the pure and infinite consciousness, the Brahman, which is the God, more than once. This world had pulled him back from the spiritual path he was destined to follow. He felt the presence of the past in his unconscious mind, and it eluded him more and more.

The vision Sukhatma had seen a week before while in trance had unsettled him quite a bit. He had tried to wipe out the past with years and years of meditation and punishment. However, he realized that he was being pulled into the quagmire of his earlier life, trying to find out about the parents as Mohan would do. Sukhatma was waking up to the fact that Mohan was able to divert his mind and lead him into those unwanted explorations. Allowing Mohan to reemerge felt like a failing on his part.

In the beginning, he had immersed himself in the Murudi River at all hours to cling to his transformed self—

to Sukhatma. However, lately, his mind had been skipping to its earlier childhood memories of the time he had spent along the river when he visited his grandparents. He had felt the touch of his mother's hand, long forgotten, when he ate the food brought by Gopal. He had no memory of the young man who had devoted all his time to keeping him comfortable but, nevertheless, was distracting. Sukhatma's unwelcome awareness of Gopal sometimes imposed itself on him, pushing him to find the connection between Gopal and Mohan.

To suppress these thoughts, he had punished himself by forgoing food for days, by meditating in the water for hours at a time, and by reading the Holy Scriptures in silence, day after day. It had worked until he had felt a tug in his heart that day. The place smelled of bygones, permeating his senses, as he kept reading the book. The food remained untouched.

After reading the Upanishad, Sukhatma sat meditating for the whole afternoon, and at night the light appeared again. This time, he knew that it was Swami Saralananda, and he concentrated hard to hear his every word.

"Tell me who you are?" the swami asked.

"I'm Sukhatma, Swami," Sukhatma replied without hesitation. He was already floating, soaring into the ether like a bird. The speck of light danced ahead, and Sukhatma followed it.

"Do you remember the house?" the swami asked.

"Yes. But they are not there," Sukhatma replied. He remembered his last vision in which Mohan could not find his parents at the house.

"Where are they? What happened to them, do you think?" the swami's voice persisted.

"They are dead. They died from broken hearts,

Swami." Sukhatma's sad voice was carried by the wind and scattered over the village.

"You didn't eat the food today, either," the swami told him in an accusing voice.

Sukhatma didn't reply to this, at first. He was confused again. He was Sukhatma, and the food reminded him of Mohan. "But only Mohan could relish the food. It wasn't meant for Sukhatma, Swami. Who would send food for Mohan?" he asked.

"That is for you to find out," the swami said as the light disappeared from Sukhatma's view. He woke up from meditation and ate the food brought by Gopal in the afternoon. With each bite he took, his body felt a shiver passing through it, almost like an electric current, as if something from the past had scorched his nerves. During the previous times, too, the food and water had reminded him of Mohan and his mother. However, he kept on eating. That was his guru's command.

Finally, he understood the purpose behind his guru's order to return to this village. To find moksha from this life, he had to face the past and remember everything that had happened to him. Then, before transcending wholly to the other world, he had to consciously let go of this world, no matter what he found or whom he found in it. It would be his ultimate test to confirm that he had renounced this world. His visions, especially the one in which he had tried to find out about the whereabouts of the parents, made him realize this.

Sukhatma left the hut and walked to the river. A crescent moon and countless stars helped light the dark path. He sat at the river's edge and closed his eyes, and once again, went into deep meditation. In the soft breeze, as he lost his consciousness and went into trance, he floated in the thin air and wandered toward the village. He saw the houses in half dark and concentrated even more to find the house he had gone to last time. Then he remembered that only the uncle and his family lived in that place, the one that once belonged to his parents.

He went around the house, but it was locked from all sides. That was the last place he had seen his parents when he visited India. They must have moved away from that place, but they were there in the village, somewhere. He knew it because of the food he'd eaten and the ice-cold water he'd drunk. The taste of them—only one person held the secret to it.

Nevertheless, he could not go looking for them in person. He remembered that he was banished by his father, never to set foot in his parents' house again. He was a sannyasi who had given up the world, and he could not go and impose on anyone.

That was when he heard his guru's voice again. "How did you get to that house the time before?"

"I trailed Neel, my cousin's son, Swami."

"You don't know what happened after you left home, do you? To find whatever you are looking for, you have to begin where you stopped last time." The swami sounded more like a friend than a guru.

As the voice faded, Sukhatma found himself awake and walked into the river. He immersed himself in the knee-deep water and took the lotus position to meditate. The moon had already disappeared, and in the dark, he went into deep meditation.

While Sukhatma's body swayed in the water, he saw Mohan leaving his parents' house for the last time. After that, in his vision, Sukhatma could not see anything for a while. Then, all of a sudden, he saw people going back and forth from that house, carrying things that looked like furniture and clothing and household items. Soon after, he saw two figures really looking sad follow the others and leave the house.

***

Right after Mohan had left, his uncle, who had chided him for not taking care of his parents, who hadn't even come to see him while he was there, had become a regular visitor at his parents' house. His wife had often cooked food and sent it with him. Unlike the other villagers, they restrained themselves from talking ill of Mohan or berating his parents in front of others for having a self-centered son. After all, the shame was theirs also, since they were part of the family.

However, as the months passed and as the parents' wounds grew deeper and deeper, forming scabs on the surface so that they looked healed to others, the uncle and aunt murmured to each other. They looked at the newly built brick house and sighed, "Such unfortunate people. What good is this big house?" They never thought about the hardship the older brother had gone through to build that dwelling or considered that he had given up his share of the old house to them.

It became a habit with the uncle and aunt to complain day and night. They complained about not having enough light for their grandson to do his homework and said that their house was too hot or too cold from lack of sunlight or too much sunlight. They openly discussed how they would never be able to build a brick house, like the one next door. Their whispered discontent became louder and spread the seed of guilt in the older brother's mind.

"They are right. We don't need this house. What is it good for, if no one is here to enjoy it?" he asked his wife. "He isn't coming back. Who is going to inherit the house?" he added, without uttering his son's name.

Then one day, after coming home from the paddy fields, he sat his wife down and said, "I've thought about giving this house to my brother and his family. The two of us don't need so many rooms."

"Do as you please" was all she said, and she went about the house finishing chores. She didn't care about the house after Mohan had gone away. It had been built for Mohan and his wife and for the grandchildren to come. She thought that giving the house away would be a good deed, which might bring her son home.

So, they built a modest house at the edge of the village, just at the bend where Mohan had stood and looked back at his mother before taking the path through the bamboo groves. The younger brother and his family counted their blessings and kept saying, "We are just the keeper of the house. Mohan can have it anytime he returns." For a change, they wished him plenty of luck in the foreign country as they said it, hoping that he would never return. Eventually, they added another floor to it.

***

All this had happened so long ago that it had taken a significant amount of time to be recaptured in Sukhatma's vision. He woke up from the meditation as he felt the water rushing underneath him. His body had become lighter because it had directed all its energy to gathering the information, and he was almost floating. He could not proceed anymore with his concentration to find out where the two figures had headed. However, the familiar aroma of the food and the flavor of the water Mohan was so acquainted with made Sukhatma restless. Not only that, someone else's presence, other than Gopal's, had disturbed him that day.

Chapter Five

The day after she had gone with Gopal to visit the sannyasi, she wanted to accompany him again. She had cooked their simple lunch with great care and put a little bit of everything on a banana leaf. She was aware that the sannyasi wouldn't be meeting her, but she wanted to hear his voice while he meditated. Then to her disappointment, she remembered that the holy man would not be talking for a week. A week wasn't that long, she rationalized, compared to the past thirty years, and after Gopal left, she set out to collect the dry clothes from the clothesline.

Gopal waited at the same spot as the day before for Sukhatma to finish his morning meditation in the river. The sadhu wasn't chanting, "*Om Tat Sat*" at the top of his lungs. Under the afternoon sun, everything was hot and quiet around him. The place seemed dead—no barking of dogs, no crows, and no wind either.

It was the middle of June, and in a month the river would rise, overflowing its banks from the constant rain. Sometimes it covered the natural spring and came toward the bamboo grove. He wondered if the sadhu would be still there then, and his instinct told him that he would be. Unlike the other sadhus, he had made the river and the groves his retreat, as if he had been there all along. Gopal worried about who would bring the sadhu food once he left for college.

Slowly, the sun moved from the zenith toward the horizon, and the sadhu still remained in the water. Gopal dozed off but woke up to the rumbling sound of the bus. It seemed that the bus stopped near the village for longer than usual. From a distance, he could see people getting out one by one, and at last, someone got off wearing a saree. Meanwhile, the bus conductor brought down a couple of suitcases from the top of the bus and left them on the side of the road. Whereas, the other passengers started walking toward the bridge, the woman and a party of three men waited until the bus pulled out.

Gopal stood to watch the three men carrying the suitcases and the woman walking behind them. Right away he knew that it was Hena with her father and two brothers. It felt strange to him that all of them had gone to bring her from her in-laws' house, and where was her husband? It was customary for the husband to accompany the wife on her first visit to her parents' house after the marriage. In any case, she hadn't been due to arrive for another month.

It was almost evening by the time Sukhatma walked toward the hut. Gopal had waited the whole afternoon for him and was eager to get back home. When he arrived at home, his father was sitting on the veranda.

"What took you so long?" his father asked him in a rather gentle voice. Recently, Gopal had noticed a gradual change in the household. Instead of retreating to their own corners, his parents were trying to communicate with each other. While his mother devoted her time to keeping the house extra clean and put more effort into cooking food, her husband offered her help in any way he could. He wiped dust from the pictures and peeled potatoes in the kitchen. Sometimes they even had tea together in the veranda. Gopal knew that the change in their attitudes had to do with the sadhu's coming.

"The sadhu meditated for the whole afternoon," Gopal replied.

Usually, his father never discussed the sadhu, but to Gopal's surprise, he said, "I hear he is observing silence for a week," to which Gopal didn't reply, but he felt a normalcy in the old man's demeanor. Unlike Gopal's mother, who was actively searching for her long-gone son, his father must have secretly entertained the hope of seeing his firstborn.

Gopal's mother was in the kitchen, making the afternoon tea. "Is something the matter?" she asked her son when he came in to get the tea. He had always looked cheerful and content when he had returned home from visiting the sadhu, and his mother knew that something was bothering him that day.

"I'm just tired," Gopal replied, as he carried the tray with three cups of tea on it. The sight of Hena weighed heavily on his mind. Nonetheless, he decided not to mention anything to his mother. For all he knew, his mother had not gotten the news yet.

Next morning, Gopal overheard the conversation between his mother and the maid, who came rather early that day.

"Do you know?" the maid volunteered as she scrubbed the pans. "Hena is back."

"Wasn't she supposed to visit her parents, soon?" Gopal heard his mother ask.

"No, she has come back for good. I hear her husband gets drunk and beats her. Not only that, the mother-in law harassed her day and night, asking for more dowry," she added.

"Poor child. What happens to these men?" Gopal heard his mother say.

"Hena sent a message to her mother: if they didn't

bring her home, she would kill herself. At least these people had the sense to bring her back," the maid said, and poured water on the pan to wash it.

Gopal didn't wait to hear more. He understood that these things still happened to girls in India. They were treated as property by the whole family—easily owned and easily discarded at the owners' discretion. He thought about his parents and felt bitter about the way they had let go of his brother because he wanted to marry a Christian. All this time, his brother had been a myth to Gopal. However, he felt that "the undeserving son" deserved respect from him for leaving his parents and taking care of someone he loved.

As his mother cooked the midday meal, Gopal went about the house unmindfully, worrying about Hena. He felt sad that she'd had to endure abuses, at all. Yet he was happy that she had returned home without harming herself. A ray of hope flashed in his mind when he realized that she had left her husband. Nevertheless, he knew that his hope would be short-lived.

That afternoon, after giving food to the sadhu, Gopal headed toward the river. He hadn't taken a dip in it since the holy man had started meditating there. On his way, as he passed the thorny *kia* bushes, he thought about Hena, and his heart became heavy. They had played together along the riverbanks and near the *kia* clumps since their childhood.

***

Hena's father was the village dhobi. Once a week, he came with his wife to collect the bedsheets and washed them in the river. Their two older children, both boys, never came with them, but they always brought the little baby, Hena. She was hardly walking when Gopal, himself barely three or four, first saw her. Her wide and curious eyes roamed around the place while her parents were busy collecting bedding. Usually, Gopal was busy writing his alphabet when they came, but his mother would let him play with the baby for a little while before they left. Before long, Gopal wanted to accompany them to the river.

In the beginning, his mother didn't let him go with them. "Who would watch you when they are busy washing the sheets?" she'd ask him after they left. "In my old age, I don't want to lose you to the river," she'd say, as he cried at the top of his lungs. At her age, she had lost all the patience to comfort a howling child, and after a while, she said that he could go.

At the river, while the dhobi and his wife washed the sheets and lay them on the grass to dry, Gopal was the one who looked after Hena. He was careful not to go into the water and sat on the wet sand with the baby. He dug holes in the sand with his hands, and to the little girl's surprise, water came oozing from those holes. After a couple of hours, when he got tired of playing, he'd ask to go home, and one of Hena's parents would happily oblige and walk with him, thanking him for being such a good boy.

Even after Gopal started going to school when he was five years old, he still wanted to go to the river with the washerman and his family. He cried hard to skip class on those days, but his mother did not yield to him. The only times he could go with them were on holidays or Sundays. By that time, he didn't like to play with the sand anymore and ran around with Hena all over the riverbank. She would hold a long stick in her small hands and chase him around the clumps of *kia*. Sometimes, he heard her parents' yelling, "Don't go too close. There are cobras hiding there." His mother told him later that the snakes were attracted to the fragrant flowers.

As they grew older, sometimes Hena challenged him to break a flower from the *kia* stalk, reminding him that there were snakes in there. He'd then grab the stick from her hand and beat the bushes with it while quickly breaking a flower from the cluster. One time, he almost stepped on a snake slithering between the plants and, screaming in horror, he tumbled back and fell on the grass. After he collected himself, he handed her the flower as if it were a trophy he had won.

They played together until Hena was about ten years old and her parents decided that it was unbecoming of her to run around with him. There was a different kind of pressure on Gopal. Although he was told at home that he had too much homework to waste his time at the river, this only disguised the true complexity of the problem. He was barred from mingling with a dhobi girl when the right time came. Afterward, when Hena came with her parents to pick up the sheets, usually she stood outside with them. If they saw each other, the old familiarity was gone. Both of them headed into their adolescence, with the knowledge that the mind had lost its innocence to the arbitrary rules set by the society.

Gopal had often thought about Hena. For more than eight years, he had considered her as a friend. At school and in the village, he hardly played with anyone. However, he always looked forward to the days when his mother pulled the sheets from the beds and collected them with her tired hands. When he and Hena played with each other, there had been no expectations, just the pure joy that two children happened to experience.

Then, after a couple of years, Hena accompanied her parents less and less, until she stopped coming altogether. If his mother asked about her, her parents replied, "It is time she learned to take care of the household chores," which implied that they were grooming her for marriage.

The last time Gopal had seen Hena up close was at the village temple. His mother didn't get out of the house at all, but once in a while, on special occasions, she sent her husband to do the puja. It had been after the harvest. She had put all the different kinds of new crops in a bamboo tray to be offered to Lakshmi, the goddess of wealth. Gopal was home from college for break, and the old man wanted him to come with him, saying, "It won't be too long before I'm gone. You might as well learn to do these things."

The temple was really crowded. The whole village was there to offer its samples of abundant crops and to ask for more in the coming year. There were some men, but mostly women and children were everywhere. As Gopal climbed the steps to the temple, his eyes caught a group of women outside, at the farthest corner of the building. He saw Hena standing with her mother and a bunch of ladies. Being untouchables, they were not allowed inside the temple. They could worship the deities which were outside. Hena was clad in a yellow saree. Her long hair was pulled back into a bun, and red kumkum powder adorned her forehead. She was all grown up and looked fresh and beautiful. As their eyes met for a brief moment, she blushed and turned away.

On his way out, Gopal's eyes searched for her, but she had already left. He had thought about her often, and the feelings he had for her were more than friendship. Subconsciously, even as a child, he had liked her. After seeing her that day, he knew that he had always loved her. He could love her for the rest of his life. At night, he imagined his head resting on her soft breasts, and he fell asleep.

Gopal's winter break neared its end. Since the time he saw Hena at the temple, the thought of her had tormented him. Then he heard the beat of drums and a small procession of people heading toward her house. A man walked in the middle, flanked by her two brothers. Gopal realized the reason for her visit to the temple. She was getting married. Next morning, when he heard the drums again, he knew it was time for her to leave for her in-laws' house, and most likely, he would never see her again. He hurried across the bamboo grove and watched Hena as she crossed the river with the other people and waited for the bus. He stood there, motionless, until the bus had come and left, as it had done before, irrespective of what happened to people.

***

Preoccupied with the memory, Gopal stood in the knee-deep water while his childhood unwound in front of him, but the river brought him back to the present. It had been flowing since time immemorial. It had absorbed the countless sorrows of the human hearts and turned them into the unceasing songs of its life. It was ever present, washing away the past, devoid of the future. When someone stepped into its water, it was a single point of time that encompassed the person, with no beginning and no end. As the water flowed around his ankles, sending the sensation of gentle strokes throughout his body, for a moment, Gopal forgot his own existence. He remained in the river for the longest time, listening to its eternal songs.

On his way home, he stopped near the sadhu's hut. The place was really quiet, leaving aside a couple of crows fighting over the empty banana leaf at a distance. He poured the water he had carried from the river around the marigolds, and plucked the dead flowers from the plants.

In five more days, his mother would expect the sadhu to end his silence, and Gopal was thinking of ways to ask him to see his mother.

"I hope the sadhu likes our food," the old man said to Gopal, as they ate their supper that night. His wife had been cooking food for the holy man tirelessly, for more than a month, but the old man had pretended not to notice anything. He bought extra vegetables when he went to the village market and asked the milkman to give them a little more milk than he usually delivered, as if anticipating someone's arrival but not wanting to acknowledge the fact that the guest had been there for a while. He used to do these things when his first child came home from college or when he had come to visit them from America. That had happened a long time ago, and after that, he had never entertained the thought of doing the same thing for anybody else.

Unlike before, Madhuri didn't retire to her room in the evening. She had to plan for the next day's lunch and keep the place clean. Gopal cleared the table after dinner and waited for his mother to finish hers. Nowadays, she ate the evening meal but, as usual, she ate alone. To Gopal's surprise, sometimes the old man and his wife even engaged in small talks. She passed on the news she got from the maid to him. He mostly complained about his younger brother and his family—how they had never offered to give the house back after Gopal was born and how they had prospered after moving into it.

"Hena is back, I heard." Madhuri said this to no one in particular. The news wasn't of any specific interest to her husband, and her son was a grown man, who had left his childhood play, far behind. She thought it was safe to discuss this in front of them. "Poor child. I hear she is . . ." She stopped short of finishing the sentence.

Gopal got up on the pretext of going over one of his syllabi for the coming year. He was sure that neither of his parents knew the depth of his feelings for Hena. Even if they knew, it was unlikely that they would ever acknowledge them, and they would expect him to learn from the past mistakes in the family history. To them, an untouchable was as unacceptable as a Christian. He tried to fill in the blanks of what his mother left unsaid. She is going back. She is not going back. She is pregnant. The way his mother had hesitated and stopped, it was more probable that it was the last one.

Gopal loved her, but it was an abstract feeling, which he could experience on many levels yet didn't know how to put into words. The love was without expectation or remorse. He could love her and admire her from a distance, but as soon as he thought of getting close to her, the forced and ever-visible sign of "outcast" placed on her by the society formed a cocoon around her, barring him to go any further. He could break the cocoon as his brother had, but he didn't think he was brave enough to abandon the only place he knew.

However, he made it a point to go and visit Hena the following day. Occasionally, he had gone to her house before to let her father know that his mother had more washing that week. Usually, he didn't see Hena during those short visits; she was always busy with chores. That day, on his way from bringing food to the sadhu, instead of going home, Gopal kept walking toward the outskirts of the village, and soon he was near the thatched hut. It was late afternoon. From a distance, he saw Hena sitting alone on a cot, her back toward the village. As he got nearer, he could see that she was mending a pillowcase.

"Hena," he called. His heart was beating hard, as if

it would jump out of his chest at any moment. The house was rather quiet. He thought that her parents might be out on errands.

Hena recognized his voice and turned around. Their eyes met for a brief moment. Gopal felt as if he was the last person she was expecting to see. He didn't think of the fact that his presence might draw unwarranted attention from her neighbors. "Baba isn't home. I'll ask him to come over to your house," Hena told him as she went back to stitching the cloth.

"I came to see you," Gopal replied hesitantly. "I saw you getting off the bus." His own words sounded odd to him.

"So, you have heard," he heard her say without looking at him, while her hands kept busy with the needle, going back and forth in the cloth. "What difference does it make to you?" she asked him after a while. He understood that their childhood years were a thing of the past, and life had taken its natural course. He didn't know how to alter it.

Gopal had no answers to her question. He could tell that the brief yet tortured life at her in-laws' house had matured Hena beyond her age. Words escaped him because the kind of love that asked for sacrifice and commitment, he didn't think he felt. If anything, he felt small and scared in front of her.

"Don't come again. There is no point," she told Gopal as she folded the pillowcase and got up from the cot. "It will only cause problems."

Gopal watched her as she gathered herself and walked toward the door. He saw her looking one last time at him and disappearing into the room. Even though she had wrapped herself carefully with the saree, he couldn't help but notice her swollen belly.

Once again, after the visit to Hena, Gopal turned all his attention to the sadhu. Somehow, he liked the holy man's unencumbered life. No physical or emotional bondage held him back from his devotion to his God. He had no need for a home to shelter him or need for food to sustain his body. If he remained silent for days, that was because he was in communication with his God, asking him how to leave this mortal world and proceed to the next. It seemed so hard, but Gopal could see himself trading this world for the one where there would be neither joy nor sorrow. He wished he knew how it felt to find the true Almighty—not in the temples, but inside his own conscious mind.

While Sukhatma remained silent, Gopal spent more and more time around him. After bringing the lunch, he'd sit at a quiet place looking at the river and try to keep his mind uncluttered as long as he could. If the thought of Hena came to his mind, he'd keep saying, "Om," until the thought was replaced by the sound. If he felt bitter toward his parents, he chanted the word to calm him down. He found magic in that single word. It brought him closer to the sannyasi.

Gopal could not wait for the sannyasi to break his silence. He would certainly be able to tell Gopal's mother about her older son. For the past ten years, the old man had written letters to his son asking him to come back and visit them, asking for forgiveness, but to no avail, as if their son had left this planet to avoid any contact with his parents and settled somewhere else in the galaxy. Gopal had seen the returned letters piling up in the old man's room, and he had even read a couple of them. Once his older brother was found, Gopal would be free to leave this place. Life felt too burdensome to him.

Chapter Six

It was a strange relationship that existed between Gopal and his parents. They loved their son, but there was a void in that love. The disparity in age they had with their son made them feel deficient as parents and they could not do anything about it. Not only that, their broken hearts could not find ways to make their love for their child whole. The awkwardness they felt toward this child was compounded by the impossibility of his birth and the fact that this child had replaced someone who was still alive and should never have been replaced.

After their only son was banished from home for marrying a foreigner, both the parents had given up on life. Their newly built home had stood in the village like a prison, and the prying eyes and wagging tongues of neighbors had reduced them to self-imposed incarceration.

In the beginning, the mother sat on the veranda, a distant look in her eyes, not remembering that there were chores that needed to be taken care of. Women, young and old, came to visit her to show her sympathy, and asked her, "How could a son do this?" their words cutting into her like barbed wire. After a while, she stopped sitting on the veranda.

The father had built the house thinking that after his retirement from the police constable job, he would relax in the village and take care of the vast farmlands his own father had left behind. No one worked in the fields by themselves. They had Dalits who worked for them. Before, when his son was studying in America, he'd had employed Dalits to do the job. He'd just supervised them. He had told them when to sow the seeds and when to harvest them, although they knew all that by heart. He would go every day to see which parcel of land was dry and which held more rainwater. Then he'd tell them to dig interconnecting channels between the plot of lands so that the water would seep into all of them.

When the sun reached the zenith, he would come home to a freshly cooked lunch of curry and rice. He would tell his wife about the lush green fields and how he looked forward to this retired life. His wife would sit there with a handheld fan, made of palm leaves, and move her hand around to keep the air cool, as well as to wave away the flies that hovered around his food. They would talk about their son, their only child, and their hearts would swell with pride.

After asking the son not to come back, the father went to the paddy fields and toiled the whole day with the laborers, which he didn't have to do. He didn't come home for lunch. If he got too tired, he sat under an umbrella and looked at the dirt road longingly, hoping his son would appear from around the bend—not with his untouchable wife, but just by himself.

The father had given up their beautiful big house to his brother and his family. When he returned at dusk, the interior of their modest new home would look dark from outside, and once he opened the door and went inside, he would see his wife sitting quietly in front of the deities, an earthen lamp flickering in the evening breeze. She would sit like that for a while as he went to the bathroom and poured water all over himself, cleansing away another day from his life.

"I will warm up the food soon," she would say as he finished washing, and slowly she'd get up to go to the kitchen. She didn't cook twice anymore. She prepared a single meal whenever she felt like it, usually before sunset. Some days, she struggled to remember what she had eaten that day or the day before.

"Are there any letters?" he would ask her indifferently, knowing well that he did not care to read them. Recently, they started getting letters from relatives who, out of jealousy, had never kept in touch with them. These relatives had never understood how a lowly constable like him had such a brilliant son who could go to a foreign country for higher studies. Now they felt superior in their social standing and wrote condescending letters to these unfortunate parents, sending their heartfelt sympathy, as if the son had not merely married a foreigner but been subjected to some kind of death. The letters read like condolences, and after a while he started tossing them in the wastebasket, unopened.

Nevertheless, he kept asking about them every day. There was a chance, he thought, that there would be a letter from his son telling them that he would be returning home soon. While working in the paddy fields with the laborers, he would secretly keep an eye on the dirt road, waiting for the postman. He would feel a momentary elation if the man turned the bike at the bend and went toward Anantpur. But disappointment would set in once he realized that there were so many other houses in that village like his.

It wasn't that his son didn't write any letters to them. In fact, he wrote to them every month. However, the father waited eagerly for the news that his son would return home. When that news didn't come, he stopped reading the letters, even though he still waited for the mailman. His wife quietly took the blue aerograms and put them away before he could throw them out, as he did with the letters from the relatives.

At times, there rose a sense of bitterness from the pit of his stomach, bitterness toward his wife. He thought that she had been an accomplice with him in sending their son away. He wished that she had not asked him all those questions at night. She was his mother. She could have simply said, "He is getting married," and if he'd asked, "Whom, where, when?" she could have answered, "Does it matter?"

Yet it mattered to both of them. As soon as they tried to forgive their son, a renewed anger caught hold of them. How could they have given life to someone who forgot who he was or where he came from? They had toiled for his sake, giving him opportunities others could not afford. In the end, all that mattered to him was his own happiness. They both felt inadequate at expressing their feelings, now that they hardly spoke to each other. That was how nine years had passed.

Then, like a river changing its course and flowing, divided, in two different directions, their joint life abruptly separated. One isolated night, after years of existence without the urge to comprehend the others needs, their naked body had entwined like dried vines. She tried to revive the long-forgotten passion. However, her body failed to recall the unencumbered rhythms of the bygone days.

Her dried heart could not squeeze even a drop of love into the act. All she felt was pain. It traveled through the base of her abdomen and seared her already scorched soul. She held on to him in utter despair, trying to find a way to diminish the distance between them. After it ended abruptly, her thighs wet from the warm and sticky liquid flowing from him, they both lay still in bed. She stared into the dark and tears rolled down her cheeks.

That was the last time they shared the bed. In their sorrow, neither of them had the strength to sustain the other. They both knew that their thirty-six years of married life had concluded that night. They would live like strangers under the same roof, but sharing the same bed did not make sense to her.

One day, not too long after that, as she sat down in front of the deities, suddenly she felt something moving inside her. She had reached an age when her womb was dry like the autumn leaves. Her period had been irregular for a while. At night, heat permeated her body from head to toe, and she would wake up from sleep, sweat pouring from all over. Soon after, her body would feel cold like ice, and she would scramble for a blanket. She thought that from her parched body, dry like the riverbeds in summer, it was impossible that a life would sprout again. Yet she did not know what to think of the slight nudge in her belly.

She prayed fervently to the gods to take her from this earth. She assumed that it was a tumor in her stomach that had acquired life and was going to deliver her from the misery. Somehow, the thought of dying made her feel strong. Death would be her salvation—revenge upon the people she loved, a chasm they could never obliterate.

A month passed. The multiplying cells in her body that she thought were a tumor made their presence known in strange ways. She did not feel sick like before, and a new energy propelled her dormant life to seek things she had forgotten about—some out-of-season fruits or some freshwater fish, which weren't available then.

Before long, her body could not fool her. The living thing stole breath from her, while moving inside her at odd hours. Slowly but surely, her belly was growing, taking the form of an alien, demanding to be noticed.

Now in her wildest imagination, she could never comprehend the hands she had been dealt with. After her first child was born, she had prayed day and night for another child. The fear that something bad might happen to their only son had made her restless. What if the gods became jealous of one another while giving all their attention to protecting him? What if one of them took their son to be near him?

When their son was a year old, she had conceived again. They had thought that the gods had smiled on them, but her happiness was short-lived. She had delivered a stillborn baby at the end of seven months, and she had almost bled to death.

After that, they had made love feverishly at odd times, as if that was also an offering—a prayer to the gods. Yet nothing came out of it. Every month, she'd waited expectantly, hoping to miss her period. Months had passed into years, but her body could not produce another life.

The thought of the night, she had sex with her husband, made her sick. She could not have imagined a more loveless act, let alone a life sprouting out of that union. She was just about fifty years old, an age when the women she knew were having grandchildren. She felt ashamed at the thought of giving birth at such an inappropriate time in her life. What would people think? What would her son think?

Eventually, she could not hide it from the village women. When they dropped in to borrow a cup of rice flour or a handful of red lentils, they saw her belly, big under the folds of the saree. In the beginning, they did not know what to think of her unnatural middle, growing like a pumpkin. They whispered, "It might be some stomach ailment she is suffering from. Who knows how many days are left?" They took pity that she did not have a son or daughter-in-law to take care of her, and brought some cooked meal every now and then.

Her husband did not notice her growing stomach at all. She hid it well with the help of the six-yard long saree that she wrapped around herself with extra care. He went to the paddy fields in the morning as usual and came back at dusk. Now that they didn't share the same bed, she remained in her room most of the time. When he returned home, she'd emerge from the semi-dark space to warm up the food, she'd cooked during the lonesome hours of the day. He had stopped asking about the letters. He'd eat silently as she sat in the corner, the tablecloth hiding her belly.

Soon the whole village was talking about the arrival of an unexpected baby, although they did not know when it would be. The women, who had shown her sympathy thinking that she was about to die, felt an unmatched contempt toward her. They envied her fertile body and envisioned the tender love the husband and wife must have had for each other.

The men took it in good stride. They talked about God being good to the Samantas after their son had left them for a Christian, an untouchable. "Life must go on," they said. "God had no intention of giving them two children, but look: once one left, the other one was sent, just like that," they said as they went about their lives.

If her husband heard any talk of a new baby, he didn't pay any attention. After all, young men and girls in his village were getting married every year, so it was only natural to expect babies. Since his son had deprived them of that happiness, he couldn't join the others in the news, and kept to himself as he went back and forth from the paddy fields.

Then one day, as he was going home in the evening, he saw his younger brother standing with some other villagers. After his son had gone abroad to study, and after he had built the brick house in the village, he had noticed a restrained jealousy from his brother. But that had changed after he had given away the house to his brother's family. However, even though they still lived in the same village since he had moved away from the house, they never sat down together like two brothers and discussed their family, or anything else.

As he approached the group, they stopped talking, and his brother looked him up and down and said, "I hope *Bhabi* is doing well," referring respectfully to his sister-in-law, not knowing what else to say.

The comment made him nervous. He wondered whether the neighbors had found out about the little secrets of their lives— they having separate bedrooms and their lives falling apart. He knew that his wife had too much pride to tell anybody, but he also knew the prying mouths of the women in the village. They were capable of making the dead talk.

"Why shouldn't she be?" he said, looking at no one in particular. "It is her nerves, you know." He looked directly at his brother as he said it. For some reason, he wanted to hang around with them for a while and wanted to share his sadness. There was no life either at home or at the paddy fields. At the same time, he did not want their sympathy, which sounded hollow to him.

"We are so happy for you. God gives as he takes," said one man as Samanta proceeded toward his house.

All the way home, he pondered the meaning of God's taking and giving. By all means, his son was still alive. No matter; he wasn't with them. And what had God given him, other than heartache? Yet the words of the villagers prodded him. His wife had not talked to him for the last five months. He wondered if everything was all right with her.

As he got closer to home, he felt an emptiness encompassing him like the surrounding darkness. He had forgotten that once their home had held much happiness, even without their son. His wife's presence had filled the house. All of a sudden, he missed her laughter and the way she'd moved around, happy and proud, taking care of everything. He wondered what she did these days, other than cooking the only meal.

He switched on the light as he entered the house. His wife was nowhere to be seen. The door to her room was slightly open, and a faint light escaped through the opening. She did not make any attempt to come out, as she did every evening when he came home. This made him afraid, and he slowly walked toward the room. "Is everything all right?" he asked from outside, gathering courage.

He hadn't been to her room for the last five months. She hardly used the electric light overhead. From outside, he could see the outline of her body on the bed, her back toward the door. A soft light flickered from the lamp on the floor and, in one corner of the room, he saw the deities she'd brought from the room they'd shared together, put neatly on a small stand.

"Madhuri, I'm home." He called out her name this time, and an intimate familiarity overwhelmed him. He did not know how it was possible that they lived like two strangers under the same roof. He stood in the same spot a little longer, then, entered her room.

She turned slowly toward him, her bulging abdomen presenting itself like an unfamiliar beast. His eyes rested on her belly, taking in the information, but his brain was not able to process it because it went into shock. He could see without doubt that she was pregnant.

"See what has become of me?" she said in a rage, sitting up in the bed abruptly. Her eyes glinted in the dim light like a wounded animal's. For the first time, he noticed that her hair had turned gray. The crow's-feet under her eyes and harsh lines across her face made her look much older than she was. Other than her belly, her body looked emaciated—starving for a life she wished for, feeding a life she did not want. She had lost all her elegance, and the child growing within her had turned her into something ugly. She started weeping.

He sat down there on the floor, his head reeling. So, this was what God had given them in their old age. He remembered that night. In their entire married life, that particular night stood out for its utter indifference to whatever little was left between them. He hadn't felt any passion or love for her for a while now. He could not understand what evil possessed them to initiate the act. He was baffled by the irony of the pregnancy. He felt as if God was punishing him in the worst possible way—forcing him to take care of a child rather than be taken care of by one.

"What should we do?" he finally asked his wife as he got up and cautiously went and stood near her. "You can always . . ." He stopped in midsentence, realizing from the shape of her belly that it was too late to abort the baby. She was the only thing he was left with. It was too dangerous a procedure at such a late stage.

"I wish it was a tumor. I thought it was a tumor. That would have been the end of everything," she said as she tried to get down from the bed. She put one foot on a stepstool and lowered her body slowly and put the other foot on the floor. She snatched herself away from him, saying, "Leave me alone," when he tried to help her.

The baby was born with great difficulty. She remained in labor for a day and a half. The midwife gave her all kinds of drinks, infused with herbs, to lessen her discomfort. She howled intermittently from the pain, then things got quiet for a while, and then the cycle started again. In the beginning, her husband retreated to the veranda, but when he could not stand her screams, he went to the cowshed with a cot. He remained there, hidden from the women coming and going from his house to see if the midwife needed anything. Finally, the next day after nightfall, when he was all exhausted from waiting, he heard the baby cry. One of the women blew the conch twice to let the villagers know of the birth and that all was well.

He did not see the baby until morning, and he didn't mind. He felt disconnected from the new life he had been tossed into. Everything about his life—his wife, their house and the newborn child—reminded him of his unfulfilled dreams. For a brief moment, the anger for his firstborn gave in to mourning. His heart felt a tug, and then it was all dark and empty.

When the midwife brought the baby, swaddled in a thin cotton cloth, Samanta was just getting up from bed. By then, he had moved his cot from the cowshed back to the veranda. The sun was about to rise, and in the soft light of the dawn, she held the baby and stood to one side. He wanted to ask how his wife was doing but decided not to. The midwife would have let him know if something went wrong with her.

The baby was asleep. He could tell that it was tiny. Clumps of black hair covered its round head. It was apparent that the midwife had cleaned the baby well. There was not a patch of dried mucus either on the body or on the head. He wondered whether it was a boy or a girl because he could not tell from the face. He had forgotten how his son had looked right after his birth. It had been more than thirty years since then.

"He looks just like the other one," the midwife said without uttering the older son's name, as if his name would ruin the auspicious birth of the younger one. "The older one was so much easier. He was just waiting to come out," she said. Then in a hurry, she put the baby on the cot because the baby had peed on her. She wiped him and gave him to Samanta to hold, while she wiped herself.

He looked at the baby's face to see any resemblance with his older son. The baby's skin was darker like his, whereas his older son was fair, the color of milk and honey, just like his mother. The baby's forehead was narrow like his brother's—the characteristic they both shared with their mother. The baby was asleep, so he could not see his eyes, but from their outline, he could tell that they were big and shaped like almonds. The baby's limbs were small, unlike his brother's.

"Babu, let me go and see how *Bibiji* is doing. You can hold your son a little while longer." Saying this, the midwife left to tend to his wife. Samanta felt stranded with the baby, who did not feel anything like his son. It felt strange to him to address this child as his son. He thought that if it were not for fate, he would be holding his grandson. Resentment crept over him. He wanted to be left alone to mourn his life's labor lost, and to blame his son for that. He did not want to be entangled with another son at his age. It would take an additional twenty years to raise the child. He simply didn't feel capable of doing that.

He walked back and forth on the veranda, holding

the baby in an awkward position. At times, it felt as if his sixty-year-old legs would buckle under the baby's weight. He walked around furtively, so that nobody could see him from the road. He knew that as soon as the sun was up, the whole village would be at his doorstep to have a look at the new baby. Their words would be a mix of praise and pity, "What a beautiful baby. Hope this one does not run away like the other son." Then they would advise him not to educate this child, just as they had with the older son.

After what seemed like a long time, the midwife came back to get the baby. "How is Madhuri?" he asked her finally. He felt miserable at the thought of her—the trauma her body had gone through.

"She is sleeping. Poor thing . . . after all that pain." She took the baby from him as she said this. "But you know . . . God is kind to give this baby. Don't let him get out of your sight," she said, while walking toward his wife's room. He understood the implication of her words, but there was nothing for him to reply. He had always respected her for her age and experience. She was at least ten years older than him and was still summoned to deliver babies in the neighboring villages. Sometimes she went to the nearby town. The kids she had delivered when she was a young woman were grown up men and women, and she was delivering their kids now.

After a while the midwife left, telling him that she would be back in the evening to massage his wife and give her more herbal drinks to reduce her discomfort. Women had come and gone—some with a pot of cooked vegetables or dal, a few with raw papaya or other fruits from their gardens. They told him how to warm up the food before giving it to his wife.

They named the baby, Gopal. It was another name for

Lord Krishna, as Mohan was. They didn't have the usual ceremony to name the baby. They didn't distribute any sweetmeats this time around; partly because his mother was too weak to do any of these things and his father did not care. Nevertheless, the baby occupied their days and nights. Samanta stopped going to the paddy fields so he could help his wife with the baby. She had no milk in her dry sagging breasts. He added enough water to the milk from the cow to make it thin, just as her milk would have been. He boiled it carefully and divided it into small glass jars. He did this twice—in the morning for the whole day and then in the evening for the night. He even got up at night to feed the baby so that she could sleep.

As the baby grew, he could not cure their discontent. If anything, he became a symbol of their resentments toward each other. After their first son's departure, their known world had vanished with him. There was no desire in them to recognize the life they had built together, let alone get attached to a baby from their passionless, hurried encounter. When his first birthday came, they did not celebrate that either. They felt too ashamed to celebrate their son's birthday when other people in the village were celebrating the birthdays of their grandchildren.

Chapter Seven

As Gopal turned the bend and walked toward the bamboo grove, he heard the sound "Om" and hastened his steps. When he reached the hut, he saw Sukhatma meditating in the open, and a book of scriptures lay next to him. He had stayed in the river since the early dawn, chanting, "*Om Tat Sat*," and had settled down to read the scriptures. For the past week, Gopal had left the hut right after he put the food on the blanket, but that day, he sat at a distance until the sadhu woke up from his meditation.

When Sukhatma came back to himself, Gopal opened the banana leaf and the aroma from the food drifted all around. After he put his hand on Gopal's head to bless him, the sadhu first offered food to God and then, as usual, scattered some for the dogs and the crows. Whatever was left, he ate it without reservation. He had been training his mind to consciously look back and recall the past, as his guru wanted him to do.

Gopal waited for Sukhatma to finish. He would have to come out with his request before the sadhu started reading the scripture once more.

"Baba," he addressed the sannyasi finally gathering the courage, and waited for Sukhatma's response. When Sukhatma raised his eyes and looked at him, Gopal continued, "My mother wishes very much to get your blessings."

"Give me a day or two. I need to talk to my guru," Sukhatma replied. Then he read aloud from the Bhagavad

Gita: "Fear not what is not real, never was and never will be. What is real always was and cannot be destroyed."

While going home, Gopal was puzzled about the sannyasi having a guru. For the past three weeks, he had never seen anyone else in that remote corner of the bamboo grove. He wondered whether the guru visited the holy man at night. The thought of spending the night at the grove to take a glimpse of the guru occurred to him, but he discarded the unclean notion right away. At home, he told his mother that she would have to wait a couple of days more.

That night, she saw the sannyasi in a dream. The holy man had come to their house. He looked so small, almost like a child. She sat on the veranda, her dry breasts hanging from her skinny chest. The sannyasi suckled from them as he became smaller and smaller and after a while disappeared into her. "Where is my son?" she kept asking. The child in the saffron robe appeared from between her legs and danced around her, saying, "Here I am. Here I am." She woke up in a sweat and switched on the light. There was no one there. She took the dream as a good omen that the sannyasi would be able to tell her about her son.

That same night, Sukhatma went into deep meditation to summon Guru Saralananda. He had been in that place for three weeks. The river, the bamboo grove, the food he ate, and the water he drank—each one of them had tempted him to forgo the *sannyas* life and merge into the past. He knew that the food he ate was from his mother. Nevertheless, he had controlled his mind and proceeded only in one direction, the path he had been familiar with for the past seventeen years. He hadn't thought about his father, or wanted to know who the young man was who looked after him so diligently every day. However, he knew that he had to face the past to advance to the next stage.

"You don't recognize your mother?" Sukhatma heard his guru's voice, every word trying to penetrate and shatter his concentration.

"I am confused, Swami," Sukhatma replied, as he remained still and tried hard to concentrate. "It is the young man's mother. It is impossible."

"You have never thought about the young man?" the guru asked.

"No, Swami. He is just someone who brings food," Sukhatma replied.

"Then you must find out." Sukhatma waited for the voice to continue, but it had vanished without notice.

Next day, after eating, Sukhatma was about to read the Bhagavad Gita but remembered his guru's order. "I'll see Mother tomorrow," he said it to Gopal, and opened the pages of the book.

That day, Gopal went home as soon as possible. He was excited at the prospect of the swami meeting his mother. "The sannyasi addressed you as 'Mother' and said you can come tomorrow to get his blessing," he told her.

"The sannyasis call all women 'Mother,' including little girls, out of reverence," she said. She did not wish any son the life of *sannyas*, let alone her own son returning as one, and calling her "Mother." She thought about the dream she'd had the night before, and her heart filled with anticipation.

"Get me some turmeric leaves from the backyard," she asked her husband, as she soaked rice in water. She boiled the milk that had been delivered in the morning and squeezed enough lemon into it to make curds. She had known this meeting was coming. She had asked her husband to get sugar and coconut from the village market the previous day. She grated the coconut and cooked it with the curds and sugar in ghee. After supper, she ground the rice with water into a thick paste and spread the rice batter on the open turmeric leaves and put the cooked condiment in the center. Then she folded the leaves gently, tying threads around them. She cooked them in steam for more than an hour. After one batch was done, she cooked another batch.

It took her the whole night to prepare the special rice cakes for the sannyasi, the cakes her son used to love so much. She hoped that this way the sannyasi would get a notion about her son and it would be easier for him to locate him. She had heard that sadhus got a vibe when they came across anything that was familiar to the person they were searching for.

***

Sukhatma had been meditating in the river since nightfall. In his meditation, he had followed the young man and entered the house with him. The two figures, Sukhatma had seen previously moving away from the big house, were sitting there. They looked old and haggard. He heard the young man call them "Ma" and "Baba," just as Mohan used to call them. He had never noticed the resemblance of the young man to Mohan, but once inside the house, he realized that the young man was indeed Mohan's younger brother. They were all getting excited about something.

Leaving them alone, Sukhatma roamed from room to room but didn't find any trace of Mohan—not a picture of him, not a single memento. Then, in one corner of the room that must have been the old man's, he saw a pile of letters addressed to the old man's son in America. Sukhatma went to the other room, full of deities. In the soft light from the lamp, he saw another pile of letters from Mohan, which the old lady was hoarding.

After Sukhatma woke up from the meditation, his body shook like the thin reeds at the water's edge. He heard thunder and saw lightning just above the water, coming from all directions but not touching him. He could feel the pull between the two worlds, the one he had left but that wanted to claim him back and the other, which he was afraid would lose him. At the top of his lungs, he recited the Bhagavad Gita and repeated, "Om," to get back to his spiritual abode. After a while, all was quiet as a beam of white light entered his body, and he saw reflections of thousands of stars in the calm water, and he went back to his meditation.

***

She woke Gopal up early in the morning to take a bath and get ready. She had immersed herself in the cold water from the well and cleansed her body thoroughly. She put on a saree that had been bought by her husband, after they got the news that their son had gotten admission to graduate school in America. That had been so long ago. It was a simple, off-white cotton saree with orange borders. She had never been able to look at it after the son was gone. The six-yard-long garment was still in good shape, untouched by insect infestation.

She was putting vermilion on her forehead when she noticed her husband standing near the door. He hesitated for a while, then heard her say, "You can come in." For twenty-one years, they had retreated to their separate corners of the house, and it felt strange to him to enter her room. He looked at her from head to toe. Her face looked happy and bright. He remembered the saree she was wearing, and a sudden sadness gripped him. He had wasted everybody's life, he thought with a sigh. He wondered how his son and his family were doing. He had been writing to him for the last ten years and understood that it was his son's turn not to reply to him.

"Do you think I should come?" he asked her. He didn't want to impose himself and spoil her preparation. After all, she was the one who had cooked food for the sannyasi, earning good karma, and he felt that she should be the one to visit him first.

"Maybe not this time. The sadhu will be here for some more days, I'm sure," she replied while wrapping herself with a shawl. She was afraid that her husband would carry his unconscious tension with him, which would hamper the sannyasi's prediction.

The mother and son were on their way, just as the dawn was breaking with red and orange colors. Gopal was holding the fresh jug of milk, and she put the basket of rice cakes on her hip, as if she were holding a child. On a small plate, she had put flowers and sandalwood paste as an offering to the sannyasi. It felt as if she were going to the temple again, after all these years. The old man stood near the door and kept watching them until he couldn't see them anymore.

The sound of "Om" resonated from the river to the bamboo groves. The stray dogs followed them silently. She saw the crows flying from branch to branch but without making the "caw, caw" noise, which always irritated her. Then, on one of the branches, she saw a blue jay skipping around. She hadn't seen a blue jay for a long time and remembered hearing that it brought good luck. She walked hurriedly toward the spot from which she had observed the sannyasi the last time. That was when Gopal came upon the cobra, lurking near the termite mound under a thicket of bamboo bush.

"Watch out," he cried out, as he pushed his mother

in the opposite direction. As she looked with horror at the brass-colored serpent, swaying with its hood expanded, she felt that their eyes met and she shivered inside. Then the reptile slithered away into the mound.

"You should not have killed that snake the day the sannyasi arrived," she said when she thought about the conversation the father and son had had on that day. "The snake always remembers," she said. Until then, all the signs she had come across had been auspicious. However, she reasoned that the snake is associated with Lord Shiva; hence, it could be considered a favorable symbol. They proceeded to an open space away from the grove and waited as the whole place became lit with sunlight, lifting the fog from the water.

At the break of dawn, Sukhatma rose from the water and with folded hands prayed to the Sun god. As he walked up the riverbank and approached the hut, he felt someone else's footsteps, weightier than his, treading on the same ground. He kneeled down and touched the earth with his bent head. The air around him felt heavy, as if it were saturated with the burden he thought he had shaken off years before. Nevertheless, he plodded along in his saffron robe and wooden sandals.

She followed Gopal cautiously toward the hut, leaving enough space between them and the sannyasi. Sukhatma went inside and after a while emerged with the Bhagavad Gita in hand. She observed him from head to toe from the corner of her eye. He had a thin face with a sharp nose. His hair was long and disheveled and hung loosely over his shoulders. His beard covered half of his face. A saffron robe draped his skeletal body and long hands. He wore a garland made out of *rudraksha* beads. She could not help but notice his forehead. Then she looked at her younger son.

"Baba, my mother would like to have your blessings," Gopal said.

She was about to touch Sukhatma's feet, but he moved away so that her hands fell on the Gita. He knew he should never let his parents touch his feet, even after becoming a sannyasi.

"Mother, please sit down," said the sannyasi, as he took a seat in the shade. His recognition of her made him ill at ease for a brief moment, but he composed himself.

His voice caught her off guard. She had heard him chanting from afar and hadn't been sure. Then she thought that she was thinking too much about her son. She opened the basket and offered the rice cakes to him, saying, "Baba, I've made these for you. Our son liked this very much."

The sannyasi took the cakes and rolled up the sleeves of his tunic to sprinkle water around them, offering first to God, then to the dogs and the crows, who had crowded the place. He didn't eat any. That was when she saw the deep indentation on his right arm. The wound from the dog bite had healed after much effort, but the mark had remained as a ghastly reminder, even after her son had grown up.

She didn't have to ask about her son anymore. Her son was sitting in front of her. There was nothing that could hold her back. Her grief was unleashed, like water through a broken dam.

"Manu. You are Manu," she wailed. "I have been looking for you all over. I've waited for you all these years. You cannot recognize your own mother. Son, what has happened to you?" Gopal held her back as she hit her hands on her head and cried.

"I'm Sukhatma, Mother. The Manu you are looking for has transformed to this life." The swami said this and looked at her with compassion.

"God must be blind," she replied with anger and glanced upward to the sky, toward the God whom she had prayed to day and night, to no avail. She wasn't looking for the son who sat in front of her but did not think about her in her old age. "Son, what happened to your wife? Where are your children?" she asked, her voice muffled by crying. "Come back to us. We have gotten old waiting for you."

"I don't belong to this material world anymore, Mother. What you see now is the reality," Sukhatma said, as he felt this world pulling him back.

Gopal listened to them, thinking that his mother had lost her mind. Certainly, the sannyasi could not be his brother. His brother would not give up the world leaving behind a wife, for whom he had once given up his parents. Gopal waited patiently for the two lives in front of him to unfold, exposing the wounds that were still bleeding, but his mother was the only one who claimed she was the mother, without any reciprocation from the supposed son.

"Son, I don't want to lose you again," she sobbed.

Momentarily, Sukhatma was swayed by the old woman's pain. Then he collected himself and tried to console the grief-stricken mother through the dialogues between Lord Krishna and Arjuna in the Bhagavad Gita. After that, he quoted what Buddha had preached thousands of years back after he found enlightenment: "The root of suffering is attachment." This time, he looked at her and said, "Mother, let go of the attachment that brought you so much pain."

Hearing this, she cried even more. "I gave you birth, my son. How can you deny the attachment I would have to you?"

Sukhatma looked at the Gita in front of him. No quote from it would suffice to quench the truth behind those poignant words. However, he replied, "Detachment is not that you own nothing; detachment is that nothing owns you." Saying this, he extended his hand and gently touched hers. "You still have the son, Mother, even though he isn't what you expected, but don't let his decision distort the course of your life," he added.

She looked up at her son's face, her eyes blurry with tears. Years of punishing his body with hunger and meditating under harsh conditions had reduced his body to a skeleton and made his skin dark and lusterless. Yet she could feel the divine touch bestowed upon him, which had washed away all his bitterness, giving him peace. His face glowed with eternal bliss. "We have been really unfair to you, my son. Forgive us for what happened." She said this as if she were talking to a guest, while wiping her face with her saree. "My heart breaks to see you like this. Leave this life behind, and come back to us."

Sukhatma tried to remain calm in the face of her moving appeal to him. Years and years of meditation had taught him to shun emotion. Yet he felt his heart flutter a bit before it settled down. He quoted the Bhagavad Gita again, telling her, "Whatever happened, happened for the good. Whatever is happening is happening for the good. Whatever will happen, will also happen for the good. You need not have any regrets for the past. You need not worry for the future. The present is happening. Live in the present."

"No matter; you are still our son. Don't you know our lives are completely destroyed? It is in emptiness we live," she said, as she looked at her other son. She had forgotten all about him.

"You can still hear songs in your decayed hearts, in the ruins of your life, Mother," Sukhatma said, as his guru, Swami Saralananda, had told him once. "Listen to the Bhagavad Gita. It is the song of everlasting joy. The song will make you whole again. It is like this river—ever present. It will wash away your sorrow and unite you with your true self." Then Sukhatma put the Bhagavad Gita near her feet and touched them with both hands. "You must return home now." As he said this, he got up and slowly retreated to his hut.

"Are these your last words, Baba?" she asked the sannyasi, as she held the book to her heart and cried inconsolably, but by that time, Sukhatma had already closed the little door to the hut.

After a while, she stopped crying. The sun beat hard on them, and with help from her other son, she got up and took a few steps. Her head felt light and her legs wobbly. She had put the copy of the Bhagavad Gita in the basket. She bent down to pick it up and said, "Let's go." As she walked toward home, she didn't look back. Gopal followed her, like a ghost.

"There is no need for you to tell your father about the sannyasi or who he is," she told Gopal as she walked sluggishly alongside him. Gopal had been quiet the whole time. He had always been invisible to her. He realized that even when she had talked to the sannyasi, she had never mentioned him, not once. In his presence, she had uttered the raw truth of leading an empty life in spite of his being there and taking care of her and his father.

"It is not my position to say anything. He is your son. I don't even know him other than what he is, a sannyasi," Gopal said, as he looked ahead in anger.

"You would never know how it has been all these years," she said in the hope of being understood.

"You kept waiting for a shadow on the wall to come to life while I disappeared behind the shadow. You could never love me. Why wasn't I able to fill up your empty life? It must be that you never wanted me."

She didn't reply to him at first. Then she said, "I was too old to take care of you."

As they walked silently the rest of the way, mother and son became engrossed in their own thoughts. The wind of change had blown over them, carrying the past with it. There was nothing to salvage from it. Just as the sannyasi had said, it was the present that mattered. However, they were not sure of what that meant.

When she arrived home, her husband could not wait to get the news about their son. "What did the sannyasi say? Where is he?" he asked impatiently. He had been pacing back and forth on the veranda the entire morning. When she didn't reply, he asked her, "Did you know how to describe our son? Does he know what our son likes?" Then, talking to himself, he said, "Maybe I should have gone."

"There was no need for you to go," she said after a while. "This is what the sannyasi gave to me," she said, and took out the Bhagavad Gita from the basket, and laid it in front of him.

"But, what about our son? Where is he?" he asked desperately.

"Mohan is dead," she answered without hesitation or tears in her eyes. "That is what the sannyasi said."

"Did he say when? How?" he asked, looking at her in surprise. There was no sadness in her. He thought that her mind had become numb with the pain she had endured throughout her life.

She didn't say anything to this at first. She was equally responsible for banishing their only child. Now that she had seen him, she wanted to make the pain only hers. It was an atonement she was willing to impose on herself.

Let her husband grieve for the son who was really theirs, but the person whom she had met was entirely someone else. She felt sadness in her heart all over again. "No. He didn't say anything like that. It must have been more than ten years ago, since the time you have been writing to him," she said finally, and went to prepare lunch for them. "We have mourned his absence for a long time now," she added.

As he followed her to the kitchen, surprised at her indifference, he asked, "Are you sure the sannyasi knows?"

"I'm sure of that. It seems he knows," she answered him, while chopping vegetables and onions. She believed every word of what she said. After all, Mohan had to be dead in order for the sannyasi to occupy his mind.

He left her alone and went to the veranda. Now that he had lost Mohan, there was nothing to think about, no looking back. Her few words, true or false, had wiped out the past. He himself was alarmed at the lack of agony in his heart. But then he thought that his heart had taken years to forget what it once loved.

That afternoon, she thought that there was no need to send food for the sannyasi, since he had not eaten the rice cakes that day. After cooking, she went about finishing the chores that had piled up from the morning. The day seemed so long to her, yet she had hardly finished anything. She gathered some clothes, already dry in the sun, and brought them in. Then, "Lunch is ready," she called out.

The old man came and took his place. "Gopal, are you coming?" he asked, and waited. There was no response. As she brought food in two plates and put them on the table, the old man called his son's name once more. The silence acquired its own voice and echoed from all around him, within him. He got up to check Gopal's room. He wasn't there. "Wasn't he supposed to come back with you?"

Samanta asked his wife. He had been so engrossed in his inquiry about Mohan that he didn't remember seeing Gopal.

"He went to his room right in front of you. Let me see." Saying this, she looked inside all the rooms, thinking that he could have fallen asleep. Then she went to the backyard and he was there, sitting under the banana plant. "We've been looking for you," she said.

"Here you are," the old man said, relieved. He had followed his wife to the backyard. "It has been a long day. You must be hungry," he added.

***

Sukhatma stayed in the hut and read the other copy of the Bhagavad Gita, given to him by his guru on his deathbed. His mind had lost its serenity, in spite of years and years of practice. Until then, he had consciously tried to forget his past and avoid everything associated with it—the food, the water, and his memories. Nevertheless, he hadn't been able to move past the fact that the place still had a claim on him. Mohan clung to Sukhatma like a shadow, waiting to pull him back to the world he thought he had left behind. Sukhatma was beyond the desire Mohan had once had to return to the village. However, now that he was there, Sukhatma would have to fulfill Mohan's wish to find closure with his parents.

That night, Sukhatma went into trance after a lengthy meditation. He saw the same bright light, a thousand times brighter than the sun, illuminating the whole place. He knew that his guru, Swami Saralananda, was there.

"Swami, I feel lost," Sukhatma said, as the light danced around him. He was floating, soaring like a bird, trying to stay in the path of the light.

The light gradually diminished, and just before the darkness returned, Sukhatma heard his guru's voice: "*You have to decide.*"

Sukhatma woke up from the meditation and headed toward the river in the middle of the night. The sound of "Om" filled the air. As he waded into the water and sat motionless, the past flashed in his mind, and then everything became quiet, except for one scene. He saw Mohan leaving his parents' house on his last visit. His mother stood near their house, her eyes following him every step of the way. As Mohan reached the bend, he turned around and saw his mother waving at him. That was the omen Mohan was waiting for. One day he would return to the place.

***

She was up before daybreak and finished her daily rituals. She hadn't slept well at night thinking about her son, the sannyasi. Amid the heartbreak, she was happy to know that he was still alive. As she went into the kitchen, she was overcome by a sudden emotion—the guilt of depriving her husband of knowing about his son. As she put the rice cakes she had made for the sannyasi, in a steamer, she wondered if he was still there.

"Did he like them?" the old man asked. He was up before his usual time.

"He didn't eat any," she answered, and thought that her husband must not have slept at night, just like her, thinking about their son.

"Maybe you can send some today. The death of our son must have upset the sannyasi," he said. That was when he noticed someone coming toward the house. The sun wasn't up yet. As the figure came nearer and nearer, he could see the long saffron robe. "Madhuri," he said, uttering her name for the first time in so many years. "I think the sannyasi is here." He said it, unable to believe his eyes. He could see the sannyasi's long hair extending to his waist.

She ran out of the kitchen, equally surprised. She'd had no hope of seeing Sukhatma again. No matter who he claimed to be, it was Mohan she would be seeing. She wondered how to explain the sannyasi to her husband.

"Baba, welcome to our house," the old man said with excitement. He was about to touch the sannyasi's feet but Sukhatma held him back.

"I've come for your blessings, Baba." Saying this, Sukhatma touched his father's feet.

By this time, the sun was up. However, the old man didn't need light to see the sannyasi. He knew Mohan's voice by heart. It had resonated in him for years and years. At night, when he couldn't sleep thinking about his son, the old man held silent conversations with him. Each time, before he could ask Mohan for his forgiveness, he imagined hearing his son's voice asking for his blessings. In his aloneness, as the words dissolved, weaving hopes more fragile than the night before, the old man would succumb to a deep sleep, lulled by the gentle voice. He would wait eagerly for the next night, hoping for the words to become alive and enclose him in their embrace and not disappear.

"You said our son is dead . . . Mohan is dead." He turned toward his wife, speaking to her accusingly. He was stunned to see his son standing in front of him. He kept looking at Sukhatma's face and tried to find Mohan's, hidden behind the long beard and hair. The face had lost its fullness. It had grown old. However, his voice held the same calmness the old man was familiar with.

"Ma is right. Mohan is dead, in a way," the sannyasi told the old man. Nevertheless, he had called them "Ma" and "Baba," as Mohan would have done. "I'm Sukhatma. I've come for both of your blessings." Saying this, he proceeded to touch his mother's feet.

The old man felt as if everything moved around him in a circular motion, and he held on to the doorframe. His son's voice took him on a merry-go-round. Mohan was standing there in person, alive. The shapeless voice that put the old man to sleep every night took shape, waking him up from the throes of despair, making his every vein pulsate with life. Yet he understood the mockery of fate. While his mind was getting adjusted to Mohan's death, the son had returned. However, once he realized the altered state of his son, nothing could have been farther than what the old man had hoped for. The sight of the sannyasi reminded him of the last words he had uttered to Mohan before he'd left.

The old man kept looking at Sukhatma, trying to find words. If he had known that it was Mohan who had been living in the bamboo groves for the last three weeks, he would have done anything to bring his son home. He wished that he could reverse time, peeling the years back from Sukhatma, layer by layer, to reveal Mohan. He hoped that it wasn't too late. "We have been waiting for you all our lives. Please, Son, don't go," he pleaded. He held Sukhatma's hand and started crying. His wife stood next to him with renewed anticipation. She hoped that Sukhatma would relent.

"Baba, forgive me. There is no return from the path I've chosen. I came for your blessings, which Mohan didn't get." Saying this, the sannyasi gently let go of the old man's hand.

"Even if you have renounced the world and everyone in it, you are still our son," the old man said, his voice heavy with the weight of each word he spoke. He knew that his wife must have tried the day before to deter their son from the path he had taken. She hadn't succeeded in breaking his resolve. He thought of giving it another try. At least, he could convince him to stay around, if not to give up the *sannyas* life. "You don't have to leave this place," he told his son, full of hope. "We promise not to impose on you in any way," he added.

The old man blamed himself for not inquiring about the sadhu, who unlike others, had stayed on in their village for more than three weeks. In fact, the whole village had paid no attention to him. The thought that the villagers must have felt relieved at not having to hand out charity to someone, day after day, crossed his mind and made his heart weep. He looked at his son's famished body and worried about where he would get food from once he left the place. "The only time we would come to the grove would be to bring food for you, after Gopal returns to college." He became silent after saying this and waited.

"I'm sorry, Baba. I must leave now. Wish me well in my next journey." Saying this, Sukhatma hugged the old man. "You have another son. You have Gopal," he added, and turned around to leave.

Sukhatma's touch had made the old man's heart lighter, even though he understood that his attempt at persuading the sannyasi had been futile. Mohan's visit meant that he had forgiven them. The old man could not have asked for anything more from a sannyasi. He was glad that he could see his long-gone son one last time. Finally, there was an end to his waiting.

"Son, take these rice cakes for the road," Madhuri said. She had slipped into the kitchen and wrapped two rice cakes in a banana leaf, just the way she used to send food for Sukhatma. She put the packet in his half-opened palms, like giving alms to a sannyasi.

Sukhatma opened his saffron bag and gently put the rice cake with his books, saying, "*Om Tat Sat.*" As he walked away, the parents stood there until he disappeared into the bamboo groves. This time around, he didn't turn back to see if anyone was standing to wave at him. For him, there would be no return. He crossed the river to the other side and waited for the bus.

***

After Sukhatma left, the husband and wife sat on the veranda for a long time and kept looking in the direction of the bamboo groves, still hoping that he might turn back. However, this time, they knew that he would never return. At the same time, they were grateful that Mohan had come back to visit them in their old age, even as a sannyasi. The arrival of Sukhatma had made their household come alive, even though they hadn't known that he was their son. They told each other that it was a miracle that every one of them, including Gopal, had done what the heart told them to do, as if the heart knew. They looked at each other. Like wild vines, the years had gotten hold of them. The old rage and pain had given way to a new understanding about life. Sukhatma had reminded them of their other son.

"Aren't you going to send food for the swami?" they heard Gopal asking. He had slept through the sannyasi's visit. They both looked up at him as if they were seeing him for the first time in their lives, and through the soft glow of the morning sun, they became aware of a grown man, whose childhood they did not remember. They thought of this son as the most obedient child, who had never asked for anything, and they had made him disappear in the shadows of his older brother.

"The sannyasi has left." They both said it at the same time. They told him that the sannyasi had visited the house, asking for their blessings.

"Let me go and see if the rice cakes are heated by now." Saying this, Madhuri got up. "You set a place for me for breakfast, with you two." She looked at Gopal as she said this before entering the kitchen. Once she had left, Gopal and the old man sat quietly on the veranda, each lost in their own thoughts.

"When is college starting?" his father asked. He thought about the loneliness he would experience once Gopal left for college.

"In another month, Baba," Gopal replied.

"Have you thought about visiting Hena?" he asked his son.

Gopal didn't reply to this. He thought about Sukhatma. It must have been something really sad that had driven his brother to a life of *sannyas*. However, he thought about the peace and contentment his brother had given them in the last three weeks he had been there. He tried to understand the pain and heartbreak his parents must have gone through and their lifelong wait to see their son again. He was happy that they had finally been able to see him. He thought about his own life in the context of his parents' existence. He thought he could understand their hopes and disappointments. In spite of years and years of indifference on their part, he thought that he could show some compassion to them.

"You were childhood friends. You should go and see how she is doing." The old man meant it when he said this to Gopal.

"Have you set the table, Son? Don't forget to set a place for me," Gopal heard his mother say as he got up.

∎

Black Eagle Books

www.blackeaglebooks.org
info@blackeaglebooks.org

Black Eagle Books, an independent publisher, was founded
as a nonprofit organization in April, 2019. It is our mission
to connect and engage the Indian diaspora and the world at
large with the best of works of world literature published on
a collaborative platform, with special emphasis on
foregrounding Contemporary Classics and New Writing.

CPSIA information can be obtained
at www.ICGtesting.com
Printed in the USA
BVHW042148100822
644333BV00014B/95